THE HOLLOW HUSBAND

COLE BAXTER

INKUBATOR
BOOKS

Published by Inkubator Books
www.inkubatorbooks.com

Copyright © 2023 by Cole Baxter

Cole Baxter has asserted his right to be identified as the
author of this work.

ISBN (eBook): 978-1-83756-287-9
ISBN (Paperback): 978-1-83756-288-6
ISBN (Hardback): 978-1-83756-289-3

1

I sipped my champagne as I watched the wealthy couple my husband was talking to. They were eating up his words, nodding along with him the whole time. It wasn't particularly surprising. Most people reacted to David that way. And why wouldn't they? He was the stereotypical tall, dark, handsome man. His eyes were so dark blue they were almost black, and his jet-black hair lacked a single strand of gray. He stood at over six feet tall, and a mere glance at him told a person he worked out. Of course, it didn't hurt that he was one of them – rich and successful; he and his twin brother, Dalton, ran their own tech company.

In truth, I didn't really fit in with this world. I wasn't a lady of leisure, for starters. Although David had made it clear on many occasions that I didn't have to work, I chose to work. I worked because I loved my job as a marketing specialist. And, despite the fact that I was desperately happy in my marriage, it never hurt to remain financially independent.

It seemed to make David proud that I was successful in

my field, and he often bragged about me to his friends and their wives. At first, his bragging embarrassed me a little, but now I'd become used to it and just smiled. Truth be told, I liked that he thought of me as an equal instead of a good little wifey who sat at home sipping cocktails and popping Valium.

A waiter breezed toward us carrying a tray filled with drinks. It made me realize that my own glass was empty, and I lifted it slightly, showing the waiter my need for a fresh one. He smiled politely and came over to me. I put my empty glass down on the tray, took a new one, and thanked him. I turned back to the company.

"What do you think, Stella?" David asked me as I tuned back in. "Are smart devices going to become even bigger over the next few years?"

"Oh yes," I replied without hesitation. He had told me about their continual growth many times over the last few weeks, and if there was one area David knew better than anyone, it was technology. "They are only going to get bigger and better as they develop."

David nodded and gave me a wink.

I glanced from him to Dalton, who was watching us, and when he saw me look at him, he gave me a smile. It was identical to David's, but it didn't make the butterflies in my stomach dance. Of course, there wasn't any chemistry with Dalton like there was with David. Still, Dalton was a good guy, and I was glad he and David had each other. I smiled back.

"Stella's right," Dalton said.

"I couldn't agree more," Simon – an old friend of David and Dalton's – said.

"See, I think people are going to go the other way,"

Andrea, Simon's partner, put in. "They're going to get sick of having devices and apps for everything and go back to the days when we could switch our own lights on and close our own curtains."

I took a sip of my drink to hide my shock. It wasn't so much the fact that I thought Andrea was wrong, it was more that she had just blatantly disagreed with Simon in public. It seemed kind of rude to me that she should embarrass her partner like that, but Simon didn't seem fazed by it. He rolled his eyes and laughed good-naturedly.

"Next you'll be saying everyone is going to revert to snail mail and landlines," he said. "Maybe even fax machines. Or are they too advanced?"

"Well, you never know." Andrea laughed.

We exchanged a few more pleasantries, and then we all moved on, going our separate ways. For a moment it was just the three of us, and I glanced at David and Dalton.

"I can't believe Andrea said those things," I murmured, careful to keep my voice low enough so that only David and Dalton could hear me.

"I know," David agreed.

"Simon is spineless that way. He lets Andrea say the strangest things in company." Dalton glanced toward them across the room and shook his head, then turned back to us. "I think I'm gonna head out. Catch you two later."

"I'll see you tomorrow," David said with a pat on his brother's shoulder.

"Bye, Dalton," I said. As I drank the last of my champagne, I caught the eye of another waiter.

As he approached, David put his hand on the small of my back and leaned in so close that when he spoke, I could feel his breath on my ear. "Maybe it's time for you to switch to something nonalcoholic," he said. "Don't forget we have dinner with your parents after this."

"Yes. You're right," I said. I'd had two glasses of champagne already, and while I would have quite liked another one, it wasn't ladylike to get drunk at these kinds of cocktail parties. And I would only be self-conscious if we turned up at my parents' house and I was drunk. "Thank you for the advice."

I took a glass of water from the waiter, and David exchanged his whiskey for another one.

A couple I didn't know approached us from the center of the room.

"David, it's good to see you," the man said.

"Kevin, Marina, you just missed Dalton. This is Stella, my wife," David said, putting his hand on the small of my back once more. "Stella, this is my friend Kevin Jones and his better half, Marina."

We all smiled, nodded at each other, and said our I'm pleased to meet yous.

I couldn't help but feel a warm glow of pride when David introduced me as his wife. Of course, it was true, but it was still so new to me that it made me smile every time I heard it.

We had definitely had what people would describe as a whirlwind romance. On our third date, David asked me to move in with him. Two weeks later, we were engaged, and then a month after that, we were married. I'd been David's wife for just over three months now, and I had never been happier.

"Sorry we missed Dalton. I wanted to speak to him about that new project," Kevin said.

"You know Dalton, he's always off doing his own thing," David said with a chuckle.

The four of us chatted for a while. Marina hung on David's every word. She laughed a little too loudly at his jokes, curling her hair around her finger and occasionally brushing his arm with her hand.

The fact that David kept his hand on my back, his fingers lightly caressing me through the green silk of my dress, helped me not to feel too jealous of Marina. In fact, I kind of pitied her. She obviously didn't have a great relationship with Kevin, because if she did, she would only have eyes for him. I couldn't imagine wanting to flirt with someone so blatantly while I had David as my husband.

For his part, Kevin didn't seem to notice Marina's inappropriate behavior. He seemed to be every bit as smitten with David as she was, although he didn't show it in quite such a tactile manner.

"It's a bit stuffy in here. Should we go and get a breath of fresh air?" David murmured to me after a while, motioning toward the balcony doors that stood open, letting cool air into the hot room.

"Yes, that would be great," I answered with a grateful smile.

"We'll see you two later." David gave them a nod, then led me through the crowd toward the open doors.

I crossed my arms over my chest as we drew closer, feeling the nip in the air. I didn't stop, though. I had already agreed to go out there now.

Just as we reached the balcony doors, a man who had been blocking my view of the end of the room moved, and I could see right to the exit. What I saw made my blood run cold, and I stopped dead in my tracks.

Andrew.

Andrew was the opposite to David in many ways. Where

David was tall, Andrew was considerably shorter, at five feet ten. Where David was dark haired and dark eyed, Andrew had brown hair and pale brown eyes. Where David was toned and athletic, Andrew was muscular and bulky. And perhaps most importantly, where David was my husband, Andrew was my ex.

I had loved Andrew once, I supposed. But he had eradicated any feelings I had for him when I found out he was cheating on me. I left him immediately, and it was only a couple of days later that I met David. Talk about falling up. Once Andrew realized I was serious about us being over, he began to hound me. At first it was just online, stalking my social media profiles, emailing me. Then he started calling me, and when I blocked his number on my cell phone, he started calling me at work or on my office number at home. God knew how he had gotten that number. And now his latest trick was following me in person. He seemed to think that if he stalked me and turned up wherever I was, I would somehow decide I was missing out and get back with him.

It wasn't going to happen, but no matter how much I told him that, he didn't give up. If anything, it seemed only to encourage him, like he saw it as a challenge. The last thing I needed was for him to be here now.

I was glad I had been open with David about everything. He knew exactly who Andrew was and that he was harassing me. He had promised me he would sort it out if Andrew tried anything. I trusted David to keep his word, but it still didn't stop me from feeling a moment of fear when I saw that Andrew was here.

"Stella? Stella? What's wrong?" David asked.

I glanced at him and then looked back at Andrew. I didn't

want to let him out of my sight for even a second, scared of what he might do.

"I ... I'm sorry," I said. I opened my mouth to tell him Andrew was here, but as I did, Andrew turned around, and it wasn't Andrew at all. He sure fit the bill for his height and build, and his hair was the right color and style, but his face wasn't even similar to Andrew's. I felt relief flood through me, and I was smiling when I spoke again. "Oh, I thought I saw Andrew, but it was a false alarm. It isn't him."

David stiffened beside me, concern and a little anger written all over his face.

I frowned. "What's wrong?"

"You were afraid," he said, his face a mask of consternation.

"I was shocked to see him here, that's all," I said.

"Sweetheart, you don't need to fear this Andrew guy or anyone else ever again. I vowed that I wouldn't let Andrew hurt you." He touched my cheek and looked deep into my eyes, but something hard in them made my stomach tighten. "I won't let anyone hurt what is mine," David said.

His voice was almost as hard as the look in his eyes, and for a fleeting second, I wondered if maybe I should be afraid of *him*. The moment passed by so quickly that I was left wondering if I had imagined it. Yes, of course I must have imagined it. As if I should be scared of David. He would never hurt me, though he might hurt someone else for hurting me, and that prospect was pretty scary too.

"If you ever see Andrew, you let me know, and I'll make sure he doesn't show his face around you again," David promised.

I nodded, but inside I wondered how he would do that. Andrew was a bully, and he was too stupid to know when to quit. He wouldn't do something just because David told him to. He would only respond to violence, and I worried about what that might mean. I didn't want David acting in a way that would lead to him being taken away from me.

"You don't look convinced." He frowned at me, his brow low over his eyes. "Do you think I'm incapable of taking care of you?"

This wasn't the time or place for me to try to explain my thoughts, which I wasn't even sure of at this point. At least I wasn't sure how to put into words what I wanted to convey without upsetting my husband more. Besides, I didn't doubt for a moment that he could protect me.

"Of course not," I said. "I know you can protect me. I was just upset because I thought if you had to cause a scene and it was my fault, I would embarrass you."

David's face softened instantly. He put his arm around me and pulled me to his side. He kissed the top of my head. "Making sure you're safe from the unwanted attention of losers like him would never embarrass me. In fact, you know what? I've shown my face; let's blow this cocktail party off and go to your parents' place now. No one will be able to upset you there."

I nodded again. I liked that he was always so thoughtful. Thinking I had spotted Andrew had left me shaken up, and I had a feeling that, if we stayed, David and I would end up arguing, and that was the last thing I wanted us to do.

As David swept me toward the exit, people came over to say their goodbyes, and I was reminded once more of David's charm and popularity. I felt foolish for thinking we would have argued over something so silly. All he would have had to do was speak with one of the waitstaff to get onto security, and it would have been sorted without anyone even knowing anything had gone down.

By the time we left the party, I had calmed down and forgotten all about the guy I'd thought was Andrew. I didn't want to think of him anymore ever; I needed to learn to put him out of my thoughts. I glanced at David, my strong, caring, loving husband, and smiled. He would protect me.

David was the best husband I could have ever wished for. If I ever needed reminding of that, I only had to watch the way his brother, his peers and their partners treated him with such open adoration.

2

"Would anyone like more dessert?" my mom asked once we had all finished eating.

I leaned back in my seat, rubbed my stomach, and shook my head. "Not for me, I'm stuffed. This dress is pretty unforgiving on second helpings."

"Perry? David?" my mom said.

My dad shook his head.

"As delicious as it was, Maria, I really couldn't eat any more," David said.

"Let's go to the living room, then," my mom said. "I'll make us all some coffee."

We moved through to the living room, and my dad and David chatted about my dad's blog. My dad used to be a marketing specialist like me. It was he who showed me the ropes and got me interested, and now that he had retired, he still liked to keep his finger on the pulse a little bit, so he wrote an independent blog about marketing research and different studies about consumer trends. He was telling David about how he was thinking of changing some of the site layout, and David was advising on what might work best for him.

My mom came into the living room with the coffee and tutted at my dad. "Now stop bending David's ear. He's not at work now; let him enjoy his time off, for goodness' sake."

"It's fine, Maria, honestly. I don't mind helping." David's smile lit his eyes and made the blue of them brighten.

My mom returned his smile and began handing out the coffees.

My dad rolled his eyes as my mom turned her back, and then he went back to talking to David, which made me chuckle.

Once we all had our coffees and my mom finally sat down, my dad turned his attention to me. "Anything interesting on the horizon for you at work?"

"I've just finished my final ad on the Jackson campaign," I said. "It'll be going out in tomorrow's edition. Front page." I was so proud of the ad I'd created for them. It was the biggest campaign I'd worked on so far in my career.

"Nice," he said with a smile at me, and then he focused back on David. "What do you think about that campaign? Don't you think Stella's done a good job for them?"

"Yes, of course, Stella has been brilliant." David smiled over at me and patted my knee. "She showed me the work she's done, and I think Jackson was lucky to have her as their marketing specialist. Pretty soon all the big names will be asking her to do work for them, and she'll be too busy to focus on such a small campaign." His grin widened.

I blushed at his attention. His faith in me was much greater than the faith I had in myself. And to call the Jackson campaign small made me laugh. The company had offices in fifteen states. That kind of business was nothing to sneeze at.

We chatted a bit more, and then my father brought up the recent news on the Garrett abduction. I really loved that my parents enjoyed seeking David's opinion. It showed they respected him, and that made me happy.

"What do you think about that, David?" my father asked.

"Well, it's a tragedy of course," he said. "But it's such an old case that without a confession from the abductor now, it's hard to say with any certainty what happened, isn't it? You know, forensics are good, but are they that good? I'm just not sure."

"I thought forensics could identify criminals from years and years ago these days?" Mom questioned.

"They can in theory," David agreed. "I'm just not sure how much I would trust the results is all I'm saying. I think it needs something more to be sure, like a confession or a witness or victims who are willing to speak out."

"So how far back would you say the results are reliable?" my dad asked. "Ten years? Twenty?"

"I was thinking more in terms of months than years, to be honest," David said.

My dad shook his head. "DNA doesn't change over time. I think it's always going to be accurate despite its age. I can maybe understand it being a little bit less accurate if you're going back a couple of decades simply because you've got no guarantee the sample was collected properly or stored properly. But only a year ago? The process would be pretty much the same as it is now."

"Imagine if David is right, and these historic cases the police think they've solved all have the wrong person doing time," my mom said. "That would be one hell of a lawsuit when the truth came out."

"And for that reason alone, I don't believe it's worth the

risk relying totally on DNA and other forensic evidence so long down the line," David said. "It can be corrupted. Especially if it's sat for so long."

"So what about that girl who went missing?" my dad asked. "Olive someone, was it?"

"Casden," I put in. "Olive Casden."

"Yeah, that's her. Do you think that any evidence in her case would be corrupted at this point?" he asked David.

"How old is the case? A year? A year and a half or so, right?" David said.

My dad nodded. "I think it's been about eighteen months since she was reported missing."

"I'd say it's borderline at best," David said with a shrug. "But let's not be hasty. Olive Casden is missing, that's true enough, but she may well be alive somewhere, you never know."

"Surely she would have come forward when she saw how many people were looking for her," my mom said, her eyes widened in surprise.

"Why would she have to?" David replied. "We don't know her circumstances. Maybe she was fleeing a violent ex. Maybe she decided to start over somewhere. Maybe she committed a crime, and she changed her identity. Or maybe she's in witness protection, and the police aren't telling us that. Maybe she went somewhere so far off the grid she doesn't even know she's considered to be a missing person."

"Or maybe she was actually murdered, and the longer the police bumble around treating the case like a missing persons case instead of a homicide, the more likely it is that her killer will get away without being punished," I suggested with a shiver.

David looked at me, and for a second, his eyes took on

that hard, almost angry look again. He blinked, and the effect was gone. He grinned. "Yeah, but where's the fun in not speculating, huh?"

I laughed and nodded my agreement when my parents did, but in truth, I didn't think there was any fun to be found in a young woman vanishing, perhaps being killed. I actually found it kind of scary because, being a woman, I knew the statistics weren't in our favor.

"I feel sorry for her family," my mom said after a break in the conversation. "Her mom in particular; I keep imagining how I would feel if it were Stella missing. It must be heart-breaking to lose a child, but imagine how hard it would be not knowing if she is gone or if she just decided to up and move without a word to them."

David reached out, squeezed my mom's hand, and smiled at her. "Don't worry. I'll make sure this one contacts you if she ever decides to 'go to find herself' or whatever," he joked.

I bristled slightly, but only inside. Why would I ever do such a ridiculous thing? I knew who I was already, and even if I did decide to go traveling, I would be more than capable of letting my parents know my whereabouts without David making me call them.

I knew I was being ridiculous. He didn't mean anything by it. He was just trying to lighten the mood and reassure my mom at the same time. It seemed to have worked too, because my mom was laughing and telling him how I would never do that to her anyway.

"And I'd hope Stella would do the same," my mom said. "Get you to call your parents and brother if you go flitting off."

"Oh, there'll be no flitting from me," David said. "Not

that my parents would know or care if I disappeared." He sighed. "But Dalton might."

I felt myself sitting up a tiny bit straighter as I started to really pay attention. I had never really heard David talk about his parents before. When we were discussing the guest list for our wedding, he had simply said he had no family other than Dalton whom he wished to invite, and when I tried to ask questions, he just smiled and told me we should stick to planning our wedding instead of talking about miserable stuff.

"Oh, David, I'm sure that's not true," my mom said.

"I don't like to talk about my family much, as I'm sure you've figured out." David shrugged. "But I'll explain a little. My mother is dead, she died when Dalton and I were about thirteen, and my father's chronically ill and lives in a private medical facility. I suppose he might notice that the bill is no longer being paid, but that would be it."

"You pay for his care?" my mom said.

David nodded. "Dalton and I do." He looked at his watch and then at me. "As much as I hate to end this discussion and our evening together, I think we had better be going. It's getting late, and we've both got an early start in the morning," he said.

It was barely eleven o'clock, but I figured he wanted to get away from the probing questions about his parents, so I nodded and put my hand over my mouth, feigning a yawn.

"Yeah, you're right," I said, getting to my feet.

David and my mom and dad all got up too.

"David, I hope we didn't upset or offend you by talking about your parents," my mom said, worry in her eyes.

"No, no, of course not," David said, smiling warmly at her. "It's simply the joy of an early morning start. And as to parents, well, mine might not have been the best, but I now have you both in my life, and that's wonderful." David hugged my mom and then shook hands with my dad.

"And we're lucky to have you as our new son," my mom said, a bright smile on her lips.

I hugged both of my parents. "I'll call you soon," I said with a matching smile.

We said our goodbyes, and then David and I were outside and heading for the car. I knew that in theory David had probably had a little too much to drink, but he seemed sober enough. Still, I thought I should bring it up.

"We could call a cab if you don't feel like driving," I said, not wanting to outright accuse him of anything.

"No, I'm fine. I need the car for in the morning," David said. He flashed me that hard, angry look again. He sighed, and though his words were gentle, he remained stiff. "Don't worry, sweetheart, I'm not drunk or even tipsy."

"I mean, I can see you're not, like, falling-over drunk, but I think technically you would be over the limit if we got pulled over. I just don't want you to get into trouble, that's all," I explained.

David's stiffness faded away to a smile; then he wrapped an arm around me and hugged me close. "You're so sweet worrying about me," he said. "But you don't have to worry. The cops will be looking for people driving erratically or for potential stolen vehicles. We're good."

I smiled up at him, and I felt myself nodding my agreement. He wasn't that drunk, and he'd eaten quite a bit, so that had probably soaked up most of the alcohol. I was just being overly cautious. David wouldn't get behind the wheel if he thought he'd get pulled over or we'd have an accident.

He was too responsible to do something that stupid. I let him lead me to the passenger side of the car.

He unlocked it and opened my door for me. He held it wide and gestured for me to get in. "M'lady," he said, giving a mock bow.

"Why, thank you, kind sir," I said, playing along.

David closed my door, walked around the car, and got in the driver's seat. He started the engine and pulled away, leaving my parents' driveway and heading for home.

We had gone a couple of blocks when I decided to try to find out a little bit more about his dad.

"I'm sorry to hear about your dad being ill," I said, testing the waters.

David made a grunting sound and kept his eyes fixed firmly on the road.

"I didn't even know he was still alive. You never talk about him, and you said you had no family other than Dalton when we were planning the wedding," I pointed out.

"I meant technically I had no other family healthy enough to attend the wedding. I didn't want to say that and bring down the mood. We were so excited to be planning our wedding. Do you remember?" David said with a side glance at me.

"Of course I remember." I smiled. "We went cake tasting after doing the seating chart, and we both agreed that we would pretend we weren't sure on the cake so we could have extra samples because it was all so damned good."

We were both laughing at the memory.

"That really was good cake," David said as our laughter trailed off. "We chose well."

"It was," I agreed. "Did you or Dalton at least take a piece for your dad?"

David shook his head, but he didn't elaborate.

I decided to try one more time. "I'd love to go and visit him with you and get to know him," I said.

"Listen, you don't want to do that. The man is poison. I know you're being nice, but here's the thing. Dalton and I tell people we have no family because our dad is the only family we have left, and we don't get on with him. We pay for his medical expenses and make sure he gets the best care because we owe him that much for him doing the same for us as children. Neither of us have any intention of playing happy families with him. There are things you don't know, Stella. Things I don't want to talk about. Can you just trust me when I say my dad is not a good person?"

"Yeah, sure, if that's what you want," I replied.

I was so curious though. I had a thousand more questions about this elusive man, but I could see that David was getting uncomfortable, and he had made it more than clear that he didn't want to discuss him anymore. So for the sake of us not ending up in an argument, I made sure to keep my questions inside.

3

As soon as I walked into the office, I felt the buzz of energy floating in the air. I had no idea what was going on, but instinct told me that whatever it was, it was something big. It felt like the day I came into the office to be told I would be covering the Jackson campaign because they'd been impressed by the idea I'd drawn up for them. The atmosphere had been charged with this feeling of excitement with an undertone of envy.

Most of the staff here were more suited to working on minor accounts of local ambulance-chasing lawyers than a national brand looking for brilliant ad copy, so they had been relieved when I said I would take on the Jackson campaign and draw up a proposal campaign to maximize their sales. It made me wonder if maybe there was another top corporation on the horizon. But this was Gull Island not New York City. Surely, the Jackson Candy Corporation would be the biggest client this place would ever see.

"Stella, Lonnie said she wants to see you as soon as you come in. This very second, not after a coffee, not after

checking email, not after chatting to half of the office. Immediately," Charlie Banks, one of the junior executives, called
over to me as I made my way toward my desk. "Her words
not mine." He was wearing a small smile, like he knew something I didn't and was excited about it.

"Thanks, Charlie," I said, dropping my purse on my desk.
I changed course slightly so that I was heading for Lonnie's
office instead of sitting down at my desk. As I passed by
Charlie, I saw him make a beeline toward my friend Brittany.
He leaned against her desk, and they chatted softly.

I refocused my attention on Lonnie's office. Lonnie was
the top executive at Master Marketing LLC. She knew every
job we did, having done most of them herself, but now she
was the CEO, and she was my work mentor. I loved working
for her.

Although I kept telling myself nothing ever happened
here on Gull Island and it couldn't possibly be another big
client coming my way, I couldn't help but enjoy the tingling
feeling in the pit of my stomach as I approached Lonnie's
office. I tapped on the door and waited.

"Come in!" Lonnie called out.

I pushed the door open and stepped inside. "Charlie said
you wanted to see me," I said.

Lonnie was already nodding and gesturing to the chair
opposite hers. "Yes. Sit down. Quickly now." She almost
always got straight to the point. She was a no-nonsense kind
of person.

I sat down and looked expectantly at Lonnie.

"I've got a big one for you," she said, a bright sparkle in
her eye as she picked up a folder.

That was when I knew for definite this was a major deal.
Her excitement was palpable, and I couldn't wait to see what

she was about to give me. Earning the right to work on the Jackson campaign had been a big step in my career, and I couldn't wait to do more, to show off my skills. I was really hoping this would be another chance to do that.

"The good news is everyone has heard of this client. And I'm pretty sure you know our contact, since they mentioned you and your work by name."

That was surprising. I had no idea whom she was talking about. "Really? Who?"

"Max Jordan. I believe you went to high school with him?"

I nodded. Max had been in my year at school, but we'd never been friends or dated or anything. He'd been one of the popular guys, the ones everyone knew, but I was just a peon who'd never made it into his circle of friends. So to realize he now knew who I was, that felt a little thrilling to say the least. "Yes, I know Max enough to say hello, wouldn't say it went beyond that though."

"He said as much."

"So who's the client, and what's the bad news?"

"The client is Wally's Chocolates. The bad news is they've fired their advertising company, and they're shopping around for a new one, so we're one of many they've come to. Apparently, Max Jordan was incredibly impressed with your on-brand marketing for the Jackson Candy Company, whom, as I'm sure you know, they sell to, which is how he came across your work. So he wanted to give you a shot since you're from the same area and went to the same high school."

My emotions danced inside me, and I couldn't decide if I was more excited at the prospect of creating a campaign for the well-known chocolate company or at the thought of getting to sample their newest candy. Honestly, it was a toss-up because that chocolate was amazing. Who didn't love a good milky chocolate with a creamy, salted caramel center? My mouth watered just thinking about it.

"Seriously?" I asked, almost afraid to believe it. This was much bigger than the Jackson account. Wally's Chocolates were sold around the world. To earn their business would be huge not just for Master Marketing, but for me too. It would put me on the map in the advertising and marketing world. I wanted the opportunity badly.

"Yes," Lonnie said, a big grin on her lips. "Do you want to try for it?"

"Hell yeah," I said without thinking twice.

"Good," Lonnie said with a laugh. "Because you're one of the few marketing specialists I have here who has even a remote chance of landing the campaign. Max Jordan said that he really hoped you could impress him with a campaign that would show off more talent from around Gull Island."

"So what does Max Jordan do for Wally's?"

"He's the CEO. They fired their marketing department and decided to outsource it, which is where we come in."

"Wow, so why did they fire their team?" I didn't want to make any mistakes that would remind Jordan of them.

"He didn't say, and I wasn't going to look a gift horse in the mouth," Lonnie said with another grin. "You're up to the task, right? You don't need a break? I know the Jackson campaign took up a lot of time and energy for you."

"No, I'm good."

"Okay then," Lonnie said. She pushed a piece of paper across the desk at me. "There's the details for a meeting that's been set up, where you can meet Jordan to discuss the particulars."

I took the paper and stood up. "Thanks, boss," I said.

"Stella?" Lonnie said as I reached the door.

I turned back, and she smiled.

"Whatever happens, this agency was here before this chance, and it will be here after, and there will be other top-dollar companies in the future. You put together a campaign we can be proud of. That's all I can ask."

"Got it," I said. "I won't let you down."

I looked at the address and saw it was for a high-end hotel here on the island. The meeting was to take place in an hour, in the hotel's restaurant. I figured if I left now, I'd be able to get a coffee and relax a little, gather my thoughts before the meeting.

I picked up my purse from my desk and walked straight back out of the office. I went down in the elevator, left the building, and drove to the hotel.

Unfortunately, when I arrived, there were cop cars everywhere. I immediately saw the crime scene tape at the side of the building, blocking off the narrow alley between the hotel and the next building. The area was quiet for a crime scene, I thought; only a few policemen, the coroner and an ambulance were in the vicinity. I didn't see any reporters.

I had always been a crime junkie. I loved looking into old crimes and dissecting them. It was a hobby I shared with my dad. So I was really curious about what was going on. Looking around, I noticed the parking lot wasn't very full. It was past the typical breakfast time and a little before lunch, and I supposed that during the week, the hotel restaurant didn't do a lot of brunch business.

I was pretty early, so I decided to let my curiosity run free and went over to the crime scene tape. Nobody was paying attention to me, so I slipped under it and started walking toward where there was a cluster of people gathered by a doorway. I could see a friend of my dad's in the group of patrol officers. Alan Kettleman was a detective, and if he was here, that meant this was a homicide.

"I'm sorry, miss, you can't be in here," a young officer said from behind me.

I turned around and put my hand on my hip. "Is that so? Because it would appear that I am," I said. The young policeman started trying to speak again, but I cut him off. "Save it, kid. I'm here with Alan Kellerman. Call him over here if you want, but I guarantee he won't be happy with the interruption," I lied smoothly, praying he'd buy it.

"Umm, no. That's fine. You go on over. I'm sorry," the young policeman said.

"No need to apologize. I realize that you are just doing your job, Officer," I said.

I flashed him a quick smile and started toward the group by the doorway. The group moved into the building, and I went to follow. It turned out the doorway led to the hotel fitness area. I'd never been in this gym, nor any gym in some time, because the last time I'd gone to one, Andrew showed up and harassed me. I'd avoided gyms after that, afraid that he would find me and do it again. That was before I met David, though.

I shook that memory away, focusing on what was going on around me. I could smell the chemical smell of chlorine drifting in from the pool, which was right next door and could be seen through the glass window. There was another smell too, a tangy, coppery smell that took me a moment to decipher. It hit me like a train when it came to me. The smell was blood.

For the air to be filled with it this way, I knew I had to be walking into some real carnage, and I hesitated. I shouldn't be here. The problem was, I couldn't stop my feet from going forward. It was like a car crash you couldn't look away from. I had to know what had happened.

I followed the group and soon found that I was in the main gym area. Straight away I knew this was where the body was. The smell of blood here was so strong it was like being inside a butcher's shop on a hot day. I swallowed and tried to breathe through my mouth. It didn't eradicate the smell entirely, but it definitely helped.

The gym was L-shaped, and the part I was in was clear. I started to walk toward the bend where the officers had gone, bracing myself for what I was about to see. I'd never been to a live, active crime scene before. I reached the bend and turned. Nothing could have prepared me for the scene I stepped into.

The body of a man was laid on the ground in the center of the floor. His torso and stomach had been split open and pulled wide apart, and his penis and testicles had been pushed into the split in the stomach region. His legs were both bent outwards, snapped at the knee and arranged like a parody of a sprinter. His arms had been removed and placed near the body with one severed hand pushed into his hair and the other one touching his pectoral muscle just above where the split down his center started.

The effect was instant and horrifying, and it was made a thousand times worse because of its location. The gym walls were all mirrors, so everywhere I looked, the body bounced back at me in multiples of its gory self. I felt my gorge rising, nausea making me sweat slightly.

I took my attention off the corpse and instead focused on the African American detective who was crouched beside the body, talking to a guy in a crime scene investigations jacket. Alan must have sensed my presence, felt my eyes on him. He glanced over his shoulder and noticed me. I felt relieved. As he straightened up and started walking toward me, his face grim, I swallowed as hard as I could, praying it would be enough to stop me from retching. I forced a smile at him.

Normally, my smile at the man was genuine. I had known him since I was a teenager, and he was one of the more amiable men my dad was friends with, and he often indulged us with cold cases to dissect. He didn't look happy to see me, though. In fact, he looked downright pissed off.

"What are you doing here, Stella? How did you get in?" Alan demanded. He suddenly seemed more than imposing in his role as a Gull Island police detective.

"Well, hi, Alan. It's a pleasure to see you too. How are you doing?" I responded with as much of a smile as I could muster.

Alan shook his head and sighed. "I can see that curious nature of yours got the better of you. But, seriously, how did you get in here? If there's an unattended door or something, I need to know about it."

"If I tell you, will you answer a few questions?" I asked.

Alan nodded, resigned to the dance we were about to complete. "But I don't want you posting about this on social media, Stella. You shouldn't even be here. And this is not how the victim's family needs to see him, and to be honest, it's not how anyone needs to see him," he added with a glance back toward the body.

I nodded.

"So? How did you get in?" he asked me again, raising an eyebrow.

"I told the kid on the door I was with you," I said.

"So you just walked in the front door?" he clarified. "Why would you do that? This isn't ... the poor bastard's been murdered in a very gruesome manner, as you can plainly see; you can't just insinuate yourself in a crime scene."

"I know. I didn't intend to. I was here to meet a possible new client, saw you, and my curiosity was piqued. Who is he?" I asked, nodding toward the body on the ground. "Don't worry, I swear I won't say anything to anyone. I'm just intrigued."

Alan sighed again, but it was a resigned sigh, the kind that told me he was exasperated with me. "You and your dad. Always sticking your noses in where you shouldn't."

"You know we're true-crime junkies," I said, swallowing a grin, knowing he was going to tell me. He'd always enjoyed getting together with us and going over those old case files. I figured this wouldn't be any different except that this case was fresh not cold.

"Fine, I'll tell you just to satisfy your nosiness and because I know you won't go posting about it. According to the hotel gym manager who found him and called us, his name is Cory Elway. He was a personal trainer."

"The hotel has personal trainers?"

"Yeah, apparently." Alan shrugged. "They offer memberships to residents on the island as well."

I glanced at the body again, and Alan moved to block my view.

"So he was one of those prima donna types who love themselves," I said, more thinking out loud than anything. "That could explain part of the pose. The way one of the hands is in the hair and the way the other one is almost showing off a pec."

Alan stared at me for a minute, then nodded. "Good theory. You could say it would seem our killer was more than a little jealous of Mr. Elway."

I wasn't sure that jealousy would be where I would have gone. I felt it was more a sign of outright hatred than jealousy, but I let it go. It would be stupid of me to argue with Alan, the actual detective, about my opinion. I wasn't a real detective; I just liked to dissect true crimes and discuss them with my dad and anyone else who would listen.

"So was this Cory liked, disliked, what?" I asked. "Because it sure looks like he had at least one serious enemy."

"I'm not entirely sure at this moment, but to me, this doesn't look like something that has been planned as such. The amount of gore and the sheer depravity makes me think it is a crime of passion. You know, someone started, and then things escalated, and they couldn't stop?"

I nodded, but my gut was telling me that this was no spur-of-the-moment thing that had gotten out of hand. As I mentioned, I was kind of a true-crime aficionado, so I'd studied crime scenes and killers, and to me, this seemed messy, yes, but also meticulous. It was almost like a ritual, or something similarly organized. And it seemed that the message the killer wanted to send wasn't one to the victim, but one to the people left behind after the victim was gone. And I firmly believed that message was about making the crime scene as disturbing as possible. For me, there was only one message in that, which was that this was just the beginning. There would be more.

"So do you have any suspects?" I asked.

"We're still at the scene, Stella." He sighed. "No suspects were on the scene when we got here, nor when the gym manager showed up, so not yet, but as I mentioned, you didn't have to be a hotel guest to make use of this gym. Residents of the island could have access to it as well."

I winced. "Well, let's hope one presents themselves soon. The last thing we need is this sort of maniac running around Gull Island," I said, directing my gaze back toward the body.

"Okay, you've seen enough," Alan said, directing me back the way I came. "It's time for you to go."

I glanced down at my phone in my hand. "Oh crap, I'm late!" I exclaimed, suddenly remembering I was here to see Max Jordan, not solve crime. "I've got a meeting in the restaurant. Bye, Alan." I practically ran from the gym area, passing through the doors and back into the hotel lobby.

4

I sighed with contentment as I snuggled up to David on the couch, a full glass of Merlot in my hand. As much as I loved my job, I was really glad it was Saturday and I had tomorrow off. Lonnie was always big on us not taking projects home with us. Work was for business hours, and if we were going to be working, it would be on their time, not ours. So the proposal I was going to create for Wally's Chocolates would be waiting for Monday.

Of course, that left me with the weekend to dig into the death of Cory Elway. I had already drawn up my own profile on the victim and on the type of person who might commit murder with a grotesque flair while David had been busy in his home office.

I had decided that I was going to spend part of tomorrow digging into Cory Elway's background and his life outside of the hotel gym. I couldn't even begin to accept that this was a stranger who just happened on Cory and took an opportunity. I knew that kind of killing happened, but I didn't think it happened quite like this. The placement of the body and everything about the attack upon it, it was all so elaborate. I couldn't shake the feeling that there was a message intended.

I wanted to find out if Cory had upset any psychopaths in his time. It seemed unlikely that there was a bona fide psychopath in our small community, but the way that body was attacked and then posed told a different story.

From what I had discovered about Cory via social media, he was well liked at the hotel. Tributes were being paid to him on the hotel's Facebook page, and there were many comments from various staff members about how loved he was and how he would be truly missed. Cory's own page was full of sorrow too. Lots of people were distraught at his death and were going to miss him, it seemed.

When I did a Facebook search on his name, though, discussions about him varied. There were the ones who thought Cory was the bee's knees, mostly women and his own clients, and then there were the ones who thought he was a bit of a showoff, which were generally men who I could see were not even close to being as in shape as he was. I figured the attitude might be a little bit of jealousy, but not one of them gave me the impression they knew anything about his murder or that they burned with seething hatred, the kind of emotion needed to fuel a murder so vicious.

There were also those who suggested Cory was a womanizer, never settling with one woman for more than a few dates. I figured this area of his life was probably what caused his death. A woman who wouldn't take no for an answer when he tried to ghost her, maybe, but the way he was murdered didn't seem like how a woman would behave. A pissed-off husband whose wife had had an affair with Cory? That could be the answer, I thought.

"Are you okay, sweetheart? You're awfully quiet," David asked, pulling me from my morbid thoughts.

His words reminded me, subconsciously, that I was supposed to be spending time with him, not dwelling on murder, of all things. "Yeah, I'm fine," I said. "I was just thinking."

"Let me guess," David said. "You were thinking about that murder."

He didn't sound angry, he sounded kind of amused, so I decided to be honest with him and nodded.

He chuckled. "I know how you love to debate these true-crime things. What is it about it that's bugging you?" David asked. "I mean, aside from finding the answer to who might have killed the guy?"

I pushed myself upright so I could face David. I took a drink of my wine and then sighed. "I just can't get past the idea that the way the body was arranged was some sort of message. Not for me, obviously, since I wasn't supposed to be there. And I don't even think it was specifically for the police. I think it was a more general message. Maybe a message to society as a whole. I'm not entirely sure. But there's something that's bugging me. And I feel like if I can work out what the message is or who it's for or maybe both, then I can tell my dad's friend, you know, Alan Kettleman? He's the detective I spoke to who's on the case," I explained.

I knew that technically I shouldn't have told David about the way the body was found or about my discussion with Alan at the scene. Really, I shouldn't have told him anything that hadn't appeared in the newspaper. But he was my husband, and I trusted him. He wasn't about to go out and tell the world I'd butted in on a crime scene and had more information than the reporters.

"Yes, of course. I remember him. You and your dad are always talking about him giving you cold cases to look at. So you think the killer is playing some sort of game?" David asked.

I thought about it before I answered. That didn't feel right either. "No, I think the killer is mentally deranged in one sense, obviously because of what they've done. But I don't think they're stupid. In fact, I think they're full of a cold and calculating intelligence. Like Rodney Alcala, the Dating Game killer," I said. "That means nothing is an accident. Like I said, I think our killer is sending a message, but I don't think it's a clue as to who might be next, assuming there's going to be another victim."

David nodded. I loved that he actively listened to me as I spoke. It was one of the many things I loved about him.

I continued, "I think it's the killer's take on art. I think they arranged the body in a way to shock, of course, but then once the shock fades and you look closer, it's almost like a picture of the victim's life spread out in gore and viscera."

I stopped talking when I saw David grinning. I felt my cheeks flush with embarrassment.

"You think I'm being stupid, don't you?" I said, looking down at the glass of Merlot.

"No. God no. Not at all. I think what you're saying is fascinating. Really, I do," David said. "I realize that sounds sarcastic, but I don't mean it that way. I genuinely don't."

"So why are you laughing at me, then?" I asked.

"I wasn't laughing at you, I was smiling. I love to see how passionate you are when you talk about making sense of these cases, that's all," he said. "As if I would laugh at you. You know how proud I am of you, Stella. I honestly think you missed your calling as a police detective, but then the marketing world would miss out on your brilliance." He leaned forward and kissed me. "Now, what do you think the killer was painting a picture of? What do you think his message about Cory's life was?"

I thought for a moment. I kind of had an idea of what I thought, but I wanted to present it in a logical way so I didn't sound like I was just rambling on, and his kisses had scrambled my thoughts for a moment, in a good way. I smiled at him.

"I think the way his arms were posed showed his vain side. His hand on his hair, like he was styling it. A hand on his chest like he was showing off his muscles. I think what was done to his genitals was a nod to his womanizing ways. And I think the message about where those parts ended up and how his arms were severed is a clear enough symbol. It's like saying if you fuck with the wrong person, you won't be a pretty boy any longer and you certainly won't be fucking anyone else. Does that make sense?"

David was quiet for a moment, and then he nodded. "Yes, it does in some ways, but keep an open mind. You don't want to miss something because you're so sure your theory is correct," he reminded me.

"You sound like maybe you have your own theory that's different to mine," I said, hopeful. I loved that he was as into it as me.

"No, not at all," David said. "I wouldn't like to posit a theory without seeing the body myself. I just don't want you getting set on one theory yet without more to go on, that's all."

"Oh, you know me," I said. "I enjoy coming up with my own theories as the investigation goes on, but I don't let my theories get in the way of the facts."

"Good," David said. "So what sort of person do you think you would be looking for?"

I thought about my original profile of the killer. The one I actually believed might be closer to accurate. "I think it's someone very petty," I said. "Someone insecure."

"Really?" David said with an eyebrow raised. "How do you come to that conclusion?"

"Well, that crime scene looked to me like whoever killed Cory really hated him. The subliminal message he left, the mirrors, the gore. It was like he wanted people to see Cory messed up like that, to see that he wasn't hot or buff or cute anymore. I think it was someone who wished they could get women like Cory could. It's probably some sad little creeper type who couldn't get it up even if he found a woman to fuck," I said.

For a second, something I couldn't place flashed in David's eyes. Then his expression shifted to one of concern and worry. He looked almost afraid or fearful. But I couldn't understand why. Not until he spoke.

"If you seriously think that personality type fits this crime, then you have to promise me that you're going to be careful, sweetheart. I know you want to play amateur detective; I can see it in your eyes. I'm worried that the kind of guy you're describing is a very angry little guy, and most of his anger will be centered on the women who reject him," David said. "Or the ones who are too gorgeous for him to even dare to approach. Like you."

I smiled despite myself at his compliment, and I took another long drink of my wine.

"Don't worry. I promise, if I do go investigate, that I'll be careful," I told him.

"You do, do you?" David said, his eyes sparkling as he looked at me.

Before I could respond, he had reached out and taken my glass from me with one hand, and with his other, he was tickling me, making me giggle and squirm.

"See, you weren't very careful there, were you?" he teased.

I sat back up, still laughing, as he stopped tickling me. He leaned in and kissed me, and I could taste the sweetness of white wine on his lips.

"Or there," he said. He began to unbutton my shirt. "Or there. It seems you're actually very careless, Stella. I think I need to take you upstairs and teach you a lesson."

I didn't need asking twice. David had barely finished his sentence, and I was up and running for the stairs, giggling as I went.

David followed me. When he caught me, he swung me into the air and carried me the rest of the way to our bedroom, where he threw me down on the bed. He scrambled on top of me, and with a flurry of flying clothes, kisses, and caresses, within seconds we were both naked, and David was making love to me. He thrust into me, and I thrust with him, enjoying the feeling of fullness, enjoying being one with him.

When I orgasmed, I called out David's name, and when it was his turn to orgasm, he pushed his face against my throat and growled my name in a low, husky voice that sent shivers of pleasure through me once more.

Afterwards, we burrowed underneath the duvet and snuggled up together. We were both asleep within minutes.

I WASN'T in the best of moods by three o'clock Sunday afternoon when I finally decided to give up on my research on Cory. There was just nothing. Or at least nothing to suggest a motive for murder from what I could find on the internet, not without paying for it, which I knew was an option, but not one I wanted to try yet. None of the women he had dated whom I had been able to track seemed to be particularly scorned by him, and none of them were married, which ruled out both of my original theories.

I supposed that took me back to my profile of the killer theory. Some sad little man who wanted to be more like Cory. So maybe Alan had been right that the motive was jealousy. I probably should trust that he'd know more than me, considering he was an actual detective, and I was just a hobbyist playing at being one.

As I waited for my computer to close down, the landline on my home desk trilled to life for the fifth time that day. The first four times, there had been no one there when I took the call, and although I suspected this one would be the same, I couldn't just ignore it. I was too curious a person to leave things be.

"Stella Greene," I said as I picked up the receiver and held it to my ear.

Of course, my name was Stella Bell now that I was married, but I'd kept my maiden name for work, because I had just started to make a name for myself, and David didn't mind.

"I still love you. You know that, don't you?" a masculine voice said.

Andrew. Great. That was all I needed. I ignored what he had said.

"Did you call a bunch of times already today?" I demanded.

"Yes," he said. "I wanted to hear your voice. I thought that would be enough. But then I couldn't resist speaking to you. Come home, baby. Please."

"I am home. Stop calling me," I said as I slammed the receiver down. What was it they said about curiosity and the cat? I sighed.

I put my notes in the top drawer, shutting it before leaving my office and going downstairs.

David was in the living room on the phone. He looked up at me and said, "Dalton, I gotta go."

I flopped down next to him and sighed.

"What's wrong?" he said. "You look flustered."

"Andrew's been calling my office phone and hanging up," I said. "The last time he spoke and admitted that he'd called a bunch of times. I guess I'm a little shaken up hearing from him again."

"You don't need to get upset by him," David said. He jumped up and stared down at me. "Honestly, Stella. I promise I'll protect you. Stop letting him get under your skin; that's what he wants. I'm going to make you a cup of tea." He headed toward the living room door.

It occurred to me that he seemed more pissed off that I was upset about this than he did about the fact it was actually happening to me.

"I don't want a cup of tea," I said.

"It'll do you good," David said, his breathing harsh. "It'll calm you down."

He left the room, and I had to wonder if what he really meant was tea would calm him down. I supposed me telling him about Andrew stalking me bothered him, and it upset him that he couldn't protect me as much as he thought. I needed to assure him that I didn't believe that. I knew he'd do anything to protect me.

He came back in with a cup of tea and put it down on the coffee table in front of me. I didn't want it, but I decided it was easier to drink it than to argue about something so silly. After all, he thought he was helping me. I picked the tea up and swallowed a mouthful. I grimaced and shook my head.

"There's sugar in it. I don't take sugar in tea," I said with a frown. He knew that I didn't, so I couldn't figure out why he'd put it in there in the first place.

"I know, but sweet tea is what you need to calm you down," David said matter-of-factly as he sipped his own tea.

I opened my mouth to say I really didn't like sweet tea, but David looked more upset than before, and I decided to let it go because I didn't want him angry at me over it. "If you think I need it," I murmured and took a gulp of the too-sweet liquid. If I had to drink it, I'd do it quickly.

"You know I just want to make you feel better. I hate that he upsets you. If I get my hands on him, he's going to regret ever having met you." He practically growled that last part.

I brought the cup to my mouth and took another gulp of the horrible tea until it was gone. "Thank you. I hope you don't think that I doubt you, David. I trust you. I know you'll protect me from him. I just hate that he's stalking me in the first place. Do you think I should report him and get a restraining order?"

David wrapped his arm around me. "You're damn right I'll protect you. I told you, sweetheart, I protect what's mine. And no, I will handle it; you don't have to worry." He leaned in and kissed my temple. "Now, why don't you go on upstairs and take a nice relaxing bath."

His suggestion sounded good, so I nodded and left him to clean up the teacups. Maybe he was right. A bath would help relax me.

5

I checked my watch. David was due home in around half an hour, so I went through to the kitchen and switched the oven on, ready to put dinner in when David arrived.

I went back to my open laptop in the living room, but I found myself staring at the screen, my mind wandering. As much as Lonnie didn't like us taking work home, I wasn't satisfied with what I'd done for the Wally's Chocolates proposal. I just couldn't get what I wanted to come together, so I thought I'd look it over to see what I was missing. But I was distracted.

I kept thinking about Cory's murder, and then Andrew's stalkerish phone calls began to bug me, and that led to David's hurt reaction and that damn sweet tea that had tasted so awful. I hated that he thought I didn't trust him. I did. That didn't mean I wasn't still pissed off about Andrew contacting me. It didn't mean he wasn't still doing that shit. I also hated that I had to defend those feelings to David and stroke his ego over the whole sorry situation.

I shouldn't have had to drink that tea. I wasn't hysterical or in shock, and even if I were, sweet tea certainly wasn't going to help. But I'd been unable to tell him I didn't want it. I'd feared he'd get angry at me over it, and I really hadn't wanted to fight with him, so I just gulped the disgusting brew. It bothered me that I hadn't stood up for myself.

David was my husband. I shouldn't have to worry about upsetting him over something like whether or not I'd drink some stupid tea he brewed if I didn't like it. It was ridiculous. As much as I loved him, I was coming to see that David had a bit of a controlling streak, and that bothered me. I wanted to be a supportive wife and all that, but I didn't want to be afraid of what he'd do if he couldn't control my actions.

A knock on the front door startled me out of my thoughts, and I jumped up, checking the time. Had I drifted off into a world of my own for so long that David was home? No. Barely five minutes had passed since I switched the oven on. David must have finished work early and forgotten his keys. I was forever telling him to keep a spare key in the car in case I was ever working later than he was, but it seemed he hadn't listened. I couldn't imagine who else it could be if it wasn't David. I hadn't ordered anything, and we weren't expecting any guests.

I was halfway down the hallway when the knock came again, more insistent this time. I opened my mouth to shout out to David to hold his damned horses, but the person on the other side of the door spoke first.

"Stella? Come on, open up," the person said through the door. "We need to talk."

I felt my stomach turn ice cold, and the tiny hairs on the back of my neck and my arms stood up on end at the sound of the voice. It wasn't David. It was Andrew, and the way he was knocking again, it didn't sound like he was in any hurry to give up and leave without talking to me.

"I know you're in there. Please talk to me, baby. I love you," Andrew shouted.

Yeah, sure. He loved me so much that he cheated on me. Wasn't I just the luckiest girl in the world?

I was debating whether to tell him to go away or whether to just slink away quietly and ignore the pounding on the door, but then the knocking changed in its intensity, and the door rattled slightly in its frame. I realized that Andrew was no longer just knocking loudly. No, now he was kicking the door. That made me angry, and before I could think through whether it was a good idea or not, I was yelling at him.

"Stop that right now, you fucking lunatic," I yelled.

The kicking stopped, and there was silence for a moment.

"Stella? Open the door," Andrew said finally.

His voice was quieter now, more reasonable, but I still wasn't going to open that door. That wasn't going to happen.

"No. I have nothing to say to you," I said.

"Then just listen to me. I know I fucked up, but I love you, and I know that you love me too," he said.

"Are you insane?" I shouted, shocked that he could even think such a thing. "Any love I felt for you died the moment you fucked that whore. I'm married now, Andrew. I want you to leave me alone."

"Married?" Andrew said.

"Yes," I replied.

"You got married?" he repeated, louder this time. "Are you shitting me? Who the fuck is he? What right does he have to be touching my woman?"

I opened my mouth to respond, to tell him that I was not

his woman and he needed to leave, but he started to kick the door so hard I was genuinely afraid he was going to kick it down.

I snatched my cell phone from my pocket. "I'm calling nine-one-one if you don't leave by the count of three," I said in a moment's pause between kicks. I dialed the number and waited, my thumb hovering over the call icon. "One ... two ... three."

I waited, listening. Andrew was no longer kicking the door, but that didn't necessarily mean that he had gone. I moved closer to the door, hardly daring to breathe, and I peered out through the peephole. The area in front of the door was clear. I looked further afield and saw that the garden and the driveway were clear too. I breathed a sigh of relief. He had gone. At least for now.

I backed away from the front door, but I stayed in the hallway. I knew it was stupid, but I felt like if I stayed there, Andrew wouldn't come back. On the flip side, I thought if I moved, I would be letting him creep back without my knowledge.

The relief I felt at seeing that Andrew had gone was short lived. It was soon replaced by a dark, foreboding feeling that ate away at me. I didn't like this new development one little bit. Andrew coming to the house meant that he knew where I lived even after I'd moved from my old address. And if he had turned up here once, I knew that he wouldn't hesitate to do it again. A shiver went through me at the thought of that, and I knew I would have to tell David what had happened. He would be so angry, but I couldn't keep this from him, not now that Andrew knew where we lived.

There was always a chance that David would find out some other way, that Andrew himself might come back and say he had been here before. If that happened, I would look guilty simply because I had kept the visit from David. I also knew I had no other way of explaining the damage to the front door – there had to be marks where Andrew had been kicking it.

A shadow passed across the peephole, and I felt my heart beating in my throat. Andrew was back. And this time, he was going to keep kicking and kicking at the door until he got inside. He would know that my threat to call the police had been a bluff or they would be here by now. I jumped so much that I made a startled little "oh" sound as the front door opened. My fear turned to relieved laughter when I saw David closing the door behind him. He turned to me and frowned slightly. I probably looked like a crazy person just standing there laughing for no apparent reason.

"What's wrong? And why are you standing in the hallway looking like a scared little rabbit?" David asked.

I shook my head and got a grip of myself, cutting off my relieved laughter. I felt better now that David was here. I felt like I was safe from Andrew and anyone else who might turn up here wanting to hurt me. Not that I exactly had a list of people wanting to harm me.

"Come on through to the kitchen, and I'll explain everything," I said, conscious of the fact that David was still a bit early, and our dinner wasn't yet in the oven. This way we could talk, and I could prepare our meal at the same time.

David was taking his jacket off and putting his briefcase on the stairs, ready to take up to his office after dinner, as I walked into the kitchen. I picked up the casserole dish with the lamb stew already inside it and popped it in the oven. I was filling a pan with water for the potatoes when David came in.

"Well?" he said.

"Andrew was here," I said.

"Andrew your ex?"

I nodded, and he frowned.

"You had your ex over here while I was at work?"

"What? No. God no," I said, shaking my head violently when I realized he thought I meant I'd invited him over. "I didn't ask him to come here. I told you that I never want to see him again. He found out where I live somehow. He was banging on the door asking me to open it, saying he still loved me and all that crap. The bastard was kicking the door when I refused to talk to him. I thought he was going to get in—"

"He doesn't know the meaning of the word love," David said, cutting me off mid-sentence. He sounded incensed, and when I looked over at him, his eyes were blazing with unbanked fury.

Emotions were running high, and the look on David's face had me worried, so I decided to try to calm him down. "Tell me about it," I agreed as I put the chopped potatoes into the pan of water. I put the covered pan on the stove. I turned the gas on, adjusted it slightly, and then I went and sat down at the table opposite David, taking his hand in mine. "He didn't know we'd gotten married until today. Maybe he'll leave me alone now." I squeezed his fingers and smiled at him.

"He had better leave you alone if he knows what's good for him," David said, his voice low and angry despite the fact he was holding my hand gently.

"I was scared, David," I said. I needed to tell him about Andrew kicking the door so he knew. I was sure he hadn't registered what I'd said a minute ago about it. I worried that he was going to be pissed off, and I didn't want to see the anger on his face as I told him, so I got up and went back to the stove, pretending to be fussing about with the potatoes. "He kept kicking the front door, and I was worried he would get inside. I was so scared of what he might do to me if he did get in. I threatened to call the police in the end to get him to go away, which he did, and then you showed up a few minutes later. You must have just missed him."

I realized David had fallen strangely quiet. That hadn't been the reaction I had been expecting at all, and I turned around to see what he was doing. Had he even heard me this time? He was still sitting at the same place at the kitchen table. He was facing me, but it didn't feel as though he was looking at me. It felt as though he was looking straight through me. As though he could see through the walls and was now glaring directly at Andrew. I could almost see the waves of anger coming off him.

His shoulders were tense, his hands balled into fists on the table. His eyes looked glassy, not like his eyes at all. The anger was intensified in them. I had never seen such fury on someone's face before. He blinked and looked at me, and suddenly it felt like that burning anger, which was so intense, was focused on me, or maybe it wasn't exactly on me, but around me, because of me.

I swallowed hard, and I was suddenly more scared than I had been when Andrew was hitting the door. I resisted the urge to take a step backwards, knowing that even if I did, there was nowhere to go except up against the stove.

"I'm ... I'm sorry," I stuttered. "I'll pay for the door to be fixed, David."

"The door?" His eyes filled with confusion for a moment, then he shook his head, and the anger was back, but again, not exactly directed at me. "I don't give a fuck about the door."

I hadn't seen that coming. I wasn't quite sure what he was so angry about if it wasn't the door. Was it the fact that Andrew had been here? I stayed quiet, waiting for him to enlighten me as I watched him with caution. It felt like I was facing off with a cobra or a mountain lion. Some predator that would take me out if I made one wrong move, but as long as I kept myself still, I'd be fine.

"Did you call them? The police?" David asked, his tone full of controlled anger. I could hear it simmering there in the timbre of his voice.

I shook my head, but he didn't seem to be seeing me despite the fact he appeared to be looking at me. I choked out, "No. I ... I just threatened to. He went away before I actually had to make the call."

David's shoulders relaxed a little, and he nodded. He let out a breath, the tenseness of his muscles melted, and he moved toward me, gently taking my elbows and drawing me toward him. "Good. I don't want the police around here, Stella." The tone of his voice had changed; he sounded almost reasonable now.

"Well, neither do I, but like I said, I was scared. I didn't know what else to do," I said, keeping my voice steady and soft. "I knew you were on your way home and driving, so you wouldn't have been able to answer."

"You should have called me anyway," David said, holding me to his chest. "But don't worry about it now." He stroked my hair, and I could feel his heart beating beneath my cheek. "I'll sort it, and I'll see that he never bothers you again. And don't worry about the door either, I'll get it fixed."

"Thank you," I whispered, finally breathing more easily.

I wanted to ask him exactly what he meant by making sure Andrew wouldn't ever bother me again, because the truth was, to me, he sounded like he was going to hurt Andrew, or at least threaten him to the point that Andrew would retaliate, and they would have some sort of fight.

Previously, if I had been worried about them fighting, it was because Andrew was huge, and he was known never to walk away from a fight until his opponent was in a serious mess. Now, after seeing the fury on David's face, I was worried he might be the one to go too far.

I didn't think it was a good time to mention this, though. The last thing I wanted was an argument with David, especially when that kind of anger was so close to the surface. I would let him calm down and then pick the right moment to talk to him about it.

David pulled back and smiled at me, the look of ire completely gone from his face, and his shoulders and his hands had relaxed. He smiled, a warm smile that, despite everything, I returned.

I couldn't believe it. It was like he'd flipped a switch, and all that rage I'd seen in him was just gone. The man had to have massive control over his emotions to do that. Honestly, it was kind of impressive, even if it was a bit scary too.

"Well, that's sorted," he said cheerily. He shook his head and gave a little chuckle. "I can't believe you thought I'd be pissed off about the door or that I would expect you to pay for it to be repaired. Honestly, Stella, anyone would think you were afraid of me." He cupped my cheek and smiled as he stared into my eyes.

I laughed along with him, but the laugh sounded hollow to my ears. For a moment there, I *had* been scared of him, not because I thought he'd hurt me, but that he'd hurt someone else, because that much rage was indeed scary. But it was easier to laugh along than to cause a fight, and anyway, why make David feel bad? He obviously knew how to control that anger in him.

Besides, it wasn't his fault I was on edge. That was all on Andrew. I was still shaken up after my earlier encounter with him. Of course, now that he'd calmed down, I was sure that David hadn't meant he was going to make Andrew disappear in any sort of permanent way. He just wanted to reassure me that Andrew wouldn't be bothering me again.

"So what's for dinner? I'm starving," David said with a grin that lit up his face, showing the joy in his expressive eyes.

It was as though the last ten minutes hadn't happened while I had put the casserole in and started cooking the potatoes. Then it dawned on me that, of course, he knew what we were having for dinner. He was just trying to change the subject, to move us onto something a bit more palatable, that was all. It wasn't like he had actually zoned out for a moment there.

6

"So what happens now?" Brittany asked me as we sat in the little sandwich bar across the street from our offices, eating chicken salad sandwiches for our lunch.

Brittany and I had been friends since high school. She was fun, had a good head on her shoulders, usually anyway, and on top of that, she shared my love of true-crime mysteries.

We'd gone to different colleges, and our paths had been very different. I had graduated and come back to Gull Island when I got on at Master Marketing, and Brittany had dropped out of college to be with her boyfriend, who'd moved her to Florida.

He'd isolated her, and for a few years, we barely kept in touch. Then Brittany's life really turned upside down when he became violent. After a couple of stays in the hospital, she escaped with her daughter, Roxy, and moved back to town. She stayed off social media and kept to herself so he could no longer threaten her.

She had finally reached out to me again a few months ago, and I had asked Lonnie if Brittany could work with us as a paid intern while she finished her degree in marketing. Lonnie, sympathetic to her situation, had agreed. In fact, Lonnie had hired a handful of interns to see if any of them would be a good fit, and I really hoped Brittany would make the cut. She had absolutely nailed it so far, providing assistance to any of us who needed it and keeping the office in order.

"What do you mean?" I asked her.

"With the murder. You know, I'm so envious you got to see the actual crime scene." She grinned.

"Well, I've been through everything on social media that I can find pertaining to him. Anything else I want to know I'm going to have to pay for. It's not exactly cheap doing that kind of thing." I sighed.

"What kind of things do you have to pay for?"

"Credit reports and criminal history, any court documents he's named in. Any marriage or divorce certificates or wills he's listed in. Anything that caused him to have gained an enemy, you know?" I dug into my sandwich. "Though it's the killer I'm more interested in at this point."

"Really? How come?" Brittany was looking at me expectantly, her sandwich halfway to her mouth. "Do you even know anything about them?"

I leaned in closer. "Because what if it's not a one-off?" I arched a brow at her. "What if it's a serial killer?" I kept my voice really low because I didn't want anyone overhearing us. I didn't want to panic anyone with my theories.

Brittany nodded. "Do you think that's possible?"

"Yeah, that crime scene ... it seemed to me he enjoyed it. That he's just getting started."

Brittany shivered. "That's a scary thought. Do you think he'll target another man like Cory Elway?"

I shrugged. "I don't know. I think it depends on if the killing was more personal or if Cory simply represented what he wanted to convey in the killing. If he's just targeting vain, body-obsessed people, there's any number of people he could go after. If he targeted Cory for a specific reason and did that in a way to mock him or humiliate him ... then it could be the guy is going after other people on his hit list, and he'll do something equally heinous to them."

"How do you know this killer is a guy?" Brittany asked, her eyes wide with curiosity.

"I don't, not really, but generally this kind of murder is done by men. You know how women generally commit murder and why they do it." I gave her a wry smile.

She laughed. "Yeah, poison and it's usually very personal. But you never know." She took another bite of her sandwich and chewed it thoughtfully before taking a sip of her drink. "I knew him, you know."

"Yeah?" I hadn't known that.

Brittany smiled, a blush creeping up her neck. "I have a membership at the hotel gym. The membership includes the pool, and they let me bring Roxy."

"Oh, that's great." I smiled. "What was he like?"

She shrugged. "He was nice, but quite a bit of a flirt. He liked to date around."

"Did you go out with him?"

She nodded. "I did once, it was nice, but he really wasn't my type." She smiled and took a bite of her sandwich. "Not to change the subject, but how's the chocolate campaign proposal coming along?" Her eyes lit up. "Do you need any help?"

I grinned at her enthusiasm, allowing her to distract me. "Not yet, but you know I'll be asking Lonnie to assign you to me when I make the proposal and they accept it."

"I love how confident you are." Brittany tilted her head at me.

"Thanks. I really think it's going to be great. I've got so many ideas. I might run it by you before I show it to Lonnie if that's okay. I have to present it on Friday."

"Sure, you know I'm dying to see it." She sipped her drink again.

"So how's Roxy?" I asked, referring back to Brittany's three-year-old daughter.

Brittany smiled and nodded slowly. "She's good. I was worried she would have trouble settling somewhere new, but she loves it here, and she seems to be making friends at her nursery, and she loves to swim. It's great to have a place with an indoor pool where we can go in any weather. Of course, after Cory's murder, I don't know when we'll be going back."

I pictured cute little Roxy with her short blonde curls and her big blue eyes, a smaller version of Brittany. Her energy was infectious, and she was always laughing. What kid wouldn't want to be friends with Roxy? And as for her mentioning the hotel pool, I couldn't blame her.

"That's great that she's making friends," I said and meant it. "David and I will have to have you two over for dinner one night."

"Yeah, that would be good," Brittany said. "How is David, anyways?"

"He's great. Doing well at work. Personally, I think he's taking on too much with the company, but what can I say that will make him actually listen?" I said with a laugh as I shook my head ruefully. "I wish Dalton would take on more, but David always excuses his absences from work."

Brittany laughed like she was going along with my humor, but I could see that her eyes weren't sparkling like they usually did when she laughed, so I hurried on to try to gloss over the strange awkwardness.

"He talks me up to all his friends and clients, telling them how brilliant I am at marketing. I swear it's like he's my agent when we go to all those charity events and stuff he attends." I grinned. "And he's great to bounce ideas off of when I'm digging into different true-crime mysteries. He likes to debate with me about killers and their motives. I like that he's not creeped out by my hobby, you know?"

"That's good," Brittany said. "That he's supportive, I mean. But don't lean on him too much, okay? Don't lose that fierce independent streak you've always had."

"Never." I smiled, a little confused, but then it dawned on me why she was saying that. She didn't want me to get trapped like she had been with her ex.

Brittany was only looking out for me. She was distrustful of pretty much all men after her last disaster of a relationship, and she now thought men were only nice until they wore you down enough to be completely dependent on them, and then they let their true colors show. She had made no secret of the fact that she didn't think much of David or Dalton. She'd told me in no uncertain terms there was something off about both of them, and she was always telling me to keep David at arm's length or to not depend on him to always be as loving and supportive as I thought he was.

I usually let it go because she was my friend. I knew she was only looking out for me and that her outlook was shaped by her own awful experiences, but to be honest, the

David bashing was getting a little old. I didn't want to argue with her about David, so I stood up quickly before she could get anything else in.

"We'd best get going, or we're going to be late," I said.

Brittany frowned at me, but she grabbed her purse, and we hurried out of the sandwich bar.

"Since when do you care about being five minutes late from lunch?" She laughed as we headed back to the office.

Since it was easier to pretend I had started to care about the time rather than hear you tear strips off my husband, I thought.

"I want to catch Lonnie before she goes off for her break at two," I replied instead. Not a lie as such, but certainly not the whole truth.

When we got back to the office, Brittany went to her desk, and I made my way to Lonnie's office. I knocked and waited for her to call out for me to come in. As soon as she did, I stepped inside the office.

"Stella, what can I do for you?" Lonnie asked, glancing at her watch.

I moved to the other side of her desk and sat down despite not being invited to do so. I smiled at Lonnie. "Don't worry," I said. "This won't take long."

Lonnie had the decency to go slightly pink when it was clear that I knew she was checking her watch to see how quickly she could get rid of me.

"Sorry," she mumbled. "What's up? Is it about the campaign proposal you're working on?"

"Yeah," I said. "I wanted to run a few ideas by you to see if they were even feasible before I added them to my official proposal."

"Are you close to having it finished?" she asked with surprise.

Grinning, I nodded. "I should have it nearly complete by Wednesday, that way you can look it over, and I can make any changes before we present it on Friday."

"That's excellent, Stella. Seriously." She leaned back in her chair and crossed her arms. "Okay, lay them on me."

We spent the next thirty minutes going over the ideas I was considering and decided to add four of the five. I'd have this proposal knocked out and ready to go by Wednesday morning even if it killed me. I wanted this job more than I wanted anything, except maybe to figure out who killed Cory Elway, an issue that was still in the back of my head and probably wouldn't go away until the case was solved. It was probably better to focus on what I could control and what I actually was paid to do instead of the murder, but that didn't stop my brain from working on the puzzle every chance it got.

7

"Thank you," I said, smiling up at the waiter as he placed my plate in front of me.

David thanked him too, and then the waiter was gone as subtly as he came, leaving David and me alone once more. I felt a tingle go through me as David took my hand in his on top of the table and squeezed it briefly before letting it go. I loved our date nights. I had been worried they would stop once we got married, but they didn't, and I was so happy about that.

"I love this," I said, smiling at David as we ate our steak and chips.

"Yeah, it's nice," David said. "But then the food is always nice here."

I laughed softly, and David looked at me, a look of mixed confusion and amusement.

"I meant this whole thing is nice," I said, gesturing around us with one hand. "You know, us being out together and having a good time and everything."

"Oh, that," David said. He grinned at me. "There's nowhere I would rather be right now."

I felt exactly the same way. There was nowhere I would rather be and no one I would rather be with. I couldn't remember ever feeling this way, and I couldn't remember any of my exes treating me this well. Andrew certainly hadn't. Even before he decided to cheat on me, the magic had fizzled out. His idea of a date night was us sitting on his couch, watching a movie, and drinking a can of beer. Of course, some nights it's nice to do that, but not every night. Maybe deep down Andrew thought the same thing and blamed me for us becoming stuck in a rut. Maybe that was why he cheated on me.

Thinking about Andrew's idea of a date night got me thinking about his recent behavior too. I hadn't heard from him since the night he tried to kick my front door down. That was on Monday. It was now Saturday, and there had been nothing. No hang-up calls, no seeing him out of the corner of my eye while I was out, no following me anywhere. He was just gone. Honestly, it was great not having him bothering me on the daily, but it was also worrying me too. Kind of like waiting for the other shoe to drop. I wasn't really worried about Andrew's personal well-being – I had stopped caring a long time ago – I was more worried about what David had done to warn him off.

It just didn't ring true that Andrew would stay away now when he hadn't for so long. At first, I thought it was because I had told him I was married, but the more I thought about that theory, the more I figured he wouldn't care about that small detail. He had shown me already that fidelity meant very little to him.

David had gotten the front door replaced where Andrew

had dented the bottom panel of it as he was kicking it. I had asked David then about what he planned to say to Andrew to get him to stay away. He had just smiled and told me not to worry about it. But I was worried about it. I didn't want him getting into trouble.

I was hoping that whatever David had done, it was legal. Maybe it was. Maybe he had sent one of his flashy, super-expensive attorneys around there to threaten Andrew with some sort of legal action. It had to be that, or he had found another way to scare him off? But what could that be? Andrew wouldn't stay away because of a few threats to punch him or something similar. He was too stubborn for that, and he always said he could look after himself in a fight. So what had David said to get his way?

"Stella?" David queried.

I looked up and saw the corners of his mouth curled up in amusement. I figured he had said my name more than once as he tried to get my attention.

"Sorry," I said. "What were you saying?"

"It wasn't important," David said with a smile. "I was just commenting on how nice the steak is. What were you thinking about?"

"Actually, I was wondering what you said to Andrew because whatever it was, it worked. He hasn't made any attempt to contact me since that day he kicked the door," I said.

David's smile disappeared, and he frowned, his mouth puckered in a stubborn mewl. His gaze grew hard, and the crease between his brows deepened. "I told you that I would, Stella. I don't understand why you would doubt me. And it kind of pisses me off that you would be thinking about him when we're here together enjoying a nice time just the two of us."

I looked down, feeling slightly ashamed, though that wasn't what I'd intended; he thought I had been thinking about Andrew, when in reality I had been worried about David getting into trouble. "That wasn't how I meant for you to take my words. It didn't come out as I intended."

"Then what did you intend? Because to me it sounded as though you were thinking about your ex-boyfriend and missing his attention." He had withdrawn his hand from mine and now sat looking at me with a mix of anger and hurt in his eyes.

I licked my lips and looked down at my plate as I spoke. "I was just wondering what exactly you said to him to get him to stay away, or if maybe you'd gotten a restraining order or something. Because it's so good not having him calling or stalking me, not having to worry that he's going to show up at our house or at my job. And I wanted to know if there was a time limit on it, like with a restraining order, or if he's going to pop back up in the future. It would be nice to know if I have to be on my guard again. And I wanted to make sure that whatever it was you did wouldn't get you into trouble, legally." I glanced up through my lashes to see if he truly understood how much I appreciated him taking care of Andrew for me.

David's face softened again, and he smiled at me as he took my hand once more and brought it to his lips, kissing my knuckles. "Don't worry, sweetheart. I promise you Andrew is out of your life forever. There is no end date to this."

My heart lightened at his words. "Thank you," I said.

I still didn't quite have the answer I was looking for, and I didn't like the way David was so certain that Andrew was gone for good. There was something creepy about his certainty. He had obviously threatened Andrew or maybe his family. I hoped he hadn't resorted to threatening his family; it wasn't their fault Andrew was an ass.

I decided to let it go. He was trying to protect me. This was David; he wouldn't get physically violent with anyone. He'd just sic his lawyers on them.

I had just picked up my fork again when I became aware of a man talking at the front of the restaurant, his voice getting gradually louder. I looked up, surprised that someone thought that level of conversation volume was appropriate in a place like this.

I wasn't so surprised anymore when I recognized James Walker. He was everything that was wrong with people who grew up rich. He was everything that David and Dalton weren't. Entitled, spoilt, arrogant. Oh, and he seemed to think that the whole world owed him something. I supposed I could see why he thought that, because even now, the hostess whom he had been yelling at only moments ago was leading him and the young woman with him through the restaurant to a table one down from David and me.

I looked at David, my eyes wide. He looked back at me and rolled his eyes, and then we were both laughing.

"God, if we ever have kids and they turn out like that, I'm sending them back." David laughed, shaking his head in disbelief. "Mind you, he's in his twenties now, isn't he? He's old enough to know much better."

I nodded in agreement, although I still couldn't help but think if his parents had brought him up better, he wouldn't be quite so obnoxious. Surely, they could have taught him that people who actually have to work for a living aren't beneath him.

"If Dalton or I had acted in such a way—" David's face closed down for a moment, and then he shook his head and smiled.

"At least while he's in here sounding off, he's not speeding through town in that awful Camaro of his," I said. "I'm surprised he hasn't killed anyone yet."

"Yeah, that's true. Because the ones like him always get away without a scratch, and the person they crash into ends up dead or badly hurt," David said. "Anyway, let's not let him ruin our night, okay?"

I knew David was right, and I turned my attention back to him and forgot all about James Walker and Andrew. Instead I focused on being here in the moment with the man I loved.

"You never did tell me how your client reacted to your proposal," David said.

"There were a few parts he couldn't see the benefit of, but I fought for a couple of them. I really think it's important for the company to have a platform on all media, as well as ones that kids are on, because let's face it, they're a big consumer of those chocolates." I grinned. "Though there were some I could see I needed to let go."

"Which ones?" David asked.

As I was about to answer him, our waiter came by to see if we were ready to order our desserts. I nodded to David, telling him that yes, I was ready, and yes, I would have my usual dessert here – a slice of the strawberry and white chocolate cheesecake. David ordered my cheesecake and his own sticky toffee pudding with custard, and then he turned back to me.

"What were you about to say?" he asked again after the waiter had gone away with our order. "I thought everything you had in that proposal was perfect."

"Oh, well, they didn't like a few of the old-school art pieces; they want to go with something a little more modern. I thought those might have a nostalgic appeal, but they want to look forward not back. I still think playing up the history of the product is a good idea, but it's more what the client wants and making sure I can deliver that, which I showed I could do."

"So this Jordan guy seemed happy with it overall?"

"He really did." I nodded. "I'm proud of what I put together, and I'm hoping they'll choose to go with us. We won't know for a few weeks."

"You should be proud." David smiled. "You know I thought it was excellent."

I felt my cheeks flushing slightly as I beamed with happiness under David's praise. As much as I was confident in my ability as a marketing specialist, it was always nice to have my talent confirmed, especially by someone I looked up to such as David.

"You really think so?" I asked.

David nodded as our waiter returned with our desserts. He put them down, and we thanked him and dug in. I moaned with pleasure as the sweet, creamy cheesecake filled my mouth. David laughed at my enjoyment, he always said I derived pleasure from the simplest of things, and it amused him. I didn't know whether to be offended or not by that, but I always took it in fun. There was nothing wrong with appreciating the simple things in life.

Once the initial hit of the dessert was over, my thoughts turned from my work to my hobby. I'd been out getting coffee for the office and had run into Alan and a couple of other detectives at the shop. I had asked about the Elway case and talked to them about my theories. It hadn't gone well. Turns out detectives don't really like it when laypeople play amateur detectives. It was kind of depressing. "I ran my theories by Alan and a couple of other detectives earlier today."

David frowned at me, confused, and I realized he had no idea I had just had a whole change of subject in my head and had switched topics on him.

"I don't understand; you went to the police station?"

"Oh, no." I shook my head. "Let me back up and explain. Sorry, my brain got ahead of my mouth." I giggled and explained about the coffee shop. "So I told them my thoughts on Elway's murder, and they were kind of dismissive of me."

"Really?" David said, his eyebrows raised. "What part did they disagree with? Because from our discussions, I'd say your theories are pretty sound."

"The part where I'm not a real detective, and I shouldn't have seen the crime scene, let alone be thinking about it or the killer or anything even pertaining to it." I rolled my eyes. "Alan, of course, wasn't as dismissive, he at least listened, but he argued with me. Said I was wrong, that the murder had to be personal when I said I thought it was more likely to be a thrill kill for the killer."

"You know cops. They don't like to think anyone else is capable of putting the pieces of something together," David said, shaking his head.

"I also told them I didn't think the guy was done. That he's more than likely just getting started. They told me I needed to mind my own business and keep my voice down because the last thing they needed was some busybody stirring up the public and making them think there was a serial killer on the loose." I sighed and took another bite of my cheesecake.

"Honestly, sweetheart, I wouldn't let that encounter get you down. They're only jealous because you're half a dozen steps ahead of them," David said. "You are far cleverer than any of those idiots on the case, and they can't stand that a woman who isn't trained in police work is better than them at their job. That's why they're angry."

I felt myself flush again under David's compliment. I loved that he was so convinced of my intelligence. He was always my cheerleader. I couldn't ask for a better husband. "You think so?"

He nodded. "My money's on you solving this before them." He winked. "Ready to head home?"

I nodded as I wolfed down my last bite of cheesecake, and he waved to the waiter for the check.

I had a feeling that we were going to see another murder soon. It was just a matter of when, not if. Maybe Alan and the other detectives would listen to me when that happened. Because, as much as I didn't want to be right, I also wanted this guy caught.

8

I couldn't help but look over to the table where James Walker and his date had been seated when James began raising his voice once more. This time, it was a waiter catching the brunt of his temper. James was clearly already intoxicated, and the waiter was trying to tell him that he was being refused any more alcohol. The couple who had been seated at the table between David and me and James and his date had left, so now we had a front-row view of James's behavior.

"I can hear you. I'm not fucking deaf. I just don't care what you think. You're here to bring me drinks not argue with me. Fuck, it's not hard, is it? And yet you're making it so," James said.

He wasn't quite shouting, but his voice was above a normal speaking volume, and the language he was using to the poor waiter was shocking. I could hear his words slurring as he spoke, and it was clear that whoever had cut off James's drinks had made the right decision. It was just a shame the waiter was getting the flak for it.

"Please refrain from swearing at me, sir," the waiter said, not raising his voice in the slightest.

"Oh, now I'm sir, am I? Not some drunken idiot you don't want to serve. And, for the record, I wouldn't be swearing at you if you could do the one thing you're here for," James hollered.

"James, stop," his date said, her voice quiet and her face red with embarrassment. "You're embarrassing yourself."

"No, I'm not. I don't give a shit what anyone thinks of me," James retorted. "Especially not some service jerkoff."

"Whatever. You're embarrassing me," his date replied. "Can't you just get a soda?"

"Fine," James huffed. He turned back to the waiter, who was looking at James's date gratefully. "I'll have a tonic water on ice. Lime. Not lemon. Do you think you can manage that?"

"I'll give it my best shot," the waiter said.

I had to bite my lip to stop myself from giggling. I knew that if James thought people were laughing at him, he would only take it out on the waiter even more, but it was funny seeing the waiter make a sarcastic comment back, but with such a genuine tone, there was no way James could complain without looking like the most petty person in the room.

"Ugh, honestly, what do women see in that rude asshole?" David said quietly to me.

"I suppose when he's trying to ask a girl out, he puts on the charm," I said.

"Do you think he's good looking?" David asked me.

"He's not my type at all," I said. "Too much fake tan and hair gel. I want a guy who likes to make an effort, but I don't want a guy who takes longer to get ready than I do."

We both laughed.

"Seriously, though," I went on, "he's not repulsive or anything. I can see the appeal if a girl is looking to be wined and dined at all the most exclusive places."

"Ahh, so that's why you married me, then," David said with a laugh. "For access to nice places to eat."

"Obviously." I grinned.

"I'd better start researching, then." David laughed some more. "In the meantime, I have to go to the men's room."

He stood up, and I couldn't help but check out his ass as he walked away. God, he was sexy. I smiled as I watched him. Maybe James Walker wasn't the only one who had had a little bit too much to drink tonight, I thought, judging from the way my thoughts were heading into the gutter.

A crashing sound caught my attention, and I looked around to see that James was up on his feet, his chair on the ground beside him where he had knocked it down. If he had noticed, he made no effort to pick it up as he swayed from side to side, his eyes narrowed into slits as he looked around. His gaze landed on me, and as his date got up to right his chair, he started toward me.

Great.

"Hey," he said.

I debated ignoring him, but I figured that if I did that, he would just get louder, so I turned to face him.

"You know, you're a good-looking woman."

I glanced at him, but didn't say anything because I was hoping he would just go away.

"Fancy a fuck?"

My mouth dropped open at that. It was shockingly forward, and it was made worse by the fact he wasn't even a little bit quiet about his proposal.

"I'm married, so that's a hard pass," I said in as nonchalant a tone as possible.

"Oh, come on. We can go to the bathroom now, bang one out, and be back before your husband even notices you're gone," he slurred.

"James, that's enough," his date said. "Sit down. You're embarrassing her."

"Shush," James said, putting his fingers to his lips but missing them and, instead, poking himself in the cheek. "I'm scoring us a three-way for tonight, babe."

"I don't think so," I replied at the same time as James's date told him, quite simply, to fuck off.

Then she got up and left the table, heading for the door, her head held high.

James watched her go and took an unsteady step after her. "Jenn. Wait," he called out.

"My fucking name is Christie," the girl hissed over her shoulder, not bothering to slow down or wait for him.

James shrugged and turned back to me. "Oops," he said.

I glared at him, hoping he could see how uncomfortable I was.

He either didn't notice or didn't care. "So she was my guaranteed fuck for tonight, and now you've caused her to leave. So I guess that means you owe me a fuck instead, right."

"Get away from me. I owe you nothing. She left because you were embarrassing her, and then you were hitting on me right in front of her. Now why don't you take yourself home before you cause any more upset," I said, anger getting the better of me and making me say more than I normally would have.

"Well, aren't you the rude one," James said. "But I'll overlook your manners because you have nice tits. Just promise me the only time you'll open your mouth is to fit my dick in it."

I stared at him, appalled, unable to even speak.

But then an arm appeared around James's neck before I could get over my shock at his crude words and tell him in no uncertain terms where he could shove his plan. The arm belonged to David. I hadn't noticed him coming back from the bathroom. He kept his arm around James's throat, and with his other arm, he forced one of James's arms up his back.

James cried out and stopped trying to wriggle free.

I could see David's face over James's shoulder. His eyes held that hard, angry fury, and I was glad to see it directed at James and not me. Not that I thought he'd be mad at me; I hadn't done anything to draw this guy's attention. I'd just been sitting here waiting for my husband to return.

"Don't you ever approach my wife again," David hissed into James's ear, his tone so deadly and menacing that it made me shiver. "Because if you do, it will be the last thing you ever do. Am I making myself clear?"

"Yes. Yes," James shrieked. "I get it. I'm sorry, man."

"Don't apologize to me. Apologize to her," David said.

"I'm sorry," James said, looking at me, his glassy eyes wide with shock and pain.

I was somewhat alarmed to see he had unshed tears glistening in his eyes. David must have had a tight grip on that arm behind his back.

"It's okay," I said, swallowing hard as I nodded, desperate for the whole scene to be over.

Instead, I heard James gasp as David pushed his arm up even higher.

I cringed, braced for the snapping sound of his arm breaking, but it didn't come. Instead, David shoved James away from him. He stumbled, but he managed to right himself, and he staggered back to his table and half sat half collapsed into his chair.

David smiled at me; the heated anger of only a moment ago was gone, as though he had thrown a switch. "Are you ready to leave, or would you like a drink or anything after having to deal with that?" he asked.

I had a feeling that if we stayed, the thing with James would end up escalating further, so I stood up and smiled at David.

"I'm ready for home," I said.

David laid a couple of bills on the table to cover what we owed, and then took my hand. We made our way outside and waited for the valet to bring David's car around. There was a light breeze, but it was refreshing rather than cold; still, I didn't object when David put his arm around my waist and pulled me close to him.

"I hope you're not tired yet," he whispered, nuzzling my neck.

"Oh, far from it," I said, meaning it.

I wanted him, and his hand resting on my hip was doing nothing to make me feel any less like I wanted to fuck his brains out right here outside the restaurant. If anyone had asked, I would have said I didn't approve of violence, even against someone as uncouth as James Walker, but the truth was, seeing David defend me like that and overpower James so easily had turned me on in a way I had never expected it to.

By the time we got home, I was even more eager. As soon as we were inside and the door was closed behind us, I took

David by the hand and practically ran him up the stairs. I led him to the bedroom, and we stripped each other, our hands all over each other's skin, our mouths finding each other and melding together.

When we were both naked, David walked me over to the bed and pushed me backwards. I fell onto the bed and scooted backwards as David climbed onto the mattress between my legs.

I reached for him, pulling him on top of me, and I gasped as he slid inside me in one hard thrust. He kept thrusting, his hips working. I moved with him, pushing him further in, my hands grabbing at his ass and then moving up his back. Pleasure flooded through my body, and before I knew it, I was coming, screaming David's name as my orgasm tore through my body. I felt myself go rigid, my back arching and pushing my chest against David's.

Another wave of pleasure washed over me, and I bit down on my bottom lip, and then it was over, and I felt as though I were floating on a warm current as I came back down to earth. David was still pumping into me, and I could tell by the raggedness of his breath that he was on the edge of climaxing himself.

He lifted one hand and cupped my cheek, and then he ran his fingers down my neck and over my collarbone. He slammed into me again, and his face contorted as he climaxed. He ran his hand back along my collarbone and onto my neck, but this time, he didn't lightly tease me with his touch. Instead, he wrapped his hand around my throat.

Any leftover urge to make love again left me in a heart-beat. I didn't like the feeling of his hand around my throat one little bit. His hand was so big, and I knew how strong he was. He wasn't putting any pressure on my throat, but I still knew that if he wanted to, he could crush my windpipe. The knowledge that he had felt the need to hold my throat that way in his moment of most intense pleasure left me feeling cold and a little bit sick. Was it turning him on more to know that he could crush the life out of me if he chose to?

Finally, David's orgasm finished, and he leaned down and ran his lips over mine, his hand still on my throat. I didn't respond to his kiss, and he frowned and then rolled off me. He lay on his side beside me, his chest heaving as he tried to get his breath back and talk at the same time.

"What's wrong?" he asked. "I didn't hurt you, did I?"

"No," I said, shaking my head against the pillow. I almost said nothing was wrong, but then he might do the hand-on-my-throat thing again, and what if he got carried away and squeezed my neck? I had to tell him, and if he got upset, well, then that was how it was going to go. "I just ... I didn't like your hand around my throat, that's all." I bit my lip as I stared up at him, waiting for him to explode.

"Oh." He frowned. "I'm sorry." He ran his finger along my hairline, then down across my lips. "I just got caught up in the moment, thought I'd try something new. I thought you might enjoy the feeling of danger when actually you know you're perfectly safe," he said.

He sounded hurt rather than angry, and I immediately felt guilty for bringing it up.

"It's okay," I said quickly. "I get what you were doing. It just isn't for me, that's all."

"Okay, sweetheart, I understand," David said. "I won't do it again."

He leaned down, and this time when he kissed me, I kissed him back. He pulled back after a lingering kiss and smiled at me.

"Well, good night, then," he said, any trace of hurt gone from his face.

Within minutes, he was underneath the duvet and asleep.

I got beneath the duvet beside him and tried to sleep, but I kept almost falling asleep and then imagining I could feel a hand around my throat before waking with a start.

I told myself I was being silly. I wasn't in any danger. I never had been. It wasn't like it was some stranger I was having a one-night stand with. It was David. My husband. The love of my life. He had tried something, I didn't like it, and he had agreed not to try it again. There was no reason for me to be so hung up on it, even if it did make me feel queasy to think he wanted that sort of power of life and death over me.

I was overthinking it. I knew I was an overthinker, and there I was, doing it again. I had to let this go. I wasn't about to let one silly little thing ruin our whole marriage. If anything, it should be David who was feeling annoyed, not me. I had rejected something he had thought I would enjoy, and I just hoped that in doing that, I hadn't made him feel like I didn't trust him. Because I did trust him. I did.

Even so, I knew he had a control streak, and I wondered if maybe that hand on my throat had been more about control than about any pleasure he wanted to give me. It had sure felt that way, and that was probably why it was bothering me so much. But he'd agreed not to do it again, so maybe everything was going to be okay.

Still, it was a long time before I felt comfortable enough to fall asleep.

9

For the next two days, I told myself over and over again that I had overreacted about him putting his hand on my throat during sex. David had tried something he thought I would like, and when I said that I in fact didn't like it, he had apologized and promised not to do it again. What more could I really ask for? How else was he meant to know if I was going to like something other than to try it? He had tried new moves in bed before, and I had always liked them. I could hardly moan too much just because this one wasn't to my taste. The problem was it was still bothering me, and I couldn't shake the disquiet I felt about it.

Thankfully, by the time we had both been to work and come home and had dinner together on Monday night, I had almost convinced myself to let it go. All I was doing by obsessing over it was upsetting myself, and, really, if that was the biggest issue in our marriage, I was winning at life, surely.

"I'm going to go upstairs and have a shower," David said once the dinner pots were all cleared away. He kissed my neck and rubbed my arms.

"Okay," I said with a laugh. "That gives me a chance to watch some trashy reality TV."

"I'll make sure to stay a while in the shower, then, so there's no danger of me accidentally catching some of it," David said, also laughing.

He went upstairs, and I wandered into the living room. I sank down on the couch with the TV remote control. Getting comfortable, I flicked the TV on and began channel hopping until I found what I was looking for – *Love Island* – and I settled back against the cushions to watch it.

I had barely gotten comfortable when David's cell phone rang. It sat on the coffee table in front of me. I debated ignoring it – he could call back whoever it was when he got out of the shower – but when I saw the name of the caller on the screen, it got my curiosity up. Sandhurst Park. It rang a bell, and it took me a second to work it out. Sandhurst Park was a psychiatric hospital, but it wasn't for any old mentally ill person. No, it was for the criminally insane, those people deemed too dangerous to walk the streets, but at the same time too mentally and physically ill to be in a standard hospital. Sandhurst had major security surrounding it. Most of the patients there had been in the system and were still required by law to be supervised at all times due to their dangerous backgrounds. Why on earth would such a place be calling David?

I couldn't stand not knowing, and I had a feeling he wouldn't tell me what this was about, or if he did, it might be a watered-down version of the truth. Before I could change my mind, I snatched up the cell phone and swiped the screen to take the call.

"Hello?" I said.

"Hi there. May I speak to David Bell, please?" a woman replied.

"He's not available right now. May I ask who is calling, please?" I said.

"My name is Elaine. I am calling from Sandhurst Park," the woman replied.

"I'm David's wife. What exactly are you calling for?" I asked.

"The nature of the call is confidential, and I'm afraid you aren't on the authorization list, Mrs. Bell. If you could have Mr. Bell call me back as a matter of urgency, that would be great," Elaine said.

It was starting to sound like some sort of sales call to me, but the fact that the number this Elaine was calling from was already saved in David's cell phone made me think that there was more to it than that. I decided to play it off like I believed it was a cold sales call and see where that got me.

"I mean I can try," I said. "But I really don't think he will call back unless I can tell him what you want. He doesn't take unsolicited calls."

"Sorry," Elaine said. "Maybe you misheard me earlier. I'm calling from Sandhurst Park, where, as I am sure you are aware as Mr. Bell's wife, Mr. Bell's father is a resident."

That changed everything. So much for confidentiality. But I felt my heart skip a beat at the mention of David's father. I knew, of course, that he was in care somewhere and that David and Dalton paid for it, but I had no idea that his care took place in an asylum for the criminally insane. What the hell had he done to end up there?

"Oh, I'm so sorry," I replied as though David's father being a Sandhurst Park resident wasn't a surprise to me. "I did mishear you earlier. I'll have David call you as soon as he's free."

"Thank you, Mrs. Bell," Elaine said.

I ended the call and sat back against the couch again, *Love Island* forgotten while I tried to get my head around what David's father could have done in the past to end up in Sandhurst Park. I knew better than to ask David outright about it. If he wanted me to know, he would tell me in his own time. Or I would find out some other way eventually, but I really didn't want to break David's trust and go behind his back.

"Elaine called from Sandhurst Park about your dad," I said as David came back down the stairs after his shower and into the living room.

"What's the old bastard done now?" David sighed.

I was slightly taken aback by that, but I ignored his insult. He obviously had his reasons for not being his dad's biggest fan. And at least he wasn't angry with me for answering the call on his cell phone.

"I don't know," I said. "I did ask her, but she wouldn't tell me. She said it was confidential."

David rolled his eyes. "I'll check in with Dalton first; maybe the woman called him and filled him in." He picked his cell phone up and went back out of the room.

I had expected him to leave the room to make his call, but I was still disappointed that he had done so. I hoped he was going to tell me what had happened once he found out what the trouble was. He couldn't just leave me in the dark about it now that I knew something had happened, could he?

He came back into the living room a few minutes later and sat down beside me. He dropped his cell phone down on the coffee table and sighed as he draped an arm across the back of the couch.

"Dad has some sort of lung infection," David said. "Dalton said it's a fifty-fifty chance of whether he will make it or not."

"Oh, David, I'm so sorry," I said as I turned into his side to comfort him.

He turned his body more toward me and gave me a weary smile. His arm dropped from the couch to my shoulders and surrounded me, pulling me close to him.

"Don't be sorry, sweetheart," he said, kissing my temple. "That's only the staff's opinion. They obviously don't know Ambrose Bell like I do. Trust me, it'll take more than a lung infection to stop that one. If there was a ninety-nine to one chance against him, I would still put my money on him winning."

"So did you talk to the woman at Sandhurst, or did you talk to Dalton?"

"Both, actually. Dalton had seen that they called, but he hadn't bothered to answer. Pretty typical of him." He smiled, as if this amused him.

THE NEXT MORNING, I went downstairs after getting showered and dressed. I made my way to the kitchen to grab a coffee before I had to leave for work. I found David already there with a mug of coffee. He must have heard me coming because, as I entered the kitchen, he was already pouring a cup for me. He held it out to me, and I took it gratefully.

"Thank you. You're wonderful."

He smiled, but he looked tired, and the smile didn't light his face up as it normally did. "Do you want some toast or anything?" he asked.

"No, I'm okay, thanks."

There was something off about him this morning that was more than him being tired, and I couldn't put my finger on what it was. When it came to me, I felt pretty stupid that it had taken me so long to notice something so obvious. Instead of him being dressed in one of the perfectly tailored suits that he usually wore when he was heading off to the office, he was wearing jeans and a more casual cream-colored shirt.

"What's with the clothes?" I asked, frowning.

"Well, if I were to go out without any clothes on, I think I might be arrested, don't you?" David said, his smile widening and finally lighting up his face.

I couldn't help but laugh even as I shook my head.

"You know what I mean," I said. "Why are you wearing casual clothes instead of work clothes?"

"Because I'm not going to work. At least not this morning. I have to go to Sandhurst Park and sign some forms and stuff for my dad," he said.

"Oh," I replied. "Give me a minute, and I'll call Lonnie and tell her I'll be in late today. You could have given me some warning."

David was already shaking his head before I had even properly finished talking.

"No, that's not necessary. You go to work, it's fine. It's a long drive, and all I'm going to be doing is signing a few papers. I'll probably see my dad for not more than five or ten

minutes. Any longer than that and we'll end up arguing,"
David said with a sigh.

"I kind of wanted to meet your dad," I confessed, wrin-
kling my nose as I looked at him over my coffee mug. "I
thought it would be nice getting to know him. He's a part of
my family too now that we're married."

"Oh God, please don't ever think of him that way," David
said, and I was sure I saw him shudder at the thought of it.
"Honestly, sweetheart, he's not a nice person. He has an
unpleasant personality – that's the politest way I can think of
to put it – and I don't want you getting hurt."

I wanted to tell him that I was a grown woman. I
wouldn't get hurt by a few harsh words. But it was obvious
that, for whatever reason, David didn't want me to go along
with him today, and I knew that I had to respect that, regard-
less of whether I agreed with him or not.

"Cool," I said after a pause. "I'll go to work as always. Call
me if you need me, yeah?"

David nodded. "Don't worry. I will," he said.

"Good," I said. I stood up and drained the last of my
coffee, and then I took the mug to the sink and left it in
there. I came back over to the table and squeezed David's
shoulder.

"Remember, he's sick. Promise me you'll be nice to him,"
I said.

David squeezed my hand and nodded, but I couldn't
help but notice that he didn't say the words *I promise.*

"David?" I questioned.

"Hmmm?" He looked up at me, his eyes haunted.

"You okay?"

His expression cleared, and he smiled again. "Yeah, I'm

all right, sweetheart, just ... thinking about some things. You have a good day."

"I love you," I said, smiling back.

"I love you too."

As I headed off to work, I couldn't help but wonder exactly what it was he'd been thinking about that put that haunted look in his eyes.

10

I sat at my desk, working on one of my more minor accounts, setting up some ads to go out over the course of the next week. My mind replayed my conversation with David, and I thought about his father and what the man could have done to have ended up in Sandhurst Park.

I wondered if whatever it was happened to be the reason for the haunted look in his eyes. How did he deal with knowing his dad was in a hospital for the criminally insane? Why hadn't he ever told me? Didn't he realize I would know what kind of place it was? I wondered if he knew he didn't have to deal with it on his own. I sighed. I supposed he didn't actually deal with it on his own since he had Dalton.

The brothers were close, being twins, but they were so different. At least to me. Where David was loving and charming, Dalton was cold and calculated. I supposed David had that side too in his business dealings, but never toward me. Dalton always seemed that way though. He just wasn't very personable. Still, ever since David and I had gotten together, Dalton had been friendly toward me. More friendly than I'd seen him with anyone else at any rate.

I wondered if it had something to do with their dad. Maybe whatever he'd done had affected David and Dalton in different ways. Maybe that was the reason Dalton was stand-offish with most people. I nodded to myself; that had to be it. Something had to have happened to him. Maybe some girl had jilted him after finding out their dad was locked up, so he closed himself off. If that was the case, I didn't blame him.

A door slammed somewhere in the office, startling me, and I blinked as I looked up. Coming out of my thoughts, I realized it was nearly noon. I glanced toward Brittany's desk, but she wasn't around. Nearly everyone was gone, I assumed to lunch, and figured I'd better go take mine too. As I left the office, I decided to head over to a café closer to the police department. I had an ulterior motive in going there, of course. I was hoping to see Alan. I knew he liked to grab lunch there too, and I wanted to get an update on the case.

When I walked in, I saw I was right. Alan was seated in a booth next to the big windows. I could see the worry lines around his mouth; he looked tired and old all of a sudden.

"Hey, Alan," I called, giving him a wave.

He looked at me warily but waved back. "Hi, Stella, you're a bit out of your usual neighborhood for lunch."

I smiled and sank down across from him. "Well, you know me ... I was hoping for an update on the case you're working." I widened my smile, hoping he'd give in and satisfy my curiosity.

Alan sighed. "We've got no new leads. The top brass are getting impatient." Alan paused as a waitress came over and took my order. "Looks like we're starting over again, trailing back through every little bit of evidence we've collected so far to see if we've missed anything."

"Do you think you have?" I questioned.

"Not really. And I've been considering your theories too, not that I've shared that with the others. Better than what we've got so far, honestly," he muttered.

His words made me smile, but it wasn't a pleasant topic for lunch, considering he was saying he was thinking I was right about it being a serial killer.

"I hate waiting around to see if he'll kill again. That scene was heinous enough."

I couldn't have agreed more. "You know I'm always around to bounce ideas off of."

Alan smirked. "You just want more info to feed that hobby of yours."

I laughed. "You're not wrong."

The waitress brought our lunches over, and we chatted about other things as we ate.

I said my goodbyes a little while later, then headed back to the office.

"Stella? Lonnie wants you," an intern named George said, coming to stand by my desk a short while later.

"Thanks," I said.

I wondered if she'd heard from Max Jordan about the Wally's Chocolates account and that was why she was calling me to her office. Excitement filled me at the thought that I could be starting on the campaign for real within the hour.

I knocked on her door and poked my head in. "You wanted to see me?"

"Come in." She smiled. "I was wondering if you'd heard from Jordan?" Lonnie asked once I sat down opposite her.

I shook my head, disappointed when it became obvious

she didn't have anything for me on it. "I was kind of hoping you'd heard from him."

"Nope, sorry. I wish I had. Still, they aren't the only client in town." She picked up a folder. "I have this one for you," she said.

"Oh, yeah?" I prompted her.

"It's the car dealership over on West and Main. They want to streamline some of their ads and add in some social media coverage. Figured you might want something to work on while we wait to hear which way the Wally's project is going to fall."

"That would be great. I can only set up so many ads for Caplin's Grocery Store at a time." I laughed, taking the file folder.

Lonnie smiled, and then her face grew serious. "Hey, have you heard of Brian Walker?"

"Well, sure," I said. "Is there anyone on Gull Island who hasn't heard of him?"

Brian Walker was a very wealthy local man. I didn't know a whole lot about his career, only that he had made his fortune in real estate. He had grown up with very little and worked his ass off to get to where he was now. He regularly donated large sums of money to various charities, was well known and well liked locally.

"Is he wanting to hire us?"

Lonnie shook her head. "No, this isn't work related. Just ... you know his son, James?"

I groaned inwardly. Everyone on Gull Island knew James Walker too, but for the opposite reasons for how they knew his father. And it hadn't been that long since that night in the restaurant when he had propositioned me.

I nodded, trying not to show my distaste, but it must have been clear on my face because Lonnie laughed.

"Don't ever play poker, Stella," she said, still laughing and shaking her head.

I didn't feel the need to explain to Lonnie why I had a personal issue with James, but I wondered why she was bringing him up. "I'm not much of a poker player." I smiled.

"Anyway, I brought it up because I just heard that James has been reported missing."

"Really? How did you hear that?"

"My husband is friends with a guy named Greg who works with Brian. He told me. Isn't that crazy? Like, how does someone so connected go missing?" Lonnie shook her head.

"He probably isn't really missing; he's probably drunk somewhere with some girl," I said, thinking of that night in the restaurant.

"I don't know. Greg was pretty shook up over it. Brian is a mess, apparently. Said they were going to the press because the cops aren't doing anything about it."

"Wow, guess it is pretty serious if they're going to the press for help." I frowned as I thought about that night again. "You know I met him. Well, sort of."

"Who? James?"

I nodded. "David and I were out for our date night, and James and a woman showed up at the same restaurant. He was drunk and loud and rude."

"I've heard he gets that way when he drinks. Greg said Brian had been trying to get him into AA."

"Anyway, David got up to use the men's room, and James decided that was a good time to hit on me." I rolled my eyes.

"What?" Lonnie gasped. "In front of his date?"

"Yeah. He made some really rude comments, and she left, but he kept it up until David returned and put a stop to it." I folded my fingers together in my lap and looked down. "I swear I thought David might break his arm with the way he was holding it behind James's back, but he didn't. He made him apologize and told him never to come near me again."

"Maybe James learned his lesson and took off for another part of the state so he'd be away from you," Lonnie said with a grin.

"Probably not." I giggled. "The guy was so drunk, I doubt he even remembered the encounter the next day."

"How is David doing?" Lonnie asked, changing the subject.

I gave her a warm smile. "He's good. We're good. We've got a fundraiser to go to this coming weekend. I'm looking forward to dressing up."

"Well, hopefully by then we'll know if we've got the Wally account."

"Fingers crossed," I said, holding up my crossed fingers with a wink. "I'm gonna go get on this account," I added, holding up the file, "unless you need anything else?"

"Nope, I'm good. Thanks, Stella."

WHEN I GOT HOME, I clicked on the TV in the kitchen and turned to the news. I was hoping there would be something about the Elway murder, or maybe about the James Walker missing case. I listened as I started prepping dinner. I decided I would make spaghetti with homemade sauce and garlic bread.

The news reporter was going over random things going on in town, talking about up-and-coming events and the like, as I started pulling out ingredients. From there they turned to sports, which I tuned out as I began adding things to the pot for the sauce.

It wasn't until the sauce was simmering that I heard the reporter say something interesting.

"Now, we bring you a press conference given by Mr. Brian Walker over his missing son, James Walker. As many of you know, Mr. Walker is well known in our community and is a big contributor here on Gull Island. Our hearts go out to him at this time. Let's take a listen."

I stopped stirring and turned to the TV to see Brian Walker, his wife, and the young woman I'd seen with James at the restaurant.

"Good evening, as many of you know, I'm Brian Walker. My wife and I are asking for your help. Our son, James, has gone missing. He was due to join us for dinner three nights ago, and from what we have been able to put together, James hasn't been seen since Monday evening."

To me that didn't mean much. So he didn't go to a family dinner? That didn't mean he was missing. He could have gone off on his own.

"We filed a report with the local police; however, I sense they aren't treating this with the appropriate urgency. I am a very wealthy man. I fear that James has been taken because of who I am. If the person who has taken James is listening, I will pay anything to get him back whole and in one piece."

I watched Brian's wife put her hand on his arm, presumably to calm him.

"Please, we implore you. If anyone has any information on the whereabouts of our son, please come forward."

A picture of James leaning against his Camaro and smiling at the camera flashed on the screen.

"The police believe that James went off on his own because his apartment was tidy and there is nothing to say that someone has taken him. However, we know our son. He wouldn't leave without letting one of us know. He wouldn't just vanish."

That I believed. James was a belligerent kind of man. He'd be vocal about where he was going.

"On top of that, his girlfriend, Christie," Brian said, indicating the woman I'd seen James with at the restaurant, "has been through his apartment, and nothing of his is missing. All of his clothes are there, all of his toiletries, everything. There's nothing to indicate that he left of his own accord."

That was interesting. What man would leave without at least taking an overnight bag with his shaving stuff, toothbrush, and the like? As I thought about that, my attention was drawn back to the sauce I was making. It was bubbling, and it needed my attention. I gave it a stir and added in the fresh basil.

The press conference ended, but I continued to think about James. I had assumed that if James had left of his own accord, there was a fair chance he was with another woman. The way she'd left him at the restaurant led me to believe that was a definite possibility. Though it did seem odd to go without his things. So I began to wonder if something nefarious had happened to him. Could he have been kidnapped? He was a grown man; how would that even happen? Had he been so drunk he made it easy for them?

I didn't know how much money Brian Walker had, but it had to be multimillions at the very least. That could be a motive, but he'd said in the press conference that James had been missing for three days. I'd have expected if it was a ransom kidnapping, they'd have heard from the kidnapper by now.

So what did that leave? I frowned as the idea of a serial killer flashed through my head, and the way that Elway's murder had been staged. I sucked in a breath. Cory Elway and James Walker were kind of similar. They were both well known for their womanizing ways.

I had said from the beginning that I didn't think Elway's murder was a one-off, that it felt like the start of something. What if I was right and Gull Island had its very own serial killer, a serial killer who had made it their purpose to rid the world of womanizing men?

I needed to call Alan and go over this idea with him. He might not listen to Mr. Walker, but maybe he'd listen to me. Or maybe I was grasping at straws to make a connection.

I sighed and went back to making dinner.

11

I heard the door open, and I hurried to slice the garlic bread. Everything was cooked to perfection, and I was ready for a nice relaxing evening in with my husband.

"Sweetheart?" David called from the hallway.

"In the kitchen," I answered as I turned to set the table.

David strode in and wrapped his arms around me from behind. "Something smells delicious."

I grinned and turned in his arms. "I made spaghetti."

"With your famous sauce?" He took a deep breath and smiled.

"Of course." I laughed as he leaned in and kissed me. "It's ready, but do you want to go up and change first?"

He shook his head, and his smile fell away. "Unfortunately, I have to go back to the office later."

I pulled from his arms and turned toward the stove. "How come?"

"New client in Japan. I need to have a Zoom call with them, and because of the time zone, well, that means going back to the office."

I sighed. I hated that. "Okay, well, we can at least enjoy dinner together, right?"

"Absolutely." He nodded. "What can I do to help?"

I shook my head. "It's all done. Just wash up and have a seat." I smiled over my shoulder at him.

"That, I can do." He chuckled as he moved to the sink and washed his hands.

A few minutes later, I set our plates down on the table and joined him. "So, other than this new client, how was your day?"

He took a bite of the spaghetti and moaned over it, which made me grin. "Better now. This is delicious."

"Did something happen?" I questioned. He seemed weary and frustrated.

"Just Dalton. He's been busy on a side project, and it's adding to my workload."

"A side project?"

"Some pet thing of his." David shook his head, dismissing the topic. "How was your day? Did you hear from the chocolate company?"

"Not yet. I worked on a new project though, for a local car dealership."

"Sounds fun," David said with a smile.

"Did you hear the news?" I asked as we continued to eat.

"What news?"

"Remember that guy from the restaurant? James Walker?"

David paused, his face becoming almost blank. "He hasn't bothered you again, has he?"

"What? No. He's missing. His family was on the news earlier."

"Hmmm," he murmured and returned to his food.

"So I started thinking."

He smiled and looked up at me. "Did you?"

I nodded. "I was thinking, what if his being missing is connected to Cory Elway's murder?"

His smile grew. "Could be. You never know."

"I mean, they are both womanizers." I paused. "So, what if this killer had a run-in with James?"

"It's a sound argument." David nodded. "Though he probably just went off on vacation without telling anyone."

"No, I don't think so. Nothing from his place was missing. Not even his toothbrush. Though his car is missing too," I said, recalling how they'd mentioned that at the tail end of the press conference as I had turned back to the sauce.

"Stella, you know he's got money coming out of his ass." David laughed. "Like, he could buy a new one."

I deflated. "Yeah, that's true. So you don't think I should call Alan and tell him my theory?" I asked as a smile twitched on my lips.

He met my gaze. "Maybe wait for more information? It's a sound theory, but it's just speculation at this point. He'll accuse you of jumping to conclusions."

I sighed. David was right. It was too soon to share my theory.

We finished dinner, and then, after we cleaned the kitchen, David returned to his office.

Later that night, I lay in the darkness, trying to sleep. It was after midnight, so it really shouldn't have been so hard to drift off, but my mind kept going to exactly where I didn't want it to go, which was wondering where David was. He had told me he had to work late so he could take a Zoom call with a potential new client in Japan. It had never really been something that happened before, so it wasn't like this pattern of behavior had always been the case.

If it was just this once, I wouldn't be worried at all, but these kind of office late nights seemed to be happening a lot lately.

David always seemed to be working late or in meetings and unavailable if I called the office nowadays. I couldn't help but wonder if he was having some sort of affair. But even as I thought about the possibility of it, I pushed the idea aside. Surely David's sex drive was too high for someone who was cheating on his partner?

He would come in after those late-night meetings, slip into bed beside me, and kiss my neck, his hand moving over my body until his fingers were between my legs, and I would wake up in pleasure to his touch. Yes, if anything, David was more passionate than usual lately. He seemed to be more into sex and more into me, and I wasn't complaining about that. After all, I was the one who got to experience the most amazing orgasms every night.

But I had to wonder what had changed. In my less paranoid moments, I thought that maybe David was using sex as a stress reliever. It would certainly make sense of how intense he was and how rough our sex had been lately.

I was beginning to think that, especially with the Cory Elway murder and now the James Walker disappearance, I had spent too much time thinking about unfaithful men. Their behavior was starting to get into my head and make me paranoid about my own relationship despite the fact that David had never done anything to make me think he was being unfaithful before. It was simply the late nights coupled with my own insecurities, that was all.

Besides, he'd said that Dalton was causing a heavier

workload for him at the office. Surely that was the reason for all of this. I was being ridiculous thinking he might be having an affair. I didn't need to worry, right? David loved me.

I heard the front door open, and I relaxed slightly. David was home. At least after he had fucked me, I figured I would relax and finally be able to get some sleep.

12

I was sitting at my desk, debating whether to call Detective Kellerman to see if I could squeeze anything at all out of him, when my phone rang.

"Stella Greene," I said as I took the call.

"Hello, Ms. Greene, this is Damien Jones. I run the restaurant Graveyard Grill, which is next door to the Laughing Pumpkin, and I was wondering if we could meet to discuss hiring your firm?"

I knew the Graveyard and the Laughing Pumpkin were both Halloween-themed businesses and drew a lot of attention, sometimes from the wrong element since it was on the edge of town and a bit out of the way. "Of course, I'd be happy to meet with you, but how did you get my office number? You know I'm just an employee—"

"Oh, sorry, I should have mentioned. I ran into your boss this morning at the coffee shop, and she told me to give you a call."

"I just wanted to be sure Lonnie knew. I'd be happy to

meet you at the Graveyard. I haven't been there in a long time."

"Well, we've got a new menu and new management, and that's part of the reason why I want to meet with you."

"That sounds great; what time suits?"

"Whenever you get the chance to come see us would be fine. I'll even serve you lunch."

"That would be nice. I'll finish some things up here and then head over there, Mr. Jones."

I got up and headed for Lonnie's office. Knocking on the door, I poked my head in and said, "You got a minute?"

"Sure, what's up?"

"Did you talk to a Damien Jones this morning?"

"Oh, yeah, I did. Did he call?"

I nodded. "I just wanted to make sure it wasn't a crank. He's asked me to meet him over at the Graveyard Grill."

"He mentioned that was his business. He's made some changes and wants to get the word out."

"I'm going to finish up on the dealership account; then I'll head over there. I don't know how long I'll be."

"Don't worry!" Lonnie smiled, reading my mind. "If I hear from Jordan, I'll call you."

"Perfect. Thanks, Lonnie."

Later, I drove toward the Graveyard Grill and the Laughing Pumpkin, which was a bit of a dive bar. It was known for being pretty rowdy. There was also a massage parlor, whose workers wore lingerie, and everyone knew they offered "happy endings" but pretended they didn't. Across from the parking lot where these businesses resided was one of those large storage lots. The kind with all the mini units that you could rent for a monthly fee. Only I would never rent one there, because the neighborhood had always been a bit suspect.

If you kept driving on the road between those businesses, you would end up at the beach. I used to make the trek on my days off to enjoy the peace of the water lapping against the shore. The beach was a nice area, but to get to it, you had to go through this rougher area where I was now, so I didn't go very often anymore.

I was just about to pull into the parking lot of the Graveyard Grill when I noticed something going on at the storage unit place. A guy I knew, Dennis Coates, who used to be a cop but had turned to private investigations, was standing there with Alan, and there was police tape around the area. I parked my car and got out, approaching them.

"Dennis?" I said, smiling hesitantly. "What are you doing here?"

"I should be asking you that, Stella. How did you find out about this?" Alan asked, his tone severe.

"Hey, Stella. Good to see you," Dennis said with a nod. "Brian Walker hired me to find his son, James. Tracked him here." He nodded to the storage unit.

I frowned. "Alive?"

"Nope. Really dead."

"Damn," I murmured and then glanced at Alan. "Same as Elway?"

Alan frowned hard at me. "Stella—"

"I've been meaning to call you. I had a theory that whoever murdered Elway had taken James Walker too."

"Good intuition, if what I heard about the Elway murder is true," Dennis answered.

"Stella, why are you even here?" Alan insisted, clearly

frustrated by how this conversation was going. "This is the opposite side of town from your office."

I shrugged. "I've got a meeting with the owner of Grave-yard Grill. Saw you two and wondered if it had anything to do with the case."

"And you were just too nosy to go about your business." Alan huffed, but I could sense him relenting a little.

"Can I see the crime scene?" I asked, chancing my luck.

"I shouldn't be letting you anywhere near it," Alan started with a resigned sigh.

"But?" I murmured, ever hopeful.

"But I know you'll badger me until I do. Fine, but the minute I hear the others arriving, you're gone, got it?"

"Of course." I grinned as I followed him and Dennis.

We reached the door and entered the unit. It was surprisingly cool inside, and I saw a large steel shutter at the other end of the building that was rolled up, leaving one wall gone, the inside of the place exposed to the elements.

"I hope you have a strong stomach, Stella," Dennis said. "Because I like to think I have, and I'm not ashamed to admit I lost my breakfast over this one."

I swallowed hard, feeling nervous but wanting to keep my cool. "Generally speaking, I'm not particularly squeamish, but never say never, right?" I said with a shaky laugh that sounded more nervous than I intended. This was only my second in-person crime scene. All the others had been photos; being there for real was so different.

We were walking as we talked, and Dennis stopped and pointed ahead. "It's that one."

"You're not coming in with us?" I asked, surprised.

He looked a little green. "Nope, I've seen enough to last me the next decade. Not gonna lie, it's grisly."

"He's not kidding, Stella." Alan handed me some gloves. "It's very disturbing."

I pulled the gloves on and looked at him. "I'll be okay. I saw Elway; how much worse can it be?"

Alan pursed his lips and shook his head as he gestured toward the door.

I pushed the door open, and the first thing to hit me was a wave of heat. The second thing was the smell. It was thick and cloying, sweet and rotten. Whatever had happened to James, it was clear he had been here for a few days. I pulled the front of my shirt up to cover my mouth and nose and stepped into the unit.

In the center of the otherwise empty unit was James's famous Camaro. It was immediately clear that the unit had been rented solely to house James's car and body. I stepped closer to the car. The windows were smeared with something, and I couldn't see inside, so I made my way slowly around it to the front so I could peer in through the windshield.

I almost wished I hadn't looked, as my gorge rose, and my stomach clenched. I looked quickly away. My mouth flooded with saliva. I swallowed and swallowed again. I kept swallowing until I was confident I wasn't going to be sick.

"I warned you it was bad."

I glanced at Alan and nodded, then turned back to the windshield. I saw instantly why I hadn't been able to see through the windows; they were smeared in blood and gore. The blood was turning brown with age; the gore had small chunks of black stuck in it.

James's body was in the driver's seat. The seat was pushed back, and it was reclined a little. James was naked, and I couldn't help but notice that his penis was blackened and blistered. It was clear it had been burned. Perhaps with a lighter? That would explain how the burns had stayed localized.

I looked away from the corpse's blackened genitals, and I was confronted instead with his head, which was resting on his stomach, his hands pressed to it to hold it in place. One eyeball hung down his cheek, attached only by a stringy red nerve. The raw hole was turning gray around the edges, where the flesh was rotting away. His two front teeth were gone, and judging from the blood on his chin, they had been pulled out either while he was still alive or quickly enough after his death that his blood was still pumping.

I didn't want to look any higher. I had seen more than enough without needing to see the stump of James's neck where his head should have been, but I couldn't help myself. It was as though my eyes had a mind of their own, and its sole purpose was to traumatize me.

I looked at the bloody stump, and that was when I lost my fight with my stomach. I ran out of the unit, brushing past Alan, made it across the walkway, bent over double and retched into the grass. I threw up twice and then I kept retching despite my stomach being empty. Finally, I felt like I was done, and I straightened up, wiping strings of saliva away from my face.

"You okay?" Alan asked as he and Dennis moved toward me.

I wiped my mouth. "That was ... something else," I said.

"You were warned," Dennis said. He smiled, and his face changed from stern to friendly. "Honestly though, hats off to you for staying in there as long as you did. I really thought you'd run out screaming in seconds."

"Oh, trust me, I wanted to," I said.

We both laughed grimly, and then we headed away from the unit. I was glad to be back in the fresh air underneath the shining sun. The one open wall didn't seem to let in enough air after what I had seen. Until I got right out of the building, I felt as though the smell of James's rotting corpse was clinging to me.

"You need to go, Stella. CSI is going to be here soon. And don't be telling any reporters what you saw. It could cost me my job." Alan glowered at me. "Hell, your dad is probably going to have my head for letting you in there to see that."

"He won't. You know we're both crime junkies." I laughed softly. "He'll probably be mad he wasn't here to see it."

"You could be right," Alan replied, laughing too.

I looked at Dennis and said, "Can I ask you a question?"

"Sure," he said.

"How did you find him?" I asked.

"You really want to know?"

I nodded.

"It wasn't that hard. No offense to the guys in blue, but with a guy like James Walker, it's a matter of finding the closest strip club or dodgy massage parlor and working outwards from there," he told me.

I glanced at Alan. "Ready to believe me about the killer now?"

He nodded. "We'll talk later. You need to get out of here."

"Okay, I have a meeting anyway." I waved to them, climbed back in my car, then drove across the street to the lot at Graveyard Grill and parked next to a couple of other cars.

I couldn't get the image of James's death pose from my head, but I did my best to keep from retching up the lunch that Damien served me during our meeting. I'd seen gruesome photos before; I needed to shove those images from today into that same category.

"So we're trying to change our image a bit, attract a slightly less rough clientele," he said, leaning forward in his keenness to convey his message. "I was hoping you could help with that."

I nodded. "I think I know exactly what you need. Let me draw up a campaign for you, and we'll meet again in a few days to discuss it. How does that sound?"

"I am excited, if I'm honest. How's the burger?"

I'd eaten about half of it. "It's really good and very filling," I replied, with a genuine smile. "I think I'm going to need to take the rest of it to go."

"I'll get you a box."

I thanked him, and then, with a promise to return in a few days with a game plan, I headed back to the office. Once there, I made a beeline to Lonnie's door. I knocked, and when she shouted for me to come in, I walked in and dropped into the chair opposite her.

"He's dead."

"What? Damien's dead?"

I shook my head. "James Walker. He's dead. Murdered. I saw him."

Lonnie sat up straighter and frowned at me. She looked at me for a few seconds, and then her frown faded away. "Dammit, you're serious, aren't you?"

"Deadly serious," I said. "I don't know if it's made the news yet or if the family's been told, so we need to keep it between us until then. But I would swear the same killer who murdered Cory Elway murdered James. It was awful." I gave her a few details of what I'd seen.

"No more. I don't want to know any more, please. This

guy is sick."

I knew exactly how she felt. "You know what this means, right?" I whispered.

Lonnie met my gaze. "Gull Island most likely has a serial killer."

"Yeah. And I'm pretty sure he's just getting started."

"You look a little pale," Lonnie observed. "Why don't you take the rest of the day off?"

I shook my head. "I promised Damien I'd have a campaign for him in a few days. I need to get started on putting it together. Any word from Jordan on Wally's?"

"Not yet, but the day isn't over."

With a sigh I got up and headed to my desk, the box with my half-finished burger still in my hand. I set it down and pulled out my phone. I sent David a text telling him what I'd seen. Not in detail, but just that I'd been at the scene, who it was, and that I was pretty sure we had a serial killer amongst us. I knew he wouldn't go blabbing it about to any reporters.

A moment later, he texted back.

> David: See. I told you that you are smarter than the cops! xoxo

I texted back a smiley emoji because I didn't really know what to say to that. Truthfully, it made me feel a little bit strange that he was praising me for guessing that a serial killer was on the loose.

I shook off the uneasy feeling and told myself sternly to stop it and just enjoy the moment. David was only texting me because he was proud of me for figuring it out before anyone else. I shouldn't have been doubting him right then. I should have been glad that he believed in me and had faith in me.

"Did you see this?" Brittany asked, showing me her phone.

I took her phone from her and read it. It was a news report about James being found. I handed it back to her. "Yeah, I already knew. I spotted Detective Kellerman at the storage unit when I went to meet with a new client."

"You met a new client at the storage unit where James Walker's body was found?"

"No, at the Graveyard Grill across the street, but I saw Alan, and, well, I went over there to see what was going on."

"They said his head was cut off," Brittany said with a shiver. "I can't even imagine having to deal with something like that in person. It makes me so grossed out, I'd probably get sick." She made a face as though she was going to vomit.

The image of James's head in his lap flashed in my brain, and I thought I might throw up again, but I managed to keep it down, thankfully. I wouldn't want to gross her out more, or have to explain why I was barfing all over her. "That's what I heard," I said cautiously, not wanting to admit to seeing it.

"I wonder who he pissed off." She shook her head. "Because they must have been really angry."

"I don't think it was personal. Not exactly. I think he was targeted because of the kind of person he was."

"So you're thinking it's more impersonal?" Brittany asked.

"Yeah. Like a serial killer. And I don't think he's done either."

"At least he's targeting men and not women," Brittany said with a grimace.

"For the moment." I glanced at her, struck by a properly scary thought. "Guess we'll have to wait and see."

13

I 'd been working on the Graveyard Grill account for nearly an hour when Brittany returned and told me that Lonnie wanted to see me in her office. I stood up and went straight there. I figured it had to do with the Wally campaign, but I wasn't nervous, surprisingly. Lonnie had been right; if they didn't go with us, then there would be others in the future. I still knocked on the office door, out of respect, even though she was expecting me. Lonnie called for me to enter, and I did. She nodded to a chair, and then her face split in a wide beam.

"Congratulations, Stella," she said as I sat down. "Jordan called, and the account is ours. Well, yours."

I felt warm pride envelop me, and I smiled back at Lonnie, unable to hide my excitement. I knew the account was going to be big for us, but I hadn't expected to feel this explosion of happiness.

"Now, don't get too cocky. To keep riding the high, your follow-up work has to be equally amazing," Lonnie said.

That kind of deflated me momentarily.

"But don't look so worried." Lonnie smiled. "I'm not expecting you to reinvent the wheel. At least not today."

I relaxed slightly, smiling at the fact that Lonnie's mind had gone to the exact same place as mine had. "That's good, because I'm not sure I've got it in me today." I laughed.

"You've done good, kid. How about you knock off a bit early? I know I just dropped a major client in your lap, and you've got a few others you're dealing with, but you deserve a small break, even if it's just a few hours."

"You sure?" I asked, my smile widening.

"You bet. Go on, get out of here. But don't be surprised if tomorrow I expect you to work through lunch." She laughed again.

"I won't even care. I'm really excited to be working on these accounts, Lonnie. Thanks for trusting me with them."

"You earned it, Stella."

"Thanks. See you tomorrow." I waved and left her office, stopping at my desk to grab my leftovers and my purse.

On my way out the door, I texted David.

> Me: I got the rest of the afternoon off as a congratulations. Lonnie got the call from Wally's. We got the account!

> David: That's fantastic, sweetheart! Wish I were off with you.

> Me: Can't you take the afternoon off? It's just a couple of hours.

> David: Sorry, but we're swamped, and Dalton's off doing his thing again.

> Me: He's always off doing his thing. When do you get a turn?

> David: Stella, this is work. I have to go. I'll see you at home later.

I could tell that he was pissed at me, and I felt a little guilty over it. Sighing, I texted him one more time.

> Me: I'm sorry. I know you're working hard. I just miss you. I'll see you at home for dinner.

I waited a few moments, frowning at my phone, but he didn't text me back. I didn't like it when he was upset.

As I drove, I thought about the two murders. I wondered if the cops had determined that I was right and the two men had been murdered by the same killer. I glanced at the clock as I drove. Alan should still be on duty. I decided to call him.

"Kellerman," he answered.

"Hey, Alan, it's Stella. I was wondering if the two murders are connected," I said as I made the turn to go toward my parents' place.

"You're not going to give me any peace until I answer, are you?" Alan said.

"Nope," I replied.

He sighed, and I knew then I had him. "Stella."

"Oh, come on, Alan. I just want to know what CSI found, please?"

"Fine," he said. "James Walker was murdered."

"No shit," I said with a laugh. "I would have been surprised if you'd said it was suicide."

Alan laughed wryly. "That would have been a surprise

indeed," he said. "All right, but this doesn't go beyond you and me, okay?"

"Who am I going to tell?" I replied, but then added, "Okay, other than David and my dad."

He chuckled at that. "So, obviously, we haven't had a full postmortem done yet, but the coroner has seen the body and given us his first assessment. The torture – the burns on his penis, the missing teeth, the loose eyeball – that was all done prior to his death. His head was removed after his death."

"So decapitation wasn't actually the cause of his death?" I said as I entered my parents' neighborhood.

"No," Alan said. "I know the scene was a mess of blood, but if he had been decapitated and died that way, there would have been so much more blood, as his heart would have kept pumping for a few seconds after his death. No, the cause of death was likely strangulation, and he was most probably unconscious from the pain and shock of his other injuries at the point of his death."

"And ...?" I prompted.

"And your initial speculation was entirely correct. We've got a serial killer on our hands, Stella," he said.

I sat up straight in my seat at that, and I felt the hairs on my arms stand up.

"Some of the smaller cuts are confirmed as having been made by the same tool as some of the cuts on Cory Elway."

"I knew it," I said.

"I know you did, and I agreed with you, but being in my position, I have to wait until forensics confirm our guess-work," Alan added.

"Maybe I should be on the payroll, then, for supplying theories for you to prove," I joked as I pulled into my parents' driveway.

We both laughed, and then I sensed Alan turning serious again as I parked the car.

"Are you all right, Stella?" he asked.

"Yeah?" I said, drawing the word out and making it a question. I turned off the engine and sat there so we could finish the rest of our conversation.

"Look, I know you're tough, but this case is ... I don't even have the words for it. It's not your run-of-the-mill stab wound or bullet hole. I have cops here who have seen enough murders to think they'd be hardened to anything a killer can throw at us, and this case is making them sick. I just ... I don't know if you should show up at any more crime scenes, Stella," Alan said.

My initial reaction was to scoff and tell him I was perfectly fine, but something stopped me. Something like a little warm glow low down in my stomach, the sort of warm glow you get when you knew someone cared about you. I bit back the sarcasm and decided to take him at face value.

"I'm not going to pretend I enjoy looking at the mess this killer is leaving behind, and I know it's not my job to be there, but I kind of feel involved now, you know? I want to help. I want him stopped."

"I know," Alan said, his voice full of understanding. "And that's the only reason I even let you anywhere near that last scene. But if another body shows up, don't be surprised if I keep you out of it. I don't want you having nightmares over this."

"Thank you," I said, knowing he was just showing he cared. "And you know I didn't turn up at the crime scene because I was following you. In both cases, I just happened to be in the area."

"I know, I know," he said. "Was there anything else?"

"Not at the moment." I laughed. "If I think of anything else, I'll call you."

"Okay, bye, Stella."

We hung up, and I got out of the car, heading up to Mom and Dad's front door. I knocked and then let myself in. "Hello? Anyone home?" I called.

Mom poked her head out of the kitchen doorway. "Stella, shouldn't you be at work?"

"Lonnie gave me the afternoon off. I won a big account for the firm, so she let me have the afternoon off as a sort of thank you."

"That's wonderful, sweetie. How's David doing?"

"He's good, just working a lot." I sighed. "Is Dad around?"

"Sure, he's in his home office; did you need him for something?"

"Not really, just thought I'd talk murder stuff with him." I shrugged playfully at her.

"You two and your macabre hobby." She shook her head with a smile. "Go ahead. Are you staying for dinner?"

"No, I told David I would cook, but thanks." I smiled and kissed her cheek.

"Okay, if you change your mind, I always make extra." She winked.

"Thanks, Mom." I passed through the kitchen to the living room and then knocked on Dad's office door. "Hey, Dad, you busy?"

"I always have time for you, honey. Is everything okay?"

"Yeah, I just got off the phone with Alan." I shared our conversation and told him my theory.

"You could very well be right." Dad nodded. "But I hate to think that we've got a serial killer operating here on Gull Island."

I shivered. "Me too."

"And I'm not sure I like you looking in on active crime scenes. It's risky, Stella. I don't want you to become a target for this killer."

"I'll be careful, Dad. Promise. And I didn't show up at them on purpose; it was all kind of a coincidence."

"That may be true, but it's still dangerous. Promise me you'll be careful."

"I will, Dad," I said and then gave him a hug. "I should head home. I've gotta get dinner started before David gets home."

"All right, drive safely." He hugged me again.

"Bye, Mom," I called as I headed for the front door.

Mom hurried out and reached the door as I did. "Did you and your dad have a talk?"

"Yeah, it's always good to share my thoughts with him." I smiled. "See you next week?"

"You know you can come by anytime. Drive safely."

"I will." I waved as I headed out to my car and set off on the drive home.

I AM IN THE DARK, a pitch-black darkness so complete that I have to touch my eyelids to see if my eyes are open or closed. I lift my hand in front of me, and I can't see it. I have no idea where I am or why it is so dark, but what I do know is that I'm afraid.

I can feel the hairs standing up on the back of my neck and on my arms. My heart is beating a little too fast and a lot too loud. My breath comes in gasping pants that I try and fail to keep silent. I feel as though I am surrounded by something — maybe people, maybe animals – and one wrong move will have them close in on me and attack me.

I want to move, but I'm too afraid. What if I walk right into one of them? And besides, where would I go? I don't know where I am, and I certainly don't know how to get out of whatever sort of place this is. I'm confident that I am indoors. There is no stirring of a breeze, no chill to the air, and the darkness is far too absolute to be completely natural. But I have no idea what sort of building I'm in or whereabouts in that building I might be. And what if I'm being paranoid and, actually, whatever dangerous thing I can sense is outside, and the building is keeping me blind but safe.

I swallow, and my dry throat betrays me, making a clicking sound that seems to be as loud as a fighter jet in the silence. I hold my breath and tense up, waiting for the attack I have triggered, but it doesn't come. I relax slightly, and I decide that I have to move. Whatever is waiting for me, sound isn't triggering it, and I need to find out where I am and how the hell I get out of here and go home.

I take a small, tentative step forward, my hands raised in front of me. I pause and listen. Nothing except for the sound of my own pulse. Boom. Boom. Boom. I take another step and then another. I am starting to get a little more confident, and I listen as I move rather than keep stopping. Finally, my hands brush against something solid.

I pull them back with a start, but then I reach out again and run my hands over the surface in front of me, confirming it is what I thought it was: a plastered wall. I turn to my right and keep my palm flat on the wall and begin to walk. For all I haven't been attacked and I am starting to think there is nothing in the room with me, I am still terrified, and I don't know why.

I move along the wall, feeling for a door or a window or anything. I don't find a door or a window, but I do find something.

A light switch. Or at least a switch that I am assuming is a light switch. I stop and think. Do I flip it?

In the end, it seems that my hand makes my decision for me, and it moves to the switch of its own accord. As my finger presses against the switch, horror fills me, and I know instinctively that nothing good can come from that light, but it's too late. I can't stop my hand from flicking the switch.

Bright, yellowy light fills the room, and for a moment, I have to close my eyes against the light. I blink slowly, and after a couple of seconds, my eyes adjust, and I can see again. What shows itself to me makes me almost wish I couldn't see again.

I am not alone, but my cellmate — because that is what this place is, a cell, three concrete walls and one made up of thick metal bars — isn't going to harm me. It would be difficult for him to do much of anything to me without his head, and his head doesn't seem to be anywhere in here. It certainly isn't attached to his neck.

His lack of a head doesn't stop him from sitting up, though, and as he does, blood pours from his neck stump and soaks into his shirt. I want to cry out, I want to scream, but I am frozen and mute. I stand on the spot, watching the headless, bloody abomination in front of me as it turns its neck this way and that, as though it can still look around, like its missing eyes can somehow still see me.

Maybe it can still somehow see, because its neck stops moving when it reaches the point where it would be looking right at me. I can almost imagine a grinning face looking at me, and I shudder with revulsion at the hunger I imagine in its eyes.

The headless body pushes itself up from the floor. As it does so, its shirt billows out, and a pile of steaming red intestines spill out onto the floor.

I can no longer hold back my scream, and it tears itself from my throat, stinging the dry skin there.

"Oops," the headless thing somehow says with no head and no mouth. It sounds amused like its insides dropping out are merely something to talk about at its next dinner party. Something to amuse its fellow guests between courses.

It turns its full body toward me and starts to walk closer. I try to back up, but I have nowhere to go. I am already at the edge of the cell, and I press myself against the wall as hard as I can, almost as though I think it might open up and let me through it if I just put enough pressure on it. It doesn't give, of course, and the headless thing is opening its jeans. It doesn't have underwear on, and its penis falls out of its jeans.

I scream again as I look at the monstrosity that is its penis. It's huge, unnaturally so. It hangs down to the creature's knees, and it's black and blistered, burned. As it gets closer to me, its penis starts to harden, and I retch when I see blisters popping and oozing as the skin stretches.

Tears blind me, and I'm screaming almost constantly now, and then the thing puts a hand on my shoulder, and I scream again, and I'm afraid I'm going to die, but I'm more afraid that I'm not going to die, and that I'm going to suffer being raped by that oozing thing.

There is a loud clanging sound, and my head turns toward it. Relief floods me as the cell door is pushed open, and the headless thing backs away from me. A man stands silhouetted in the door to the cell. He is wearing black jeans and a black T-shirt. I can't see his face because he wears a fedora with a black veil hanging over the front of it, covering his face.

"I could have saved you," the headless thing says.

It sounds like it is about to burst into tears, and I frown. How has the thing gone from being my would-be rapist to being someone who can cry because he didn't get to save me? And how does he not realize it's him I need saving from?

"Enough," the man in black says. "Look at you. You're disgusting. When will you learn that you can't have any woman you want?"

"I wanted to save her," the headless thing shouts. "I only wanted to save her. But she made the wrong choice. Just like they all do."

"Silence," the man in black orders. He moves closer to the headless thing and pulls a Taser gun out. He puts it on the headless thing's chest, and it shrieks and falls to the ground, where it lies twitching and shaking.

"Are you here to save me?" I whisper to the man in black.

"That depends," he says.

He is walking toward me, and something inside me is telling me I should fear this man even more than the headless thing.

"On what?" I manage to ask.

"On how long you continue to amuse me before I grow bored of you," he says. He holds out his arm, and I slip my hand through it without hesitation.

"I think I can be very amusing when I want to be," I say with a flirty smile.

"Oh, I'm sure that's true, Ms. Greene," the man in black says.

"It's Stella," I tell him.

I JUMPED AWAKE THEN, my heart racing and my nightgown soaked beneath me. I sat up, gasping for breath. I reached out and put my bedside lamp on. I pulled my knees up to my chest, wrapped my arms around them, and rocked slowly back and forth as I whimpered. I knew it had only been a dream, but my God, it had been an unsettling dream to say the least.

Damn it, Alan, I thought. I was okay with all of this until he made me realize just how bad it was, and now I'm having nightmares about the case.

A shudder went through my body, and then a warm hand touched my shoulder. I threw myself forward, screaming.

"Hey. Hey. It's okay, Stella, it's me," David's voice said from behind me.

I relaxed and breathed out a sigh of relief. "I'm sorry," I said.

He reached out, pulled me into his arms, and I clung to him as he stroked my hair.

"What happened? Did you have a nightmare?" he asked.

"Yes," I said, my voice muffled against his chest. "I guess finding out I was right about there being a serial killer on the loose has affected me more than I let myself believe."

"Ah, you don't have to worry about that, Stella," David said. "You're nothing like his victims."

I frowned. It was almost the same thing that Brittany had said, but from him it sounded weird. It was a strange thing to say to reassure me. I wanted to ask him to elaborate, but I was enjoying the warmth of his arms around me, the solidity of his chest, and I decided just to relax and enjoy being comforted.

14

I had finished work, come home, and put dinner on. David had decided he would have an early day since he'd missed several evenings with me over the last week. I was looking forward to us eating dinner together like a normal couple again. But the sound of his cell phone ringing from the living room sent a wave of disappointment through me. No doubt he would have to go running off to appease a disgruntled client or fix some problem at the office. I wished Dalton would take these calls, at least some of the time, so David and I could spend more time together.

I strained my ears to try to work out whom I would be losing him to this time, but he was talking too quietly for me to hear. All I caught was the word "no" said several times and the phrase "irreconcilable differences." I thought it was a bit of a weird thing for him to say about a client, but maybe it was just an excuse because he wasn't going to drop everything and run back to the office. Maybe he wasn't going to drop me to run off to work. That would be nice.

After a few minutes, David came into the kitchen.

"Is everything okay?" I asked.

"Yeah," he said.

I realized he wasn't going to elaborate, so I pushed him a little further. "You're not going to the office tonight, are you?"

"What? No, of course not," David said with a frown, which then cleared and was replaced with an expression of understanding. "Oh, you heard me on the phone. You thought the call was work. It wasn't. It was one of Dad's doctors."

"How is he doing?" I asked.

David looked somber. "The lung infection has pretty much cleared up. He wants to see me, but I told his therapist to tell him there's no chance of that happening."

"You don't want to see him?" I asked. "I get that you don't have the best relationship, but he's still your dad."

"That means something very different for me and Dalton than you," David said. "For you, your mom and dad mean love and stability. For me and Dalton, our dad means pain and heartache."

"I get that," I said. "And I can understand why you don't want to see him. I just don't want you to regret not seeing him when it's too late, that's all."

David crossed the room and pulled me into his arms. He kissed the top of my head, and when I looked up at him, he kissed the tip of my nose and then my lips.

"I love that you're looking out for me," he said.

I smiled up at him. "Of course I'm looking out for you. I always will. Do you want to talk about what happened with your dad?"

David kissed me again. "You're too good for this world, and you're certainly too good for me. But believe me, Stella, you're already having nightmares from the murder scenes you've seen. You don't need any more horrors on top of that. Honestly, I appreciate the offer, but the last thing I want to do is force you to hear about the terrible things my dad has done. Let's just say you don't need to know the depths of the depravity certain members of my family have sunk to, my dad included."

I squeezed David tighter against me. I knew he and Dalton had been abused as children, but I was starting to think that abuse had been much, much worse than David had ever let on. Dalton wouldn't even allow a word to be mentioned about it, let alone his father's name, in his presence. "I can handle it. If you need to talk to me, you can."

"Maybe you could handle it. You're pretty strong. But I don't think I could handle rehashing all that stuff. Let's just leave it, okay?" He didn't wait for an answer. Instead, he asked, "What's for dinner? It smells delicious."

15

I'd felt kind of strange the last few days. I was either nauseous to the point where I could barely bear to look at food, and the smallest hint of a food smell made me want to be sick, or I was completely ravenous and could easily eat two or three portions at a single meal. Both were kind of embarrassing. Although I could control myself and not eat and eat when I was going through that phase, if I didn't eat until I was truly full, my stomach would begin to rattle, and that was when things started to get really embarrassing, even more so than stuffing myself did.

I also kept feeling dizzy on and off, and I was so tired all the time. I couldn't even blame work. Sure, I'd been busy with the campaigns I was putting together, and I'd eaten quite a bit of chocolate, because of course I did. I needed to sample the products I was going to be creating ad copy for, right? Still, it wasn't that much chocolate, and it had never made me dizzy or tired before, so I knew that wasn't the reason. I was starting to think that I must be coming down with some sort of flu or virus.

"Stella," David said from beside me, his elbow gently jabbing me in the ribs.

I looked up at him through barely open eyes.

He studied me for a moment. "Are you okay?"

I nodded, just wanting him to stop talking so I could go back to sleep. Why couldn't he let me have a nice little nap? I could feel myself drifting, and I relaxed and let myself float away toward oblivion. David, however, had other ideas, and I felt his elbow in my ribs again. I opened my eyes for a moment, and then I let them close again. I didn't have the energy for an argument, that was for sure.

"Seriously, sweetheart," he whispered. "You're falling asleep again. We're out in public."

His tone brought me fully awake, and the urge to tear him a new one faded away when I saw where I was. We weren't at home. I wasn't in bed. We were at a brunch being thrown by someone David very much wanted to schmooze with.

"I'm so sorry." I ran a hand over my face. "I barely slept last night." This wasn't true at all, but I didn't want David to worry. "I'll go outside and get some air; that should help wake me up."

David nodded.

I stood up. The room lurched as I got to my feet, and I stumbled slightly. I caught myself on the back of my chair, hoping that my stumble hadn't been seen by anyone else.

I was halfway across the grand ballroom when a door to my right opened, and a waiter stepped out. He was carrying a large silver tray filled with scrambled eggs. The smell of the hot eggs caught in the back of my throat and made me want to retch.

Oh God no, please not here, I thought.

I pressed my hand to my mouth, being as subtle as possible. A wave of nausea washed over me, leaving me teary eyed and ready to throw up at any second. And then, just as quickly as it had come, it went away again.

Grateful for the reprieve from the flood of nausea, I took another step forward. My head exploded with dizziness, and my vision swam in and out. I had stopped walking now, and I held my hand out, a gesture that was my way of asking for help, literally reaching out for someone. But no one was there.

Another wave of dizziness hit me, and I struggled against it, but it was no use. Before I could do anything to stop it, my knees were buckling, and I felt strong hands in my armpits, lowering me to the floor instead of letting me slam down. It was a kind gesture, and I would have to thank the person responsible afterwards.

That was my last thought before dizziness overtook me, and everything went black.

I REMEMBERED A SERIES OF FLASHES. I would wake up and see David's worried face relax into a smile when he saw my eyes were open. Then there was a stranger dressed in green looking down on me. A paramedic? I vaguely remembered hearing sirens, and then I was on a wheeled gurney, and I could smell antiseptic and sickness.

I came awake properly to find myself laid on a bed on my back. A woman stood beside the bed. A nurse? Yes, a nurse. I was in the hospital. But why? I went to sit up, and the nurse smiled down at me.

"Would you like a sip of water?" she asked.

I nodded. I hadn't even realized how dry my throat was until she offered me the water.

She helped me to sit up and then poured me a beaker of water from a jug that sat on a small table beside my bed.

I drank the water and handed her the empty cup. "Thank you. What happened?"

Before she had a chance to answer, the door opened, and David rushed into the room. He came to my side and leaned down and kissed my forehead. His lips lingered for longer than they normally would have, and when he finally pulled away, I could see the worry lines on his face.

"Thank God you're okay," he said. He sat down on an orange plastic chair beside my bed and took one of my hands in his.

"I feel fine," I reassured him. "I just don't know what happened." I looked to the nurse again.

She picked up my chart and flicked through it, nodding to herself here and there. She looked back up again. "So, it seems that your blood pressure was rather low, which is why you fainted. Have you been feeling dizzy at all?"

I nodded.

"That will be the low blood pressure too. It's not low enough to be a concern right now, but we'll keep an eye on it. In the meantime, start taking some iron tablets and some folic acid. They'll help with the dizziness and any nausea you might be suffering from," she said. "But on the plus side, your baby is doing just fine."

"Baby?" David and I said together.

"Ohhh," the nurse said, her eyebrows raised. "Well, that explains why you didn't ask about it sooner." She smiled warmly at us. "Stella, you're pregnant."

"I ... I can't be. I'm on birth control pills," I said, feeling completely stunned.

"Unless one of those pills has sprung a heartbeat and moved into your uterus, I can assure you that you very much are pregnant. Around fourteen weeks," she said.

"But ..." I started and then trailed off. I shook my head. "A baby? I ..."

"I'm going to give you two a minute to talk about this and get your heads around it. I'll come back shortly, and I'll ask one of our OB nurses to have a chat with you too," the nurse said.

I watched her as she left the room. I was nervous about looking at David and seeing his expression. What if he didn't want this baby? I finally risked a glance at him, and I instantly felt better when I saw him beaming at me.

"I'm going to be a dad," he said. His grin got even wider, and he punched the air.

I nodded and found myself giggling. David's excitement at the prospect of fatherhood was catching.

"Are you happy, Stella?" he asked.

"Yes," I said, realizing all of a sudden that I really was. "Are you?"

He nodded and put his hand on my belly. "I'm happier than I ever thought I could be," he whispered.

16

I didn't know if I was being ungrateful and a tad hormonal, or if I was justified in being slightly annoyed with David. Since he had found out I was pregnant, he had worked out an agreement with Dalton and made sure that he was barely at the office so he could be home around me all of the time. I thought that part was sweet. But then there was the other side of it, the side I didn't find sweet at all.

David had spent a ton of time on Google working out what was best for me and the baby, and he was becoming almost overbearing in his mission to make sure I was doing everything I should be doing. What he didn't seem to grasp was that most of it was just guidelines and that ignoring at least some of the advice was perfectly fine. He didn't seem to understand that I knew my own body and what worked for me, and by extension, I knew what worked for the baby while it was inside me.

I knew he meant well, and I was trying my best not to get annoyed with him, but it was hard sometimes. I'd come upstairs to take a bath just to get a half an hour or so away from the nagging. I'd only been in the bathtub for about five minutes when there was a light knock at the door. If I ignored it, he would only assume I had fallen asleep and was drowning and burst in. I sighed.

"What?" I said.

The door opened a crack.

"What? That's not very nice, is it?" David said. "Can I come in?"

"I'm having a bath," I said, stating the obvious and hoping he took the hint.

He didn't go away.

"Yes, come in."

David came in and sat down on the closed lid of the toilet. He sat watching me for a moment, and then he frowned. "Why aren't you massaging your breasts?"

"Umm, because it's not your own personal porno," I joked.

David laughed, but he was soon back to serious again. "You know what I mean, Stella," he said. "It helps to bring your milk in."

"I'm only fifteen weeks pregnant," I pointed out.

"I know, but it won't hurt to get into the practice of doing it, will it?" David said.

"I haven't even said I'm breastfeeding yet," I said.

"I thought it went without saying. Breast milk is best," he said. "Why would you want to give our baby anything less than the best start in life?"

"I didn't say I wasn't going to breastfeed either," I said. "I just feel rushed and overwhelmed with it all at the minute, and honestly, it would be useful if you would relax a bit."

"I would find it easier to relax if you would do as you're told," David said.

I raised an eyebrow.

"Oh, don't get all feminist on me," he said as he sighed and flapped his hand at me. "You know what I mean."

I shrugged. "For what it's worth, of course I'm going to breastfeed, and I know how to bring my milk in when the time is right," I said, trying to be patient with him. I knew some women would kill to have a man who wanted to be this involved in their pregnancy, and it made me feel like I was being a bit of a brat pushing him away constantly. "I want this baby as much as you do, and I would never do anything to harm it."

David smiled, and I hated that I enjoyed getting his approval.

"That's my girl," he said. "Right, I'll leave you to it. Don't be too long. It's time to take your vitamins soon."

I didn't bother to argue. The sanctuary of my bath had been ruined, and I figured I would get out as soon as David had gone back downstairs. I did just that and went and sat on our bed, wrapped in a dressing gown. I waited until I felt mostly dry, and then I took the dressing gown off, hung it up, and put on a pair of sweatpants and a T-shirt. I combed my hair, tied it back out of my face, and then I went downstairs.

"In here," David called from the kitchen as I reached the bottom stair.

I went through to the kitchen to find my pills lined up on the table and a glass of water beside them. I felt torn. Part of me was annoyed that David was being so controlling once again, and part of me thought it was sweet that he had the timings all worked out and was willing to sort out this kind of stuff for me.

I sat down and took my pills. "Thank you," I said.

"Do you want some tea?" David asked.

I crinkled my nose slightly. "I would rather have coffee."

"We don't have decaf coffee, sorry," he said.

"One cup won't hurt the baby," I said.

"Probably not, but why risk it when there are so many other things you can drink?" he replied.

It frustrated me when he spoke like that. I wanted to tell him if I wanted a cup of damned coffee, then I would have a cup of damned coffee. But how could I argue with his logic without sounding like I was being selfish and not giving a shit about our baby?

"Tea will be fine," I said through gritted teeth.

"I'm having a chicken salad sandwich. Do you want one, or do you fancy something different?" David asked.

"I'll have the same, but here, let me make them," I said.

"No, it's fine," David said. "Drink your tea."

I watched as he cut and buttered two bread rolls. He grabbed a packet of cooked chicken from the fridge, lettuce, a tomato, a cucumber, and a jar of mayonnaise, and then he stood and cut up the salad and began to assemble the sandwiches. He finished by spreading a thick layer of mayonnaise on the top half of one of the buns and then closing the sandwiches. As he put the mayonnaise and the butter and the leftover chicken back in the fridge, I waited. When he was done, he picked up the sandwiches and put one on the table in front of me and then sat down opposite me.

"You've given me the wrong sandwich," I said before either of us took a bite.

David peeked inside his sandwich. "No, that's right. Mine is the one with mayo."

"I wanted mayo too." I started to stand up to rectify the situation.

But David was already shaking his head. "You know you're not allowed mayo when you're pregnant."

I rolled my eyes and stood up anyway. "This is getting ridiculous, David. I'm not a child," I said as I went to the fridge, opened it, and pulled out the jar of mayo.

"Then stop acting like one," David fired back. "You know for a fact that mayonnaise can be dangerous for the baby, and you're going to eat it anyway? If that's not the action of a child, I don't know what is."

"Fine. I won't have any," I said. I opened the fridge door again and practically threw the jar back inside. "Happy now?"

"Quite," David replied. "I'm going to assume this new snappiness is just your hormones playing up because you're pregnant. I'm going to assume that things will go back to normal once you have the baby."

"It's nothing to do with my hormones." I sat back down and took a deep breath, needing to say something. "It's because I can't stand this constant need to control me that you seem to have developed. So it depends on you. If you're going to stop making me feel claustrophobic once I've had the baby, then, yes, things will go back to normal. If you keep trying to tell me what I can eat or drink or what time I can go to bed or take a shower, then no, I genuinely can't see things going back to the way they were."

"You're being dramatic," David said. "It's not about me controlling you. It's about what's best for the baby. I had hoped that you would be on the same page as me when it comes to doing the right thing by him or her."

"Of course I want to do the right thing for the baby," I said.

"Except when it comes to something *you* want like coffee or mayonnaise?" David challenged.

"Yes. Except when it comes to something that is perfectly harmless in moderation," I said.

"You have, what, twenty-three, twenty-four weeks left. Something like that?" David asked.

I nodded, thrown by the abrupt change of topic from an argument about mayonnaise to when my due date was.

"Would it really be so awful for you to do without a few things for those few weeks just to be certain our baby is getting the best start in life? It might be stupid. But is it worth the risk?"

I sighed and shook my head. This was what I really hated about David the odd times we did argue. Not only did he like to be in control, but he always managed to word his argument in a way that would make any comebacks seem petty, like his way was the commonsense approach, and he was surprised that no one else had seen it themselves.

"No, it's not worth the risk," I said. "I promise I'll do better."

David reached out and squeezed my shoulder. "That's my girl," he said. He smiled at me and then bit into his sandwich.

I had to bite my tongue to not point out that he wasn't sacrificing anything for our baby, that maybe I would do better at being deprived of treats if he followed the same regime when it came to food and so on with me. I didn't say it because I thought there was a chance, however slim, that he would agree to go without the things I couldn't have, and

then he would make it look easy, and I would resent him
even more for it.

We finished our sandwiches in near silence, one of us
occasionally breaking it with a comment here or there.
When we had finished eating, David stood up and went and
washed the dishes and cutlery we had used.

"What are you doing this afternoon, then?" I asked.
"Have you got any meetings or anything?"

"Just one," David replied. "I scheduled it for three o'clock
so that I would be out while you had your nap. Then, if you
need anything the rest of the time, I'll be here."

"You don't have to plan your workday around me," I said.
"I can do things for myself."

I cringed inside, ready for another argument, but instead,
David turned to me and smiled.

"I know you can, but I like doing things for you and our
baby. You get to carry our baby, and that automatically
makes you useful. I am a bit of a spare part at this point, and
this is my way of feeling involved," he said.

I stood up and went to him. I wrapped my arms around
his waist and leaned my head back, and he kissed me. He
wasn't trying to control me. He really was trying to help me,
and I was too much of a bitch to see it. I kissed him again,
and then I moved back slightly.

"I'd best get to work," I said. "I have an ad for the Graveyard Grill to finish by tomorrow, so I figured I'd do a bit now
and then have my nap, and then maybe we could have an
early dinner and watch a movie or something? I can always
finish it off tomorrow."

"That sounds great." David smiled. "Don't be over-
working."

"I won't," I said.

"I'll pop in and remind you of the time as I'm leaving, so you know it's time for your nap," he said.

While his thinking he had to tell me it was nap time like I was a toddler still irked me somewhat, now that he had explained why he was being the way he was, I didn't have the heart to tell him that I was absolutely shattered now, and I would have preferred to nap before working, not after he had planned his day to be available to me.

I went upstairs into my office and fired up my partially created ad. I started to type, but then I stopped and just sat for a moment, processing everything that David and I had just said to each other. Yes, it was sweet that he wanted to be so protective of the baby, and I loved him so much for that. But, as much as I didn't want it to, it did bother me that he was perfectly happy to brush away my needs in favor of the baby's.

I was going to be a mother. I knew there would be sacrifices along the way, and I was perfectly happy to make them for my child. But I didn't want to be the thing David was okay with sacrificing. The more I tried to tell myself I was being dramatic or exaggerating the point, the more convinced I became that I wasn't being either of those. In fact, the more I thought about it, the more I began to ask myself how much did I really know about David? Probably not enough to know if he would make a good parent and a good husband at the same time.

And as much as I hated to admit it, there was a part of me that was starting to seriously question whether having a baby with David was a good idea. I decided to call my mom and ask for her take on it. She and Dad had been over the moon upon learning that we were going to have a baby, so maybe she'd have some good advice.

I picked up my cell phone and dialed Mom's number. "Hey, Mom," I said when she answered.

"How is the little mama?" she asked.

I told her how frustrated I was feeling, and she calmed me down by telling me how her mother-in-law had gone overboard with the advice and controlling behavior when she'd been pregnant with me. What she described was way worse than anything David was doing, and that made me feel better.

"Besides, everything he's doing is with the best interests of you and the baby at heart. He's excited. The two of you are going to make great parents."

"Thanks, Mom. I think I'm still just overwhelmed about it all since I wasn't expecting it, you know?"

"I understand that. Just remember, being patient with him will help you learn to be patient with the baby when the time comes and as they grow."

"That is a good point," I said with a giggle. "I'd better go. I need to get a little work in before I take a nap."

"All right, sweetie. Give my love to David."

"I will." I smiled and hung up.

Feeling much better, I got busy on designing an ad that would draw in new clientele to the Graveyard Grill. I was nearly finished with it when David strolled in.

"That looks great." He leaned down and kissed my cheek as he rubbed my shoulders. "I really like that part." He pointed at the computer screen.

I glanced up at him and smiled, then hit save before closing it down. "Mom sends her love." I stood up in his arms.

"You spoke to her?"

I nodded. "I needed her perspective because I'm still a little overwhelmed at learning I'm going to be a mom."

"I can understand that. Did talking to her help?" he asked.

"It really did." I yawned.

"I'm glad. You should take your nap now. I'm going to head off to my meeting."

"You'll be home for dinner?"

He nodded as I picked up my phone and set an alarm. "I'll make your favorite."

"Then I'll be quick so I can come home and help," he offered.

I rested a hand on his cheek. "Thank you, I appreciate everything you're doing."

He smiled and kissed me before heading out the door.

As I watched him leave our bedroom, a part of me still wanted to rebel and get back up, but he was right. A nap would be good for me, so I lay down and was asleep before the front door even closed.

17

A month had gone by since I had found out I was pregnant. Over that time, David and I had been through a bit of a rocky patch, but we had come out of the other side of it now, and things were better than ever.

I had begun to think that David and I weren't as good together as I had always believed we were, but after talking to Mom about it some more, I started to be grateful that he was so attentive. And after a while he started to chill out, and the more chill he became, the more willing I became to do the right thing without grumbling, like taking my pills on time, napping when I felt tired, and eating the right sort of food.

We settled into a new routine, one where David helped me by getting my pills out in advance, and I didn't feel controlled. Instead, I felt helped. It was the same with food. David would scour the internet to make sure every ingredient in every dish was safe for the baby, and instead of moaning that I couldn't have something if he found out it wasn't safe, then I would thank him for keeping our baby safe.

I was starting to think that David would make a hell of a good dad. Perhaps in the beginning he had been a bit nervous, and it had made him come across as somewhat overbearing, where that wasn't really the case. He just wanted to be involved, and I couldn't deny that having him around more when he was being this attentive did make my life so much easier.

I had spoken to Lonnie about my pregnancy, and she had asked me if I wanted to give up the Wally's Chocolates account. I told her no way – that account was as much my baby as my actual baby was my baby. I would never have let David hear me saying that, not even as a joke because I knew he wouldn't appreciate it, where Lonnie understood me completely. She gave me free rein to work from home whenever it suited me, and in exchange for her trust, I promised her that my pregnancy wouldn't stop me being there at the next ad copy meeting with Jordan. I would either get there, or I would send Brittany in my place if I had to.

As for the serial killer case, it had gone completely cold over the last four weeks, according to Alan. No new bodies had turned up, and no new people had been reported missing. I had wondered if the killer might have sought out someone homeless, but that seemed unlikely given the status of his first two victims.

Alan and I had discussed theories about why the killer had suddenly stopped. Neither of us really believed it marked a permanent halt to his killing spree. A person didn't start something like this and then just stop. We speculated that maybe he was extra busy at work, or maybe he had found a new hobby that kept him occupied. Or maybe he was still killing, but he had moved out of the area.

That theory gave Alan some work to do, contacting police stations in other jurisdictions to see if they had had anything similar turn up. There had been a couple that had similarities, but not obvious ones. And after some investigating, they'd turned out to be too different to say they were by the same killer. It was frustrating; I didn't like knowing this guy was still running loose out there, and neither did Alan.

There was still someone who was notable through his absence, and that was Andrew. It occurred to me that whatever David had said to him had more than worked to keep him away from me. I wasn't complaining – I was glad to have him out of my life for good – but something niggled at me. Andrew wasn't the type of guy to just give up without a fight, and I worried sometimes about what exactly David had threatened him with.

I'd avoided asking David about it again because the last time he had gotten upset. I was a big believer in not asking questions you didn't want to hear the answers to, but I suddenly felt like I was ready for those answers, so I left my office and went to find David.

He was sitting in the living room with his laptop open on the coffee table in front of him.

"Have you got a minute?" I asked.

"Of course," he said, closing the laptop. He patted the couch beside him. "Is everything okay?"

I moved to sit down. "Yes. There's just something I've been meaning to ask you about, but we're so happy and getting on so well again, and I don't want to make you mad."

"God, Stella, you make it sound like you're afraid of me," David said.

We both laughed, but maybe there was a tiny part of me that was afraid of him. I didn't believe he would hurt me, but I wasn't so certain he wouldn't have hurt Andrew.

"Come on, out with it. I promise I won't get mad."

"What did you threaten Andrew with to make him leave me alone? I'm glad it worked, but the fact that it did makes me think it was something truly terrible," I said.

"Don't you think he deserved something terrible after scaring you half to death that day he tried to get in here?" David asked.

I sort of did, but I didn't want David to be the one who did it to him. "Yes. Maybe. I don't know," I said. "I just want to know what you said or did because I don't want anything to come back on us, on you."

David smiled and put his arm around my shoulders. "I could have threatened him, but guys like Andrew don't listen to that sort of thing. They might for a little while, but they will always come crawling back. So no, I didn't threaten him with anything terrible. Dalton and I just took him for a walk on the beach and explained a few things to him, man to man, you know; then I came home to you."

I thought for a moment, then nodded. I was relieved to hear that David had warned Andrew off without turning into a monster to do it. "That was the day you came home with sand in your shoes, and you said you'd gone running on the beach?"

"It was." He smiled. "I didn't want you worried; that's why I told you I'd gone running."

"I thought it was weird." I giggled. "You hate running on the beach."

"Yeah, because that sand gets everywhere." He chuckled.

"It does," I said. I smiled playfully at him. "Do you have another minute?"

"Sure."

I maneuvered myself so that I was straddling David with my arms around his shoulders. I leaned down so my mouth was close to his ear. "Good," I whispered. "Because the idea of my man telling someone to back off because I am his really turns me on."

I ran my tongue down David's neck, and he moaned, and then his lips were on mine, and he was kissing me, and I forgot all about Andrew. All that mattered now was David and me and our unborn child.

18

I was in town shopping for groceries for dinner when my cell phone rang. I almost ignored it, but something told me not to, and with a sigh, I hefted my basket onto my arm and dug in my purse. I smiled when I saw Alan's name on the screen, my annoyance instantly forgotten.

"Hello," I greeted him.

"Stella, hi. Are you busy?" he asked.

His voice sounded higher pitched than usual, and he was slightly out of breath. My senses were already tingling when I lied to him and told him no, I wasn't busy at all.

"Remember how the last time someone went missing, I dismissed it, and you were right about them being the next victim?" Alan said. He went on without waiting for me to answer. "Well, I've learned from my mistake. And seeing as you helped to teach me that lesson, I thought I would share some information with you."

"Go on," I said.

"Do you know a man named Ryan O'Donohue? Have you ever heard of him before?"

I thought for a moment. Gull Island was a relatively small town, but I didn't know everyone. Ryan O'Donohue. Ryan O'Donohue. Why did that name seem so familiar? It came to me in a rush. Brittany was always talking about him. She had a serious crush on the man. He ran the boarding kennels and the animal rescue center. She knew him when she went looking for puppies.

"He runs the kennels, right?" I said.

"Yes," Alan answered. "And we got a call this morning that he's missing. Well, he's been missing since yesterday evening, from what the report said. I fear he's going to be our next victim."

I frowned as I thought of what I knew about Ryan from Brittany's chat.

"I don't know," I said. "I mean, yeah, the fact he's missing is obviously worrying, but he's not like the other two victims. He runs an animal shelter. People love him, from what I've heard."

"Yes, but he's similar in other ways," Alan explained. "From the few questions I've asked his family so far, it's clear that he too is a bit of a player. He isn't a cheater – he has no long-term partner – and he's open about not wanting to settle down, but he still likes to get about, if you know what I mean. We've sort of assumed at this point that the killings are a punishment for sleeping around, for hurting people. What if they're actually much simpler? What if it's someone who can't get a woman, so he's taking his anger out on men who can?"

I had to admit that sounded like a possibility, and I found myself nodding along despite the fact that Alan obviously couldn't see me. Even if it turned out we were wrong and Ryan was an adult who had chosen to go off grid for a while, until that was proved, we had to take his disappearance seriously.

"He was last seen at the animal shelter by the secretary, who had asked to leave early that day. She left at twelve fifteen, and no one has seen Ryan since then. I'm about to go over to the shelter and take a look around, see if I can turn up anything interesting," Alan told me.

"Want some company?" I asked.

"Sure, since we've no real reason to think this is an actual crime scene and I'm just giving it a look, that'd be okay."

"Great, I'll meet you there in ten minutes."

"Cool. See you then," Alan said and ended the call.

I looked down into my shopping basket. I had a packet of chicken breasts and a carton of cream among other things, and I felt like an asshole just dumping them on a shelf, but I didn't have time to make it back to the fridges and then get out and back to my car and to the animal shelter on time. I spotted a woman in the store uniform and approached her. I smiled apologetically and held out the basket to her.

"Sorry, I have to go," I said. "I don't need this anymore."

The woman glared at the basket and then at me, and I knew I needed to go a bit further.

I put my hand over my mouth and made a retching sound because I knew it would get me free of her. "Sorry, I'm pregnant, and I feel rather ill all of a sudden."

"I understand; thank you for not just dumping your things," the woman said, obviously wanting me gone now before I threw up in her store and she was left to clean it up.

I raced to my car and sped over to the animal shelter. I saw Alan sitting in his car, and I drove across the parking lot to park beside him. He saw me pulling up and got out of his car as I got out of mine. He nodded to me, and I smiled.

"Let's go," he said.

I followed him into the building where a young woman sat behind a desk. She smiled up at us as we approached.

"Sylvia?" Alan said before she could speak.

She nodded, a questioning frown on her pretty face.

"I'm Detective Kellerman. We spoke briefly on the phone earlier today?"

"Oh, of course," Sylvia said, a smile replacing her frown. "Any news on Ryan?"

"None, I'm afraid," Alan replied. "Is it okay for us to have a look around?"

"Yes, yes, of course, whatever you need, Detective," Sylvia said. "But, of course, we couldn't leave the animals unattended, so I've had to have a couple of volunteers come in to help out, so unfortunately I think any forensic evidence will be long gone. But there is something weird that I think you should know."

I felt myself leaning in closer. I liked weird. Weird was something I always looked for in the true-crime mysteries I studied. It could be said that weird was my middle name. Alan also moved in closer, nodding for Sylvia to go on.

"When I came in this morning, all of the animals had food and fresh water, which means whoever took Ryan cared enough about dogs to come back this morning before we opened to see that they were okay," she said.

"Or that Ryan fed them last thing before he left here, and whatever it is didn't happen here after all," Alan said. "Or maybe he's not missing and simply left of his own accord?"

Sylvia shook her head. "That would have been my thought too, Detective, but the front door was unlocked, and there is no way Ryan would have done that. And the cameras for the kennel's security system have all been disabled. Even if Ryan did forget to lock the door, he wouldn't have done that. There isn't a single thing recorded after two p.m. yesterday. And Ryan didn't feed the dogs before that. And we usually feed them between four thirty and five p.m. in the evenings and then again in the morning."

Alan and I shared a glance.

"So you're positive that the food they had when you came in isn't from last night's feeding?"

"Oh, no, that would be impossible. These dogs are serious about their food. They wouldn't all wait all night to eat, and we usually change out their water in the mornings, because dogs get messy with slobber and stuff."

"Yeah, I don't think they'd wait to eat either," I said, looking at Alan again.

Sylvia smiled, evidently realizing she had given us something important.

Alan thanked Sylvia, and we began to look around the place. We soon saw that Sylvia was right – any evidence of any wrongdoing would be long gone. People milled about everywhere, some with dogs on leads, some without. We left the animal shelter and headed for our cars.

"Okay, that's as far as you go," Alan said as we reached our cars.

"What do you mean?" I questioned, wondering if he meant that literally.

He smiled. "It was nice having a second set of eyes here, but now I have to go speak to the family and friends, and I can't take you with me in an official capacity."

I was disappointed, but I understood. Plus, I had grocery

shopping to get back to. "Okay, but you'll let me know what you find out?"

"Of course." He paused and shook his head with a chuckle. "I really shouldn't, you know. I figure though, if I control your access, then the captain can't get too mad, and you won't go digging around on the case on your own."

"You make a very good point." I reached out and touched him on the arm. "I'll talk to you later, Alan. Thanks for letting me tag along here."

"ANYTHING?" I asked as I answered Alan's call later on that day.

"No. Nothing useful."

"Really?" I said in surprise. "Nothing at all?"

"His friends all seem to think the same thing. Everyone really likes Ryan, and he has no enemies. Normally, I'd call bullshit on that and say his friends are trying to protect his reputation because he could be dead, or that we need to keep digging and we'll find the one person who doesn't like him. But this time, it feels different. I actually believe his friends."

"I get that. I mean, how can someone who rescues animals be hated?" I asked.

"Yeah, that's pretty much the same thing I kept getting," Alan replied. "I figured his family are going to be biased in his favor, but it looks like there is some truth to it."

"So really, we're left with two possibilities. Either our guy has made a third kill, or Ryan is perfectly fine and skipped town of his own accord. I know that is out of character for him, but we can't rule it out one hundred percent at this point," I said. "He could have had a mental breakdown or anything, for all we know."

Alan laughed.

"What's funny?" I asked. "It happens, you know. Even to people who seem to have it all together."

"Oh, I know, Stella," he said. "I'm not laughing at the idea of the man having some sort of breakdown. I'm laughing at this. Us talking. It's nice having someone to bounce theories off of, isn't it?"

"Yeah, it is," I agreed.

"Between me and you, Stella, it's like working with a competent partner for once," he added.

And I couldn't help but laugh at that. I wasn't a real detective. I just played one as a hobby.

19

I was in the office bright and early the next day. I could have continued to work from home on the chocolate campaign, but I needed access to some files, so I decided to work in the office. I had kind of missed being in the office, and, strangely, I had discovered that rather than the background noise distracting me, it actually kept me going. I found that when I was working from home and the room was silent, I kept drifting away in my head, my thoughts whirling around and inevitably landing on something other than the ad copy I was supposed to be writing or the press releases I was supposed to be setting up.

It was still early, though. Early enough that there was only a handful of people already in the office, but it was enough to get me going on the latest ad. I could hear the clicking of keyboards, the murmur of early morning greetings and phone calls and the almost constant whirr of activity.

I was almost finished with the ad when I became aware of someone heading in my direction. I looked up and smiled when I saw Brittany. She smiled back, but within a half second, her lower lip wobbled, and her smile became a sob. I stood up quickly, the ad momentarily forgotten, and enveloped Brittany in a hug. She clung to me, and then she did a big sniff and stepped back.

"Sorry," she said.

"You don't have to apologize," I told her. I sat back down and pulled a chair over from the next desk for Brittany, who sat down beside me. "What's wrong?"

"Ryan," she said after a beat. She looked down into her lap and then back up at me. "He's missing." She sniffled, and then her eyes teared up again. "He's dead, isn't he?"

"No one knows that for sure, Brit," I answered.

"But that killer is still out there," she said.

"Yes, that's true, but if you look at the two who were murdered, Ryan doesn't exactly fit."

Brittany gave another shaky sigh, and then she pulled a tissue out of the Kleenex box on my desk and wiped her nose. "But he might fit to the killer."

I hated seeing her so upset, but I couldn't lie. She was right. It was always a possibility, and I was pretty sure that she was right. "That's true. I'm sorry."

"I need to talk to Lonnie," Brittany said. "But I'm glad you're here. I didn't want you to ever think I'd gone behind your back and threw your help back in your face."

"What are you talking about? I would never think that," I said, and I meant it.

"I'm probably being paranoid, but it's just because I so appreciate you getting me in here." She sniffed, then threw her tissue in the garbage can. "I can't take it anymore, Stella. I'm not cut out for this. I'm not good at it like you are. I like doing office stuff, the day-to-day upkeep on accounts, but coming up with ads and everything ... I just don't think it's what I want to do anymore." She sighed, then took another tissue. "And my classes aren't going well."

"It's okay." I reached out and squeezed her arm. "You don't have to be like me. You could move to an administrative role. Lonnie would be thrilled to have you as an administrative assistant."

"Do you really think so? I mean, it's not why she hired me."

"Honestly, Brit. Since you've been here and taken on all that stuff, the office hasn't ever run smoother. I know that Lonnie would love to have you shift to that if it's what you really want to do."

"You're sure? You don't think anyone would be upset?"

"No. We would genuinely love to have you doing all the assistant stuff, all that is so time consuming for us and takes us away from the creative stuff, which we love – and which should be our focus," I replied with a smile.

"Okay, you've convinced me. I'll ask Lonnie if I can stay and be the office assistant even though I'm not going to pursue my degree in marketing anymore," Brittany said, her face brightening a little. "I hope you don't think less of me."

"Of course I don't," I said, meaning it. "This isn't for everyone, Brittany, and I would much rather see you happy than doing something that upsets you. At the end of the day, we need a really good assistant who's going to make sure the accounts stay on track and up to date."

Brittany smiled again, and then she stood up. "Well, I'd best go and start practicing what I'm going to say to Lonnie now that it's changed from me telling her I'm leaving," she said with a rueful shrug.

I laughed and shook my head as I watched her walk

away, but I couldn't shake the uneasy feeling that had settled over me. Brittany had been so apologetic about not following a dream that she no longer wanted, and it made me wonder again exactly how messed up her relationship had been with her ex. The guy had done a real number on her. He'd shook her confidence so bad. I hated it for her and for her daughter, Roxy.

And then to have the new guy she really liked go missing, that had to shake her confidence even more. And what would happen if Ryan really had been targeted by this serial killer? Would it bring her even lower? I hoped not.

I also hoped, a little absurdly, that if he was murdered, his death wouldn't be as gruesome as the last one. I didn't think Brit would be able to take it if it were. Just hearing how the head of the previous victim had been cut off had made her look nauseous, so I hadn't told her anything of what I'd actually seen. It made me wonder why I wasn't quite as bothered by the vile scenes as she and others were. I mean, sure, I had thrown up, but then I'd gone right back in.

Sighing, I tried to put those thoughts out of my head as I got back to work, but when my phone rang and I saw it was Alan, I decided to answer and see if he had anything new to tell me. Maybe he'd found Ryan alive and well.

"Hey, any news? Is he okay?" I asked before he could get a word in.

"I just got off the phone with his sister. She's going to the press, hoping she can either make an appeal to Ryan to come home or call if he's gone off on his own, or to the killer if they still have him alive somewhere."

"Because that worked so well for the Walkers." I knew I was being snarky and sarcastic, but I couldn't help it.

"True, but maybe we're wrong and the killer isn't involved. It's possible."

"Yeah." I sighed.

"Something wrong?" Alan asked.

My thoughts from earlier were still playing with my head, and I wondered if Alan would know. "Why don't these gruesome murders bother me?" I asked.

"Huh?" he grunted.

I knew I had to explain, or he would think I was losing my mind. "I've just been thinking about the murders and how they don't really distress me, but my friend Brittany got seriously grossed out when we were talking about some of the crime scene stuff, and before you get your panties in a bunch over me sharing details with her, I didn't. Not really."

"It's okay. I mean, I know you weren't going to advertise what happened to those men. She's not a reporter or anything, right?"

"Right. She's just my best friend, and she works here with me."

"Then no harm, no foul, and it doesn't make you weird or uncaring to not be bothered by those scenes," Alan said. "Some people have stronger stomachs than others, that's all. If everyone backed off at the sight of a bit of blood and gore, there would be no emergency services. But not stressing out over something you can't change doesn't mean you don't care. You empathize with the victims and their families, just like I do, and that empathy is the driving force, the thing that lets you see terrible things and be okay with it, because you know that seeing it is all for the greater good because you have to witness it in order to find the person responsible and serve up their justice. Not that you are actually doing that, but you have the instincts of a person who does. In another life you could have been a good detective, Stella."

"Well, when you put it that way, I feel a bit more normal," I said with a soft laugh. "Thank you."

"You're welcome," he said, his voice soft. "You've got a good head for mysteries, and I like having you to bounce theories around with."

20

Although Alan's words had soothed me somewhat, I was still feeling out of sorts that evening. I didn't really expect David to notice, but he did.

"Are you okay?" he asked as we sat down to watch a movie after we had had dinner and cleared the dishes away.

"Yes, why?" I said.

"I don't know. You're really quiet. Do you think going into the office in your condition might have been a mistake?" he said.

"No. I didn't do anything I wouldn't have done working from home," I said. "I just ... There's another guy gone missing, and I would be surprised if he isn't dead at this point. You know my friend Brittany? She knows the guy who's missing, and she was a bit of a mess at work, unsurprisingly. On top of that, she's decided to drop out of her classes, and she was going to quit, but I think I talked her into staying on as the office assistant. She was really stressed out and emotional."

"She's the one who had the abusive ex-boyfriend, right?"

"Yes, that's the one. Anyway, after we talked, I started thinking more about the murders and how she got so bothered about the gruesomeness of them, but how I wasn't."

"And is that a problem?" David asked.

I shrugged and then frowned. "I don't know. Maybe?"

He smiled for a second. "Explain it to me like I'm five."

I knew it made me sound a bit crazy, and besides, Alan had made me see it was okay to be the way I was. But I had to say something now that I had started down this avenue, and I decided to tell David the truth and see what he made of it.

"So, I've seen some pretty horrific shit over the last few weeks alone," I said. "The sort of shit you can't ever unsee. The sort of shit that would have normal people running away and never coming back. I have had the odd nightmare, the odd moment of nausea. But I can't help but think that Brittany's reaction is the more normal one. I mean, I didn't even give her basic details of the scenes I saw. I guess it makes me wonder what the hell is wrong with me that I can see this stuff and not be all that affected by it."

David smiled at me, reached out and wrapped his arm around my shoulders, then pulled me closer to him.

I snuggled against his side and rested my head on his shoulder.

"You have absolutely nothing to worry about," David said. He kissed the top of my head almost like he was proud of me. "Some people are better equipped for walking in dark places than others, that's all. It's rare to find people who are that way. People who can look at a murder scene and help figure out the who and why. I'd like to think that I am a bit like that, and that is one of the things we have in common. We can handle the dark in this world. Not everyone can. I'm so lucky to have you in my life. It's good to not feel so alone."

I frowned. I had no idea what he was talking about. He was making it sound like he thought we were a couple of emo teenagers, only this was about more than black lipstick and bad music. This was about life and death, murder, and terrible, terrible violence.

"What do you mean?" I said.

David kissed the top of my head again, and I felt a whoosh of his warm breath on my hair as he gave a soft laugh. He squeezed me tighter against him for a moment.

"I just mean that you can detach yourself from the darkness you see when you need to. You can keep your emotions out of a situation and get shit done when other people can't," he said. "It's a good thing, Stella, really, even if a lot of people don't see it that way."

I felt as though his explanation didn't really clear anything up. If anything, it raised more questions than answers, but suddenly I was afraid to ask them. Well, no, that wasn't true. I was afraid of what the answers might be, so I bit my tongue and didn't ask him anything else.

I tried instead to focus on the movie. It wasn't particularly good, and I felt myself drifting off to sleep. I didn't fight it. I let myself drift. I woke up after what felt like about ten minutes, but when I blinked and looked at the TV, the movie had finished, and a different one was on. I yawned and sat up and stretched.

"Oh, you're back with me, are you, sleepyhead?" David said with a laugh.

"Just barely," I admitted. I yawned again and leaned back against the cushions. "You should have woken me."

"The baby needs you to get plenty of rest. And besides, you looked so peaceful I didn't want to disturb you," he said. "Are you hungry?"

"No, but I'd kill for a nice cup of tea," I said.

David smiled and stood up. "Coming right up," he said.

He left the room, and I tried to think back to what he had said earlier that had left me feeling so uneasy. Oh yes, he had said that it was good I could detach my emotions from a distressing scene. I didn't let myself dig deeper than that. That was the main point; David had said so himself. I wanted to let go of the uneasy feeling in my stomach, but I couldn't. Something was gnawing away at me, and as much as I tried to, I found that I just couldn't ignore it.

David came back in and put my cup of tea on the coffee table in front of me.

I smiled and thanked him, then picked the cup up. I sipped the tea and moaned in pleasure as I sipped it again. I looked at David over the rim of my cup.

"What?" he said.

"I just ... I know I'm being weird, but it's playing on my mind. What did you mean when you said it's a good thing that I can detach my emotions when I have to?" I asked.

"You are being weird, but that's okay, I like weird," David said with a smile. "Seriously, Stella, all I meant was it's good you can switch off when you're looking over crime stuff, or you would be a nervous wreck, and you wouldn't be able to think so analytically about things or come up with the theories you do."

He was saying basically the same thing that Alan had said earlier. That I could ignore the gore and the horror and focus on seeking out answers.

But why was it that when Alan said it, it sounded like he

thought I had real empathy, yet when David said it, it sounded almost like he thought I was some sort of sociopath? And why, rather than being disturbed by the thought of me being a sociopath, did it seem almost like he was pleased by the idea?

21

I spent the morning reading the news story about Ryan's disappearance, and I noticed that the reporter had included Alan's and my speculation that he was victim number three of our not-so-friendly neighborhood serial killer. The story had become so big, hitting not only the local newspaper, but also all the local TV stations. I couldn't get away from seeing or hearing about it everywhere I went. I wished I could have a moment where I was able to think about something else.

Of course, even when I went to the office, it was buzzing with talk about Ryan being missing. I'd had to turn off the radio because it was all they were talking about on my way to the office too. And now I was sitting in a coffee shop, and the news was on the multiple screens around the place, and I knew it was only a matter of time until Ryan's face would appear again. I knew if it came on while we were here, it would be especially bad considering that I was only here because I had brought Brittany out to grab a coffee and take her mind off the fact that everyone around us was talking about Ryan like his death was a foregone conclusion.

"So how did Lonnie take your news?" I asked between small, delicious sips of my vanilla latte.

Brittany smiled, her face lighting up. "You were right. She practically kissed me when I told her I wanted to drop out of the intern program and be the office assistant," she replied.

"I told you she'd be happy to accommodate you," I said with a laugh. "You've saved her from having to make us do all that complicated admin stuff."

Brittany laughed. "Hey, I meant to tell you. The Church of Holy Mary is having a drive for its food bank. They help low-income families and pensioners, as well as homeless people. They're trying to encourage people to donate. I was thinking maybe we could do something to help them out. Maybe do an ad for free?"

I was wondering what I could draw up when she continued.

"I was thinking it might be something that would benefit the business, showing that we're a philanthropic, community-oriented company. What do you think? Do you think Lonnie would approve something like that?"

"I do think you should bring it to Lonnie." I nodded. "It would be a great opportunity to help the community and show that we're doing our part to better our town." I grinned at her, delighted by her ideas and enthusiasm.

"I'm glad you think it's a good idea. They helped me a lot when I first got back to town. I would love to give back to them." Brittany's smile widened. A moment later, her smile faded, and she looked down into her cup.

Wondering what had caused her sudden change in demeanor, I glanced over my shoulder and saw Ryan's handsome face on the TV screen. "Do you want to go?" I asked.

"No. If we go back to the office, they're only going to be talking about it there too," she said.

She was right, of course, and I did my best to keep her talking so she wasn't just sitting there staring at the screen. When we had finished our drinks, she excused herself and went to the ladies' room.

While I was alone, I turned my attention to the screen. A reporter, who had already updated the public on the fact that nothing new had turned up in this case, was now talking to members of the public, asking them their thoughts on the murders and who might be behind them. The majority of them said they didn't know. Some tried to be funny, giving her answers like Dracula, Hannibal Lecter, or Jack the Ripper. A few gave sensible, well-thought-out answers.

Two of the more convincing theories – there were a few people speculating on slightly different versions of each one – seemed to be the most popular. The first one was that the killer was a woman, either someone who had been hurt by all of the victims and was now taking matters into her own hands, or someone who had been hurt by one of the victims and went a bit nuts and kept on killing anyone who reminded her of him. It was a little farfetched, but I could see how it had become popular. There was always a lot more interest in the idea of a female serial killer than there was in a male one.

The second theory, the one closest to my own, was that some sad little incel was taking out men who had success with women, because he was riven by jealousy. I thought it went a bit deeper than that, but on the surface, I agreed.

I'd also heard it thrown around that it was a jealous boyfriend doing the killing. That the first victim had had an affair with his girlfriend, and then, like the woman who went nuts in the first theory, he got a taste for killing and kept going after men who reminded him of the one his girlfriend cheated on him with. Again, that one felt farfetched, but also like there could be elements of truth in it too.

Brittany came back from the ladies' room, and she timed it just right as the news show went to a commercial break, so we could at least gather up our things and get outside without Ryan's smiling, handsome face watching us. We headed back to the office and said our goodbyes when we got there. Brittany went off, happy again as she went to talk to Lonnie about her community-minded idea, and I went back to my own desk.

I spent the rest of the working day drawing up the Graveyard Grill ads and for Wally's Chocolates. Damien had already approved different versions of the ads I was doing, and he had given me the go-ahead to carry out a few alterations and start setting them up. Jordan was a little pickier and wanted final say over anything that went out.

When I finally got to the end of my working day, I left the office and drove home. I went inside and through to the living room, where I found David sitting watching the news. I groaned inwardly when I saw they were leading on Ryan. It seemed I really couldn't get a break from that story anywhere I went.

David looked up from the TV and smiled as I crossed the living room and sat down on an armchair opposite him.

I smiled back as I leaned down and removed my shoes, sighing at how good it felt to be out of them. I rubbed the balls of my feet.

"Long day?" David asked.

"Not really," I said. "I think I'm just getting too pregnant for heels."

David nodded toward the TV. "Have you been watching the news on this guy?"

"No, not really," I said. "It all seems like a lot of opinions and theories and speculation, but so far he hasn't been found, has he?"

"Isn't hiding the body outside of this killer's MO?" David asked.

I thought about it, but we'd only had two bodies so far, and there wasn't a pattern as far as hidden or otherwise went. "Not really," I said. "He's killed twice before, and one body was hidden, and the other one wasn't. I don't think it's about moving them or not moving them for him. I think he has in mind the perfect setting for the body. The gym was the perfect one for the first victim, so he wasn't moved."

"That makes sense," David agreed. "So which of these theories are you backing? The one where it's a woman? Equal rights and all that." He chuckled.

We both laughed, and then we turned serious again.

"I think the closest one for me is the incel one. Some jealous sad case killing off men who don't repulse women," I said as I shook my head.

David frowned, and for a second, I thought he was annoyed, but then his expression smoothed out, his frown gone.

"I think the sort of man you're talking about is too weak to do anything like this. I think it's more likely someone with a slightly more noble cause," he said.

"A noble cause?" I said, my curiosity piqued. "What cause would you think he has?"

"Ahh." David smiled. "Well, that's the sixty-four-thou-sand-dollar question, isn't it? And when your detective friend answers it, maybe he'll finally be on the right track to catch this guy."

"You think the killer is cleverer than Alan, don't you?" I said. "And me!"

"I think this killer could run rings around your detective friend," David said.

It was the second time he had referred to Alan as *my detective*, which I found a bit strange, but he didn't seem like he was insinuating anything, so I let it go.

"I don't think Alan, or any of the cops he works with, could catch this guy even if he sent them his name and address. You, though, I think you will work it out in time. I think you're just a little bit behind the killer."

He sounded proud again as he said it, and while it felt good to have him be proud of me, something niggled at me about this whole conversation. I knew David wasn't a huge fan of the police and that he generally believed they were always at least two steps behind any decent criminal, but this seemed different to that. It seemed almost personal, like he had a stake in the game. That was when it hit me.

"Oh my God," I said. "You actually admire this guy, don't you?"

"All I'm saying is that if he's got even you stumped, then he's no fool," David said.

When he said it like that, it sounded reasonable, normal. But for a moment it had sounded ... different. Like David was rooting for the killer, almost.

But that was just crazy talk, wasn't it? It must be my hormones, I decided. The pregnancy was playing havoc with my emotions, and now I was simply looking for things that weren't there.

22

I was working from home this morning, setting up various social media releases for the accounts I was working on. Lonnie had lightened my load, not giving me any new clients, but just the task of maintaining the three major accounts that were mine, and now that all the major artwork and ad copies had been completed, it was merely a matter of upkeep.

David, too, was working from home, which was nice, because it meant we could see each other throughout the day and even enjoy lunch together. As I was making us both sandwiches, my cell phone rang, and I saw it was Alan.

"Hey, Alan, what's up? Anything new with the case?"

"You're not going to believe this," he said.

"Well, don't keep me in suspense," I said as I spread mayo on David's sandwich but not my own, unfortunately.

"Ryan O'Donohue has turned up at the hospital," Alan replied.

"What? Are you sure it's him?" I asked.

"Yep," he said. "He showed his ID to the nursing staff."

"You are one hundred percent sure it's him? Not some faker looking for notoriety?"

"I can't be one hundred percent until I go over there and interview him, but I thought you might like to know and maybe join me when I speak to him?" he offered.

Excitement bubbled up inside me. "Really? Is that allowed? I mean, the captain isn't going to get mad?"

"He might, but you've been a big help to me in this case, and I'm hoping you might pick up on something I miss."

"Alan, I'm an amateur, and you know it. But if you think I can help, then I'm on my way," I assured him.

"Great, I'll meet you there."

I put my sandwich in a box to take with me, then picked up David's plate. I hurried down the hall toward his office.

"You'll never believe what's happened," I said.

"What? Are we not eating together?" he asked.

I gave him an apologetic look. "Ryan O'Donohue has turned up," I said, feeling another wave of excitement.

"Oh yeah?" David replied, sounding curious. "Where did they find the body?"

"No, you don't understand," I said. I knew I needed to get moving, but I also wanted to see David's face when I told him the news. "He's not dead. He's in the hospital. Someone tried to kill him, but he escaped."

"What?" David said, his brow scrunched in confusion. "How can he be alive?"

He sounded flabbergasted, and it seemed like a strange reaction to hearing someone was alive instead of murdered by a serial killer. "You seem almost disappointed," I said, "that the man is alive?"

He shook his head, his expression clearing. "No, not disappointed. Just shocked. Come on, Stella, you didn't believe he was going to turn up alive any more than I did," he said.

It was a fair point.

"True," I agreed. "I really didn't. Anyway, Alan's asked me to come speak to him too, see if I can pick up something that he doesn't."

David stood, a strange smile on his lips. "Well, don't disappoint that detective of yours. He probably can't survive without your input."

I rolled my eyes. "You know that's not true."

David drew me into his arms. "No, I'm serious. You're probably the best chance he has to figure out whoever is behind these murders."

His words were nice to hear, but there was something off about them, but again I didn't have time to question him on it. "I'll be back later, okay?"

"Sure thing, bye," David said, hugging me and blowing me a kiss as I hurried toward the door.

I sensed him move behind me, and I looked back over my shoulder.

He smiled and held the door for me. "Remember the guy has probably been through something pretty awful. His memory might not be one hundred percent."

"I'll be gentle with him," I said with a smile.

I stepped out of the house and got into my car. I drove to the hospital, reminding myself to stick to the speed limit. I parked and made my way toward the entrance, meeting Alan at the main doors. Adrenaline fizzed through my body. I was about to talk to a survivor. I could be mere moments away from learning who our serial killer was.

We headed into the hospital together, and Alan asked for the ward Ryan was on. The receptionist gave him the details once he showed his badge. We headed for the elevator, and I hit the button for the right floor.

"Do you know his condition?" I asked, curious.

"No. All I know is he somehow made it here and still had his wallet with him. The nurse who called it in said he was incoherent, but I'm hopeful that he'll be able to answer some questions and we'll be able to figure out who's behind all of this shit."

I nodded as the elevator dinged. We got out and headed for the ward number the receptionist had given us, but just as we reached the door, a doctor stepped out of the room.

"You can't be here," the doctor said.

"I'm Detective Kellerman." Alan showed his badge. "I need to speak with Ryan O'Donohue."

"That's not going to be possible. Ryan has been sedated; he is in a medically induced coma."

My eyes widened. "Why?"

The doctor's eyes flashed toward me, and he arched a brow.

"I'd like to know the extent of his injuries," Alan said, drawing the doctor's attention back to him.

"He's lost a lot of blood. We've had to give him a blood transfusion," the doctor said, his tone clipped. "He's had multiple lacerations, several broken ribs, and there are bite marks on his hands."

"Bite marks?" I questioned.

Again, he looked at me, but this time he answered. "Yes, he was found with a malnourished German shepherd. We called animal control for the creature, but he was pretty docile, and they were able to take him somewhere safe where he could be cared for properly."

"So they aren't going to put the dog down, right?" I asked.

"Not as far as I know." The doctor shrugged. "Anyway, you won't be able to speak to Mr. O'Donohue until tomorrow."

"I'm going to put an officer on the door," Alan informed him. "I don't want anyone else speaking to him about this, no reporters. Considering what we believe to be going on, I want to get him in a safehouse, for his own protection. Will he be able to be moved tomorrow?"

The doctor nodded. "I would say yes, probably after he's had a good rest. Though he'll need a significant amount of time to recover and should stay on bed rest for at least the next week."

Alan nodded. "I'll see to it." He tilted his head at me toward the elevator. "Thanks for your time, Doctor."

"Pleasure." He nodded and walked over to the nurses' station, speaking to them in hushed tones while glancing back at the two of us.

Alan pulled his phone from his pocket and dialed, then stopped before we reached the elevators. "Adams? I need two officers over here at Mercy General. I want round-the-clock guard duty on Ryan O'Donohue ... Yeah, he's alive, he's sedated, and we can't talk to him until tomorrow ... Right. Yes, I'm calling the captain next; just get a couple of officers over here now." He hung up and glanced at me.

"Guards and a safehouse? Do you think the killer will come here to finish him off?"

Alan shrugged. "I don't know. Maybe? We don't know why he didn't have the kind of injuries the others did. For all we know, he's not even a victim of our serial killer. And what's with the dog? That's an unusual addition, don't you think?"

I nodded. It didn't make any sense to me. I had expected

Ryan to turn up dead, but here he was still just about alive. So yes, I thought that was unusual. "I guess we'll have to wait for tomorrow to find out what happened. I suppose it's a good idea to keep an eye on him one way or another until we work it out."

"Exactly my thoughts. I'll give you a call and let you know when we have everything set up for the safehouse. I'll wait to question him once he's installed there."

"All right." I sighed. "You coming down with me or waiting for the officers?"

"I'm gonna wait; you go ahead."

"See you later." I gave Alan a wave as I stepped on the elevator, deflated that I didn't get to talk to Ryan after all, especially now that I had more questions than answers.

23

I drove home with the windows down and my music blaring out. I even sang along, not caring that I was probably way off key, and everyone could hear me. I was in a good mood despite not knowing anything more about the killer yet. With Ryan being alive, we were close to having that information. Nothing could have brought me down at that moment.

I was still singing under my breath when I got home. David shouted at me from the kitchen, where he was standing stirring a pan of something that smelled meaty and delicious.

"I guess it went well, then," he said, glancing at me over his shoulder, still stirring the pan.

"Yes. We weren't able to speak to Ryan yet, but when he's moved to a safehouse tomorrow, I can go with Alan to interview him," I explained.

"You should be careful who you tell about that," David said. "One phone call, one whisper to the press of the fact that Ryan is alive, and the killer could be tipped off."

"Are you seriously threatening to do that?" I said, shocked.

David laughed and shook his head. "No, of course not. I was just saying I hope the hospital staff know better than to open their mouths," he said.

"Oh, yeah, good point. I'm sure Alan will take care of that. He's still at the hospital, waiting on the police guards to get there."

"Would you like some beef stew?" David asked.

"Yes, please. My stomach started growling the minute I walked in the door; it smells so damn good." I sat down at the table and waited.

David spooned the stew into two bowls, carried them over, and sat down with me.

I placed the first spoonful in my mouth and was instantly met with a warm, salty richness. "Oh, that's delicious."

"Thank you." David smiled. "So, back to Ryan. You'll be going to the actual safehouse to speak to him?"

I nodded.

"Okay. That could be quite far out. I'll drive you."

It didn't sound like an offer. More like an order, and I immediately bristled, but I forced myself to be civil in my reply.

"I can drive myself," I said.

"I know you can," David said. He smiled, and suddenly it didn't seem like he was ordering me about but rather that he was trying to help me, and I was just being unreasonable again. "But you said you were too pregnant for all this running about and driving so much. I just want to take some of the pressure off for you."

"I appreciate that," I replied. "But I only meant I was too pregnant for the stilettos." I lifted my foot up and poked it out from beneath the table, showing him my sensible flat shoe. "See? Flats. I can still drive and do everything else."

"Are you sure?" David pressed me. "I don't want you exhausting yourself. It's not good for the baby."

I nodded. "Besides, Alan is being generous indulging me, and I'm pretty sure he's not going to want anyone extra tagging along."

"I'm your husband, Stella. It's not like you're handing out invites to strangers," David said. "And I just want to be sure you're not overdoing it."

"I know, and I promise I'll go easy." I smiled and reached for his hand. "I probably won't be driving anyway. Alan will probably have me meet him at the station, and he'll drive us to the safehouse."

David leaned over the table to squeeze my hand. "Okay, I trust you to know what you're doing. Just be careful? And remember to take what this guy says with a pinch of salt. He's been through the mill, and his memory might not be up to any sort of standard."

I smiled at him. It was actually quite sweet how protective of me he was. "Thank you for letting me pursue this hobby," I said. "I know it's kind of a weird one."

He chuckled. "I don't think it's all that weird. You've got a quick and intelligent mind, and I think that detective of yours is lucky to have you on his team."

I blushed at his praise, then turned back to my meal.

"Oh, I forgot to tell you, I'm probably going to have to go out to the office tonight. I've got a conference call with the Japanese investor. Dalton can't take this one."

"Will you be late?" I asked, feeling let down.

His eyes lit, and he smiled at me. "I'll make it as quick as I can. Promise."

24

"Still interested in coming with me to speak to Ryan?"

"Of course I am," I answered.

"Meet me at the mall in the orange parking lot," Alan said before he ended the call.

I hurried out to my car. I had been sitting in my home office, waiting for his promised call. I had finished up all the account work I'd needed to do for the day, getting Wally's newest revised ad out on all their accounts. Jordan had reported they'd had an uptick in sales since we'd started the campaign, and they were quite happy with everything I was doing. And once I'd finished with that, I'd sat mulling over the two murders and Ryan's disappearance. So Alan's call had been welcome. I was driving myself crazy with questions.

I arrived at the mall and drove toward the orange parking lot. I spotted Alan's car and parked beside it. I rolled my window down, and he did the same.

"Do you want me to ride with you?" I asked. "Or are you giving me the address for my GPS?"

"Actually, I thought you would ride up with me, and then I'll drop you off back here when we're done," he said.

"Not going to lie, I was hoping you'd say that." I grinned. I grabbed my purse and made sure I had my cell phone. Once I had everything I needed, I closed my window and got out of the car. I locked it and got into the passenger seat of Alan's car.

He pulled away, and we left the parking lot, heading toward the outskirts of town.

"How far away is it?" I asked. "The safehouse, I mean."

"It's not that far. About twenty minutes or so by car, about ten miles past the Walker crime scene. It's near the beach," he said.

I nodded and fell silent. I had hundreds of questions, but none of them were ones Alan would be able to answer.

We had been driving for about fifteen minutes when Alan glanced at me and started to talk, breaking the comfortable silence that had fallen between us. "There's going to be a couple of officers on duty at the safehouse. They will be staying with Ryan until we can determine what happened to him and, if he was taken, then probably until the killer is caught."

"Will the cops question me being there with you?" I asked.

"No, they are already aware. I cleared it with the captain." He sighed. "You know we're not really equipped for this kind of killer here in Gull Island, so he's pretty open to any help we can get."

"Do you think Ryan will accept me being there?"

"I'll introduce you along with myself. I doubt he'll think anything about it, don't worry."

"And if he does, I'll tell him I'm Stella Greene, homicide," I teased.

"Umm, no, you won't. It's against the law to impersonate an officer," he replied.

"Oh, you're no fun," I said, grinning at him. "Go on. I'll let you tell people you're a marketing executive." I laughed. "Think they'd believe you?"

Alan shook his head. "I wouldn't know the first thing about doing what you do."

I shrugged. "It's not all that hard."

"For you maybe." He winked. "I couldn't draw anything without a traceable."

"You know it's not all about the art, right? I use photography, videography, all mediums of art. Some of it I can do, but most of that stuff is farmed out. I do the word stuff. Creating vocally and visually appealing ads for the companies that hire us. Then I not only book newspaper space, radio and TV ad times, I do social media posts on various platforms. Most people skip TV ads now, so they aren't as viable as they once were. Now it's all about social media."

"And I don't do social media, so I haven't a clue about that stuff." He chuckled.

We pulled up outside a house, and I realized I had no real idea where I was. I had been too busy talking for the last five or so minutes of the drive to take any notice of where we were going.

The safehouse was the same as the other houses in the small cul-de-sac, only it looked a little bit bigger. It was white, and it had a wraparound porch complete with chairs and a small plastic table. A swing hung from a large tree to the side of the house. It was only when we got out of the car and walked past the end of the driveway and I was able to see between the safehouse and its neighbor that I saw what was so special about these houses. Alan hadn't been kidding when he said the house was by the beach. The backs of the houses on the cul-de-sac had small yards of grass and garden, depending on the house, and then the beach was just beyond.

"What a beautiful place to live," I remarked. "Unless you're in Ryan's situation, I guess."

"It really is beautiful." Alan nodded. "And it's ideal for us because the other houses on this street are all vacation homes. Oftentimes, out of season, the other houses are empty, and even when they are in use, the people here are used to seeing different people coming and going where the owners of the beach houses rent them out to holiday vacationers. It's a good place to be a stranger and not stand out as strange."

We went up to the house, and Alan knocked on the front door.

After a moment, I heard feet approaching. There was a pause where I assumed the person was looking out through the peephole at us, and then the door opened, and a uniformed officer smiled out at us.

"Detective Kellerman," he said, giving him a nod.

The detective nodded back, and the officer stepped aside and let us in. He nodded to me too, and I nodded back, relieved that I seemed to have made it past the first hurdle without any fuss.

"How is he, Officer Feeney?" Alan asked once we were inside and the front door had been closed and locked behind us.

"He's on and off sleeping, but when he's awake, he seems coherent enough. He's taking his medication without any arguments. Considering how this could have ended, I would say he's doing pretty damned well," Officer Feeney replied.

"Yes, he's one very lucky man," Alan agreed. He motioned to the stairs beside us. "I take it he's up there?"

Officer Feeney nodded. "The second door on the right," he said. "Can I get either of you anything? A drink maybe?"

"No, thank you," Alan said, already heading for the stairs.

I was kind of thirsty, but it wasn't exactly a raging thirst, and I didn't want to draw any attention to myself, so I shook my head. "I'm good, thanks," I said.

I followed Alan to the second door on the right, where we had been directed. He knocked lightly on it, but no answer came. He looked at me and shrugged, then pushed the door gently open.

Ryan was propped up on several pillows in the center of a large bed. His eyes were closed, his mouth was open, and he was snoring gently. His being asleep wasn't a big worry. We had as long as this took for him to wake up, and with him being asleep, it gave me a chance to have a quick look at him and the room without it being obvious.

Ryan had a small cut on his top lip, but other than that, his face was unmarked. His chest and shoulders had a few lacerations, which didn't look too bad, but his arms and hands were covered in cuts, bite marks, and scratches, several of which had stitches in them. At least one was an angry red color and swollen; I figured it might be infected. I hoped for his sake that one of the meds he was taking was a strong antibiotic to fix it.

Having learned everything that I could by assessing the

sleeping man, I went to the window purely for something to do. There were two chairs beside the bed, obviously put there for our arrival, but I didn't feel like sitting down. Not until Ryan was awake. I was too full of energy to sit quietly and wait like Alan was.

The view from the window was stunning: the deserted white sand and the ocean waves gently rolling in and lapping at the sand before lazily rolling back out to sea again. It was so peaceful, and I felt as though I could stand there looking at that view all day. That was until I heard someone cough behind me. I turned to see that Ryan was awake.

"Umm, who are you?" he asked, looking from Alan to me and back to Alan again, who was seated next to him.

I moved and sat down in the other chair beside the bed.

"I'm Detective Kellerman," Alan said. "And this is Stella Greene. I believe Officer Feeney told you I'd be coming to talk to you about what happened."

Ryan screwed his face up for a moment.

I squeezed my purse in my lap, anxious to get things started. I had so many questions I was dying to ask.

"Yeah," Ryan said after a moment. "Yeah, that's right. He did." He reached for a glass of water from the table beside his bed. He picked it up and took a long drink, and then he put it back down. "I hope you're going to catch that bastard."

I bit the inside of my mouth to keep from smiling. The venom in Ryan's voice told me that he was more than coherent and that he wouldn't care who was present in this interview as long as someone who could catch his attacker was one of them.

"I hope so too," Alan said. "And I have every reason to believe we will be able to with your help. So, to start with, if you can just tell us anything you can remember that has happened to you, in your own words."

Ryan nodded.

"Great. Whenever you're ready, Mr. O'Donohue," Alan said, pulling a notepad and a pen from his pocket, as well as a voice recorder. He looked up and said, "Do you mind if I record this?"

Ryan shook his head. "It's fine."

I sat back in my chair, ready to hear how Ryan had been abducted. And how he had managed to be the one who'd gotten away.

25

"So, you know I work at the kennels?" Ryan asked. "And that we have a section for surrenders and strays that we help adopt out, right?"

"Yes," Alan said. "Is that where you were abducted from?"

"Yes, sir. It was the middle of the afternoon, which is usually quiet for us," Ryan said, then frowned. "I don't know why. My theory has always been that anyone who wants to adopt a pet and has thought about it long and hard gets there early. Anyone who wants to adopt a pet and makes the decision on the spur of the moment seems to turn up toward closing time. And most people dropping off their pets for kenneling or picking them up are the same. They drop them off early and pick them up around closing."

I opened my mouth, ready to tell Ryan to skip to the important parts, but Alan looked at me with a stony expression on his face and shook his head firmly. I more than got the message. He didn't want me to rush him. Ryan needed to do this at his own pace.

It wasn't that I was in any hurry, I just wanted to hear the important part of the story, the part that was going to hopefully break open the case so that we'd be able to figure out who the killer was. I forced myself to be patient, and I kept listening to Ryan, accepting that I was going to have to let him tell this story his way – even if that meant him talking for two or three times longer than was strictly necessary.

"Usually during the afternoons, I potter around doing what needs doing," Ryan went on. "Walking dogs, bathing them if they need it, giving out medication, playing with the dogs and the cats, filling out paperwork, whatever is needed that day. And Sylvia, my secretary, she staffs the reception desk and gets on with her stuff. But she had asked to leave work early that day, so there was only me there."

"And that was unusual?"

He nodded. "Yes. Anyway, I had just done my medication rounds, so it must have been around two thirty, maybe three p.m., something like that. I thought I heard something out in the reception area, and I started toward it. At the same time, the door opened, and a man appeared. He apologized for the intrusion and explained there was no one in reception, and he asked if he could have a look around. He said he was looking for a dog to adopt. Obviously, I said yes to showing him around. We are always looking to place our dogs and cats in their forever homes."

"And was there anything in his behavior that seemed odd?" Alan asked.

"No, not at that moment." Ryan shook his head. "I started asking him questions about the size of dog he was interested in, the age, that kind of thing. He was very vague in his answers, but that alone wasn't enough to rouse my suspicions. Lots of people think by keeping their answers vague, they are more likely to be approved to get a dog. It's actually more likely to be true the other way, that they will be approved if they know what they want. It shows they have at least a basic understanding of a dog and its needs."

He was babbling again, but this time, I made no move to interrupt him. He must have realized for himself though, because he gave a little laugh and shook his head.

"Sorry, I think I wandered slightly off topic there," he said. "If I start giving you guys my 'why you need to adopt a dog' spiel, please tell me to shut up and move on, okay?"

"Just take your time." I smiled at him. "You've been through a lot. Talking about it has to be hard," I acknowledged.

"It is." He looked down at his bandaged hands. "Now, where was I? Oh yes. I was showing this man the dogs, trying to get him to tell me a bit about the sort of dog he wanted in an ideal world. We had only seen about a quarter of them when I realized that he wasn't by my side anymore. I thought he must have seen a dog that had taken his liking, and as I turned around to see which dog it was, he grabbed me and pressed a wet rag to my face."

I had been expecting something like this, but hearing it firsthand was startling. I nodded at Ryan to continue.

"I didn't know what it was or what was happening at the time. All I knew was I had to get him off of me. I tried to fight him off, but my limbs were growing weaker, and then I guess I fell unconscious. I'm assuming now that the rag was soaked in chloroform?" He raised a questioning eyebrow at Alan.

"We can't know for sure without the rag itself, but judging by your description, I'm guessing yes," he said.

Ryan thought for a moment, and then he went on. "Sorry, before I continue with what happened, I have to ask, are the animals okay? I mean, they were never fed that night, and I've been really worried about them. Nobody's been able to tell me."

"Yes, I'm sorry, we should have let you know," Alan said. "Sylvia is taking care of them, and she has recruited some volunteers to help her. And we're pretty sure that whoever did this to you returned to the shelter and gave each animal food and water."

Ryan laughed.

I frowned, confused. Alan looked confused too. Surely someone feeding the animals and giving them water was a good thing. I couldn't understand why Ryan was laughing.

"Sorry," Ryan said. "I was just thinking I've always said I prefer animals to people. This guy takes that to a whole new level, doesn't he?"

I was kind of shocked that his sense of humor was still intact after everything he'd been through.

"Yeah, I guess he does," Alan agreed.

Ryan fell silent, and after a few seconds, Alan spoke up again, nudging Ryan back into his story. "So, can you tell us what happened when you came back to consciousness?"

"Oh. Right. Sorry." Ryan took a deep breath, gathering himself. "I woke up and found myself in a basement. It didn't have that musty smell that abandoned properties have, but at the same time, it felt still and empty. I was in a large metal kennel, the kind people use for dogs when they have them in the car or for when they crate them while they're at work. I felt that was kind of ironic, like he had probably stolen the thing from the shelter and then used it on me."

"Aren't they easy enough to open?" I asked.

"Normally, yes, but this one was locked with a big padlock, but I wasn't worried about that – I knew I could get it open, given time. What I was worried about was the huge feral dog that was roaming free around the basement. It looked like a German shepherd – it was certainly the right size – but the poor thing was emaciated, clearly starving, and likely abused and therefore mistrusting of people."

"There was a dog in the basement with you?"

Ryan nodded. "I said 'hi' to the dog, hoping to make friends with it. He snarled at me, showing me his teeth and growling. I knew that getting the dog not to attack me wasn't going to be easy, but I also knew that I had to escape that basement, which meant freeing myself from the cage and facing the dog without the meager protection the cage gave me. I also knew that, no matter what happened, none of it was really the dog's fault and that I had to save him."

"Your first thought was to save the dog?"

"It might sound odd to you, but yes. It wasn't his fault this asshole had starved him and left him down there, thinking he'd hurt me. My abductor clearly underestimated me, because the only thing he took off of me was my cell phone. I still had my wallet and my keys. But, most importantly, I was still wearing my wristwatch. I know a lot of people don't wear them anymore, but I do. And it's good that I do. I was able to break it apart and pull out the little metal rods that hold the straps onto the watch face. I used those to open the padlock. It didn't take me very long."

"Smart. How did you learn to do that?" I asked, curious.

Alan gave me an exasperated look, but I really wanted to know.

"As a kid, I wanted to be a spy, so I used to read a lot about things like that. I taught myself how to open all kinds of locks." Ryan smiled.

Again, his good nature shone through as he spoke. "Well,

since you're here, I'm going to say it was a pretty useful skill to have learned."

"Yes, it was." He nodded. "Anyway, as soon as I was out of the cage and on my feet, the dog came toward me. He was still growling, still terrified, and I took a step toward him. He took a step back. He wasn't going to attack me. At least not fatally. He was more scared of me than anything. If he could have gotten away from me, he would have, but whoever put him in that cellar tied him up and placed him between me and the stairs."

I gestured toward his hands and arms, where the bite marks were still visible. "What about those?"

"Yes, he did nip at me a bit. It took me a couple of hours of coaxing and talking softly to the dog, then gently petting him, before he realized he could trust me. Usually, I am quicker to persuade a dog to come around to me, but usually I would have dog treats to help, and, of course, I wouldn't usually be putting off the scent of so much adrenaline and fear. That definitely made the dog skittish long after he usually would have calmed down."

"So they really can smell fear?" Alan asked.

"They can, yes." Ryan nodded. "Once he accepted me, I untied him, and I went up to the door at the top of a wooden staircase. I tried the door, but it was locked. I used the pins from my watch again, and the door opened. I went back for the dog, who was cowering at the bottom of the staircase. Maybe that was stupid, but I couldn't just leave him there. I used the rope he had been tied up with as a makeshift leash."

"Well, considering you said your first thought was to rescue the dog, it's not surprising that that's what you did." I smiled at him.

"True, I suppose. So when I got up into the main house, it had that same feeling as the basement. Not an unlived-in feeling as such, but a feeling of emptiness, like no one was home. It seemed that I had finally caught a break because if there was anyone home, they didn't make any effort to stop me from leaving."

"So you didn't stick around to explore where you were?" Alan asked.

"No, I went to the front door first, but it was locked from the outside with no way of unlocking it from the inside, which was weird, and there was no sign of any keys. The front door was much more modern than the basement door, and the lock was far too sophisticated for me to pick with watch pins, so I went to try the back door. It was locked too, but this one had the locks on the inside, so I could just undo them. The door opened, and we were free."

"So that's when you made your way toward the hospital?"

"Well, not yet. We weren't exactly free. We were in a large backyard, and surrounding it was a barbed-wire fence. No gate. My heart sank. I knew I'd be ripped to shreds getting out of that place, but I figured that was still likely better than whatever my abductor had planned for me. As you can see, I cut myself to ribbons getting the two of us out of there. I did well, though; the dog didn't have a single mark on him as far as I could tell."

"That accounts for the lacerations on your chest and arms, yes. Do you have the same on your legs?" Alan asked.

"Yes, a few," Ryan said. "Anyway, that's pretty much it. It was dark by the time I got over the fence. I checked my watch, which was still in my pocket, and confirmed it was almost five a.m. I stumbled along, looking for a house with its lights on. I knew I was losing blood from the barbed-wire cuts, and I was starting to feel light-headed. Somehow, I managed to get out of the neighborhood and figured out where I was. It wasn't too far to the hospital from there, but I'm not sure how I actually made it. I don't really remember too much after that until I woke up in that hospital room."

I thought Ryan was finished, but then he frowned.

"What happened to the dog?" he asked, looking about almost frantically. "Did he run off? Has he been found and brought to the shelter?"

"He didn't run off," Alan explained gently. "He was still with you when you were found at the entrance to the hospital. He was skittish, and the staff who found you both called animal control—"

"They didn't harm him, did they?" Ryan sat up, worry laced through his voice.

"No, he's fine," Alan reassured him. "They are taking care of him. He was docile, according to the doctor I spoke to. He didn't want to leave your side, but when I called to check on him, they said they were able to coax him with a meal and get him looked at. He's resting comfortably and receiving the care he needs."

Ryan nodded, his face a picture of relief. "I'm glad to hear that."

"Do you have any idea of the address of the house you were held captive in?" I blurted out, unable to keep my question in any longer. I waited for Alan to give me another one of his "shut the hell up" looks, but he didn't. He looked at Ryan instead of at me, seemingly as interested in the answer to that as I was.

"No, not really," Ryan said. "I know it was somewhere nice, a nice estate, I mean. All of the houses I passed after I got out of were huge, and the place had that feel to it, you know? It was fairly high up, because I could see the island sprawling out for miles from where I was; I could even see the sea in the distance. I could probably find the neighborhood, and then I would know the house again if I saw it, I think. No, I know I would."

Alan nodded thoughtfully.

I figured that once Ryan was up to it, Alan would be taking him on a long drive around the higher points of the island, hoping that he might spot the house he'd been held captive in. I half wondered if Google Earth might help, but I knew from experience that if you weren't sure what you were looking for, it didn't always help. Maybe Alan would give it a whirl though, so I mentioned it.

"It's worth a shot," Alan replied as he pulled up the app. "What do you think, Ryan?" he handed over his phone.

Ryan pulled the screen closer to his face and began to zoom in and out, looking at various parts of the island on the app. "I don't know. I was pretty disoriented. I think I may have to physically retrace my steps."

Alan sighed and gave him a nod as he took his phone back.

"It was worth a shot though; thanks for trying." I smiled at him.

Alan asked a few more questions, trying to establish a clear sense of the timeline of events.

As he continued to ask his questions, I sat there thinking things over. There was something niggling at me. I really wanted to know more about the abductor. The man who'd pretended to want a dog, but then kidnapped Ryan.

"I have a question, and please don't think I'm being rude," I started.

Alan looked at me a bit warily, but he didn't interrupt.

"Did you at no point think it was odd that someone came to adopt a dog in the middle of the afternoon with their face hidden?"

"Well, sure, that would be weird," Ryan said. "But that wasn't the case."

I felt a shock of excitement surge through me, and I finally risked a look at Detective Kellerman. He was gaping at Ryan.

"Wait. Are you telling me that you saw his face?" Alan asked.

Ryan shrugged. "Yeah."

"Sorry, but did you seriously not think that was worth mentioning?"

"I assumed you knew, when I said he came in asking to see the dogs," Ryan explained. "Like Detective Greene said, it would have been odd to come in to look at the dogs with your face hidden."

Alan winced as Ryan called me Detective Greene, but he didn't comment, and I knew I couldn't be in trouble for it. I hadn't told Ryan I was a cop, and when he had addressed me as such, he had been talking to Alan, not me. It wasn't like I had answered him and kept up the ruse. Surely correcting him at that point would have seemed nit-picky.

"I definitely would have mentioned that his face was covered," Ryan continued. "I thought it went without saying that he wasn't wearing a mask or a balaclava or something."

"Fair enough, my mistake," Alan conceded. "I suppose when you put it that way, it makes sense." He held his pen poised over his notebook. "Can you describe him for me, please?"

"Sure," Ryan said. "He was tall – I would say at least six

feet – and he was well built, but not fat. He looked like he worked out. He wasn't built like a bodybuilder, just like an average guy who worked out and kept in shape. He had dark brown hair, which was short. And he had really dark brown eyes. They were almost black. He was wearing a black suit and a pale blue shirt and a darker blue tie. I remember at the time thinking he might have been on a break from an office job somewhere."

"How old do you think he is?" Alan asked.

"Not old. Not young. Maybe thirty-five to forty, something like that," Ryan said.

"Was there anything that stood out about him?" I asked.

"No," Ryan said. "Like I said, he was well dressed, and he was good looking. He didn't look like the sort of man who might attack you, you know what I mean? He looked like a businessman."

"Did you recognize him? Even as someone you have seen in passing around the island?" Alan asked.

"No," Ryan said with a shake of his head. "Definitely not."

Alan started to close his notebook and put a cap on his pen. "I'll leave you my card, Ryan. If you think of anything else, call me, okay?"

Ryan nodded as he took the offered card.

"I'll have one of our artists come by if that's okay; that way we can get a sketch done of your assailant."

Ryan nodded again. He was starting to look tired, and as if to prove it, he yawned. "Sorry," he said.

"No need to apologize. We've taken up more than enough of your time already," Alan said. He stood up, and I did too. "Thank you for answering our questions so fully. Now, please, get some rest."

"When can I go back home?" Ryan asked as we moved to leave.

"As soon as we've caught this bastard," Alan replied, a hard edge of determination to his voice.

"And when will that be?" Ryan asked.

"Soon, I hope," Alan answered.

I thought how he sounded a whole lot more confident than I felt. While a living eyewitness was a great breakthrough, he wasn't yet up and about to go with Alan to where he'd been held prisoner. And the description he'd given of his abductor, while not exactly vague, surely it described at least fifty percent of the men who lived on Gull Island.

26

I had barely gotten through the front door when David ushered me through to the living room and tried to get me to sit down next to Dalton.

"Has something happened?" I asked, worried by his insistence that I sit down. I looked from him to Dalton.

"Hi, Stella." Dalton glanced at me sheepishly.

"No, of course not, everything's fine," David said. "But you promised me the full story when you came home, remember? And Dalton is interested too. I thought it would be nice if he joined us for dinner."

"Yes, I remember. Hi, Dalton, I'm glad to have you." I smiled at him, then turned back to David. "I kind of meant I'd share everything after I've taken my coat off, used the bathroom, and gotten a drink," I told him with a laugh.

David looked irritated for a moment, but then he and Dalton both laughed.

"Sorry. Of course you want to do all of that first. I'm just trying to show an interest, and I guess I got too involved. Here, give me your coat, and I'll go and hang it up for you, and then while you're using the bathroom, I'll make us all something to drink. How's that?"

"Good." I smiled, charmed by how interested the two of them seemed in what I'd learned.

I shrugged out of my coat and gave it to David; then I went upstairs. I used the bathroom and splashed some water on my face. I brushed my teeth and then went into the bedroom, where I changed into a pair of lounge pants and a comfy top. I came back down to find David and Dalton in the living room, drinking cups of coffee. David had made me a tea and set it on the table.

"Thanks," I said, sitting down next to David and picking up the cup. It wasn't as good as coffee, but with the baby, I still wasn't drinking much coffee. I took a long drink and made an "ahh" sound. The tea felt good after my throat being dry for so long.

"You changed your clothes?" Dalton asked, eyeing me.

"Yeah, I just wanted to be relaxed. The baby, you know?" I smiled, patting my growing stomach as I wriggled on the couch, getting more comfortable.

"So what happened?" David asked me. "How did this guy escape our killer?"

"And how come you were able to go with this detective?" Dalton asked, his voice curious.

I explained about my connection to Alan.

"I've told you that Stella likes to dig through true-crime stories. She's damn good at it too," David said proudly.

I blushed at his words.

"How did that lead to actually getting involved in this?" Dalton asked, staring at me intensely. "Isn't it dangerous?"

I shrugged. "It was kind of by accident." I explained how

I'd come upon the two murder scenes and how Alan had agreed to let me help.

"So it's not dangerous if she's there after the fact," David said, his voice almost hard as he spoke directly to his brother.

I frowned as I looked between him and Dalton.

"She's as good a detective if not better than the local PD. Stella could run circles around them if she decided to change her career."

"Hmmm," Dalton murmured noncommittally.

I gave him a tight smile and then looked at David.

"So? Tell us what happened," David encouraged.

I ran through the story of Ryan picking the lock on the cage door, getting the feral dog to trust him, and then picking the lock on the basement door, going out the back door, before finally climbing the barbed-wire fence despite it ripping him to shreds.

"Who is this guy?" David said. "Rambo?"

I frowned at him, and Dalton started laughing, which made David laugh too. I relaxed. For a second there, it had sounded almost like David was pissed that Ryan had escaped.

"So do you or Detective Donut have any leads?" David asked.

"Don't call him that," I protested. "He's a good detective."

David rolled his eyes. "Yes, but you're better."

I decided to answer his question instead of getting into an argument about what he should or shouldn't call Alan.

"Why Detective Donut?" Dalton asked curiously.

David rolled his eyes again. "Ever seen Detective Kellerman?"

Dalton shook his head.

"He's a big guy."

I frowned. Before they could continue that conversation, I decided to jump in. "No, we don't have any leads. I mean, we have a description of the man who took Ryan, but all it really does is rule out women, Black men, obvious Middle Eastern, Asian, and Hispanic men, and blond-haired men. Even ruling those groups out, it leaves one hell of a large pool behind. I think it's all going to come back to the dog."

"The dog? You said it was feral. It's not likely to be chipped or anything," Dalton said.

"No, I know. I don't mean that. What I mean is, where on earth would someone find a feral dog? That's got to be a clue, right? It's not like stray dogs just wander the streets here," I said.

"No, you're right, they don't," David said thoughtfully. "I think they have the sense to avoid residential areas for the most part. But I know I've seen some on the outskirts of the island. There's plenty of them wandering around out there, probably from irresponsible owners letting them go."

"Oh," I said, a little bit deflated, thinking I had found a way to help Alan track the guy.

"Sorry, I didn't mean to shoot down your idea," David said, looking apologetic. "But I don't want you to waste your time chasing a tail that isn't attached to the dog you're after."

"No, I'm glad you told me," I said.

"Could have been brought onto the island from anywhere though, really," Dalton added.

I sighed. "Yeah, I guess you're right."

"So this poor guy must have been held somewhere pretty rough, then, for feral dogs to be roaming around," David said, bringing us back to the main topic.

I shook my head. "He didn't know exactly what the

neighborhood he was in was called, but he did say that the houses he passed after escaping were all huge and well-tended. He also said the neighborhood was high up with good views across the island right down to the sea, and it wasn't too far from the hospital," I said. "I reckon the dog was caught and left in the basement in advance."

"Yeah, you're probably right." Dalton stared at me over the rim of his coffee cup.

"It's funny, you don't imagine someone being abducted or whatever and left for dead in an upmarket estate, do you?" David said with a frown as he glanced at his brother, then back to me.

"No, definitely not. Even after hearing Ryan describe it, I have to keep stopping myself from picturing a dive," I said.

"It'll be quite a step down for him now, then, I imagine," David said.

"What do you mean?" I asked.

"I was just thinking about the safehouse. Most of them are in the parts of town that make the descriptor 'safe' a bit of a joke," he said. "Isn't that how it is in the movies?"

"The safehouse is actually gorgeous. It's out somewhere on the beach and ..." I realized I had said too much, and I stopped talking.

David frowned, and then he seemed to realize what had happened. "Oh, come on, Stella. We're all family here. You can tell us stuff, and it won't go any further, you know that," he said wryly.

This was someone's life, though. If the location got out, Ryan could be killed. But then I told myself I was being too cautious. As if David or Dalton were going to go around telling people where to find Ryan.

"I know, I'm sorry," I said, shaking my head. "Where was

I? Oh yeah. It's right on the beachfront with private access. I don't know a lot about real estate, but even I know those houses don't come cheap. It's not like he's going to be surrounded by riffraff."

"Won't that draw attention to him? Like the neighbors in those kinds of places always want to introduce themselves and gossip and whatnot," David said, grinning. "Or is that just on TV?"

"I think that's just on TV," I replied, also smiling. "But seriously, that's the beauty of this place. There's a row of these beach houses, and all of them are listed as holiday homes, so they're people's second properties. And some of them are rentals too. As Alan put it, it's a good place to be a stranger without standing out as strange."

"Yeah, it sounds like it," David said.

"It must be costing us taxpayers a pretty penny," Dalton put in.

"The guy was almost killed. I think people might have a bit of compassion and not care too much about that," I said, frowning at him.

"Maybe. Maybe not," David said, sounding a little annoyed.

"Second to the dog, I think the next best clue is going to be the house where Ryan was held," I said, trying to move away from the taxpayer thing that was obviously aggravating David for some reason. "Up until now, the killer has been clever. There have been no traces of DNA evidence at any of the scenes. But surely no one can live in a house and not leave any trace of themselves."

"Yes, that's true," David agreed.

"But I thought you said earlier he didn't know where he was," Dalton questioned.

"Yeah, that's the thing. He said that he would know the estate and the house if he saw them again, but, at the moment, he's on bed rest and not allowed to leave the house. Alan can't really do anything about the house until Ryan is deemed well enough to be allowed to go with him to find it," I said. "And then finally, this monster will be caught, and these awful killings can stop."

"I don't get why you're so concerned about some random Casanova, to be honest. Since when did we start caring about these annoying neighbors and drama queens?" David said.

I frowned and studied his face for a moment. His expression was unreadable, and I couldn't decide if he was joking or not. Either way, it was a distasteful thing to say. I looked from him to Dalton, who wore a similar expression. It was very strange.

"I would have thought you would care. You have friends who might fit the profile for the next victim," I said.

"Yes, I do realize that. The question is, though, why do *you* care about them so much?" he said quietly.

I realized then he wasn't joking so much as one of his insecurities coming to the surface. He wasn't really saying we shouldn't care that there was a serial killer on the loose. He was wondering if I was so invested because I was hanging around with womanizers, maybe even cheating on him with one.

"I don't care about them like that," I said. "Of course not. But I don't have to know the victims personally to have compassion for them. They might not all be the nicest people, but they are still people."

David smiled then. "You are so cute," he said.

It felt like he was patronizing me, but I didn't want to

start any arguments, so I decided to take it at face value and tell myself it was a compliment.

"My sweet little Stella, always seeing the good in people, even when it's damned hard to find," David said, and Dalton chuckled darkly, adding to the discomfort I felt.

I gave him a look, then said, "I'll go start dinner." I got up and headed for the kitchen.

"You know, I think I'm going to skip dinner, if you don't mind," Dalton said. "Not really feeling all that great."

I paused and looked at him, then to David. They seemed to be having one of those private twin conversations that were just a series of looks instead of words, so that you never quite knew what had passed between them. "Are you sure?" I asked hesitantly. "You know you're welcome, right?"

Dalton looked at me, but it was almost as if he was looking through me instead. Then he blinked and smiled. "I know, and I really appreciate how welcoming you've been, Stella. I couldn't ask for a better sister-in-law." He smiled as he came over and hugged me awkwardly.

"I feel the same for you, Dalton." I looked at David and smiled as we broke apart.

"I'll see you at the office tomorrow, right?" David questioned.

"Of course." Dalton nodded.

A moment later he was gone.

27

I got to the office the next morning and ran into Brittany, who looked away from me and down at her feet as she sat at her desk, letting her hair fall forward, hiding her face.

I frowned as I started toward her. "Everything okay?" I asked.

She nodded, keeping her face from me.

"Brit? Look at me, please."

She shook her head, keeping her face from me.

"Are you angry with me over something? Did I do something to upset you?"

"No, I'm fine; everything's fine."

I squatted down next to her desk and brushed her hair aside. I drew in a sharp breath as I noticed the large purple bruise on her cheek. "What the hell? Who did this?"

She moved her head so the hair hung in front of her face again. "Who do you think?" she whispered.

"Jeff is back?" I asked in surprise. "Is Roxy okay?"

"Yeah, she was with my mom. He wanted to see her, but I said no. He did this." Her hand flashed up to her face.

"How long has he been back in town?"

"A while. He's been texting me, begging me to come back to him. I didn't want to say anything." She sniffled.

"Brit, you need to get a restraining order against him; you can't let him do this to you."

"He's Roxy's dad; how can I?"

"The bastard deserves to be in jail for how badly he beat you last time! How can you sit there and say that?" I sighed and rubbed her shoulder. "Do you want me to call my friend Alan? The detective? He can help us get a restraining order set up on Jeff so he has to stay away from you."

"I don't know, Stella." She started to cry properly now.

I pulled her up from her chair and said, "Come on, let's go to the ladies' room. Too many people here," I murmured as some of our co-workers started to arrive at the office.

She nodded and went with me.

I handed her a wad of tissues. "How did he even know you were back here?"

"I ran into one of his old friends. Andrew Corbett? I think you dated him, didn't you?" She sniffled and wiped her nose.

"Seriously? Jeff and Andrew?" I said, taken aback. I hadn't known the two of them were friends. That answered a few questions about Andrew's behavior, then. Maybe I'd been luckier than I thought that he'd cheated on me.

Brit nodded. "Yeah, from high school. They ran around together for a long time. When I got back to town and I ran into Andrew, he hit on me. I told him to fuck right off, but he must have told Jeff where I was." She sighed.

"He turned out to be such an asshole. Did I tell you he tried to kick down my door about two months ago?"

Brittany looked startled. "Jeff tried to break down your door? Why?"

"No, Andrew."

"Oh, no, you didn't."

"Yeah, scared the crap out of me. So grateful to David because he found Andrew and made him leave me alone."

"How did he do that?" Brit asked; her eyes brightened, and she looked hopeful for the first time since I'd seen her that morning.

I shrugged. "Not sure, really, he said he and Dalton had a conversation with him."

"That's it? And he's left you alone? Wow, maybe I should have them have a conversation with Jeff. Think it would work?" She gave me a half smile.

I laughed. "Maybe. In the meantime, I really think you need to organize that restraining order."

"Yeah, okay. Can you call your friend at the police department?"

"Sure, of course."

She cleaned her face, and then we headed back to our desks. "Thanks, Stella."

"Anytime, seriously."

I picked up my phone as soon as I sat down and called Alan. The phone rang steadily a few times, and then his voicemail picked up. I found that a bit odd, but I went ahead and left a message. He didn't call me back, so thirty minutes later, I tried again, and he finally answered.

"Stella, it's not a good time," he said.

"Where are you? It sounds like you're in a wind tunnel."

"At the beach," he said; his voice was strained.

"Did you take the day off?"

"No, we've got another body," he growled.

I leaned back in my chair as I gasped. "Another? Already?"

"Don't know if it's our guy. This one's a little different."

"Sooo ..." I started hesitantly. I wondered if I could come see the scene. I knew it was a long shot, I wasn't supposed to be at any of the crime scenes, but I wanted to catch this killer so bad.

"No."

"Please, Alan? Come on, I've been to all the others, and you even said I help you out when I contribute."

He sighed heavily. "Let me clear it with the captain. I'll call you back."

"Great." I hung up, feeling impatient. I raced through my morning to-do list, getting things set up to go out on various social media accounts as I waited for him to call me back. It was nearly another twenty minutes before my phone rang. "Yes?" I answered without looking.

"It's me. You can come," Alan said, then proceeded to tell me exactly where they were.

"I'm on my way. Oh, and when you have a minute, I need to talk to you about a restraining order."

"Against whom?"

"Oh, not for me, it's for my friend Brittany. Her ex, Jeff Landry."

"We'll see what we can do about that later. For now, we've got a strange one down here."

"Okay, I'll be there as soon as possible."

"Be careful. Don't want to scrape you off the highway, okay?"

"Yeah, I will." I hung up and practically ran from the

office. "Tell Lonnie I'll be back later," I said to Brit as I passed her desk. "And Alan's going to get that order for you, don't you worry."

"Thanks, Stella, I'll let Lonnie know."

I headed out to the car and drove to the beach that Alan had directed me to, and forty minutes later I parked in the lot for the beachgoers. It was a chilly day, and not many people were around, which suited me just fine. Even on a scorching hot day, most people avoided this part of the beach because of the rockiness. It was mostly dog walkers and the odd lone jogger who populated this area. That was one of the advantages of being on an island: plenty of choices as to which part of the coastline to visit.

I wandered down the uneven concrete steps to the sand and headed off in the direction of the rockiest area where Alan said he'd be waiting. I was relieved to see that the tide was on its way out not in, because when it was out, there was a thin stretch of sand to walk on to get to where I needed to be. If it had been in, I would have had to clamber over the rocks to get there, not something I relished the idea of while pregnant.

I walked quickly along the sandy strip and saw Alan up ahead. I glanced back over my shoulder to see if anyone had followed me. It was weird, but I felt like I was being watched. However, when I looked back, nobody was around. I shrugged and continued my trek forward.

I didn't have to go far. I didn't even need to go into the caves themselves. I clambered over a few tall, jagged rocks, and there Alan was, standing next to the body. Or rather part of a body. A head. Or should I say a skull with a few strands of hair still attached. The face and the thick part of the scalp were long gone, making me wonder how long the body had been here. Certainly a week or two, long enough for the tide coming in to slowly but surely erode away the corpse's face.

I couldn't help but wonder if the body had been buried there up to the neck, or if the body had been decapitated and only the head was here.

"So, is this all there is?" I asked, looking from Alan to the head.

I moved closer, barely even registering that this was indeed a dead body. After the work of the killer, the blood, gore, and violence, this seemed tame enough to be a display in a museum. I came up beside the head and looked down.

"Take a closer look." Alan nodded.

I did as he said, squatting down to get a better look. Below the head, a vertebra or two were visible, and then the spine disappeared into what looked like the chest of the body. The flesh there had been bleached gray, almost white, but there was no denying it was human flesh.

"Who the hell is this?" I murmured.

"I don't know. He isn't much of a talker," Alan said.

I looked up at him, and we both laughed at his gallows humor, but then he was all business again as he crouched down next to me and looked at the head.

"Well, hopefully there's some ID in a pocket beneath the sand because this could be anyone," he said with a sigh.

"It doesn't seem like the usual MO for our guy, does it?" I asked, thinking about the previous two murder scenes. "Of course, that's discounting Ryan, since he got away. Had he been murdered too, it would have been different as well. So maybe it's still him?" I frowned.

"Looking at this, I would say this was personal, that this

person was buried here unconscious, but would have woken in time to be awake for the tide coming in. I could be wrong, of course, but if it's our guy, the body will be a hot mess beneath the sand. And that's definitely our guy's MO."

I nodded. He stood up straight then, and I heard his knees crack as he came up. I winced, but he didn't even seem to notice.

"How did you even find this body, anyway?" I asked.

"Dog walker called it in. His dog got loose and ended up over here."

"How long before the CSI team arrives?"

"They should have beaten you here." He shook his head. "I don't know what the holdup is."

"It's Gull Island; nothing ever happens quickly, you know that," I teased.

He rolled his eyes. "You should probably head on back. I don't want to be responsible for you slipping on these rocks. Not in your condition."

"Yeah, okay."

"Oh, hey, before you go."

I turned around, and he was holding a sheet of folded paper out to me.

"I almost forgot to give you this."

"Is this the restraining order?" I asked.

"No."

I took the paper and opened it. It was a drawing of a man.

"The artist's sketch of Ryan's abductor?" I said, looking at it.

"The very same," Detective Kellerman said. "There will be a copy going out by email in the next half hour to all the news outlets, so you're best off waiting for the non-creased version. I just thought you might want a copy of it."

"Thank you," I said with a smile. "He looks familiar, but I can't place him," I said, studying the sketch. "Maybe I've seen him around town?"

"I thought the same." Alan nodded. "And about that restraining order. When I'm done here, I'll let you know, and we can arrange a time to meet up with your friend and get that taken care of."

"Thanks, Alan. I appreciate it. He gave her a black eye sometime last night. I just don't want him to hurt her again."

"We'll make sure that doesn't happen."

I smiled and then hurried back up to the parking lot, got into my car, and drove off, heading back toward the office. Something was niggling at me, even as I drove, and I struggled to put my finger on what it was, but then it hit me. I needed to look at that sketch again. I had this bee in my bonnet about it. I knew I couldn't wait.

I pulled off the main road at the next intersection and drove down a quiet residential street until I found a gap at the curb. I parked the car and pulled the sketch out of my jeans pocket. I unfolded it and studied it.

I didn't recognize the man in the picture fully, but he looked so familiar I felt like I should have known who he was. I kept staring at the sketch, first looking at the individual features and then looking at the whole picture together. I realized with a start that the man in the sketch looked similar to David and Dalton. Not exactly the same, but very similar.

The eyes weren't the right color and were slightly too far apart. The nose was too big, and the lips weren't big enough.

The jawbone wasn't sharp enough, and the little lines around the mouth that both David and Dalton had were missing. But still. This guy could be a cousin; that was how close the similarities were.

Was it possible that David or Dalton was the serial killer and the artist had just gotten those few features wrong? The thought sent a shiver through me. There were things that David had said recently that certainly seemed off, but enough to make him a suspect? No, of course not, I thought, smiling as I shook my head, dismissing the idea. God, talk about an overactive imagination. It was just a coincidence that the picture looked so close to David and Dalton. It had to be. It was like I kept saying yesterday – Ryan's description could be just about any male office worker. This picture, while narrower than that, could still be any number of people.

I put the sketch back in my pocket, started the car up, and headed back toward the office. I was determined not to let my imagination run away with me on this one, and by the time I got to the office, I had decided the man in the sketch didn't really even look anything like David or Dalton.

IT HAD BEEN A LONG DAY, and my feet were hot and burning, my back ached, and I had a headache coming on. I also felt grubby, like I needed a shower badly. I hadn't done anything particularly dirty or even physical, it was just the feeling I always got after a long day at work.

It was after six when I parked my car in the drive and headed inside the house. I had called David to tell him I was running late, and he'd said he'd pick up dinner. He was sweet like that.

I walked down the hallway and found David in the kitchen, spooning a large piece of lasagna onto a plate. I hadn't realized how hungry I was until I smelled the food, but as soon as I did, my stomach rumbled loudly.

I sat down, and David put the plate in front of me along with a knife and a fork. He kissed my cheek.

"I figured you would want to eat as soon as you got home," he said.

He sat down opposite me as I tucked in.

"You figured right. I'm starving," I said.

"So what happened today? You said your detective friend called?"

"Yes, Alan called because a body turned up down near the caves on the beach, you know the area?"

David nodded. "Oh yeah? So the killer struck again?"

I shook my head. "Well, we're not sure. I mean, yeah, there was a body, and the guy was most likely murdered, but whether it's the serial killer or not is questionable."

David raised an eyebrow. "So you're thinking there are two killers on the loose here on Gull Island?" He looked shocked.

"I know it sounds crazy. Especially for a place as tiny as Gull Island, but yeah," I replied. "This guy wasn't messed up like Elway or Walker. He was buried neck deep in the sand. The tide coming in and out basically removed his facial features, so he hasn't been identified yet."

"You don't think that's messed up?" David asked.

He didn't ask me like he was judging me, he just asked me like he was genuinely curious that I might think this was okay, but I rushed to explain anyway.

"No, I mean, obviously it had to have been a torturous kind of death. What I meant was that the actual body wasn't slashed to pieces like Elway's and Walker's," I replied.

"So you don't know who he was?" David asked.

"Not as far as I'm aware," I said. "Like I said, his face is gone. We don't even really know that the body is a 'he.' I've just been saying that. If anything had been found, a driver's license or something like that, I'm sure that Alan would have called to let me know. I think they're going to have to go off dental records to find out who he was."

"How long does that take?" David asked.

"I don't know, really. There are only two dental practices on the island, so if he's from here, it won't be hard to match their records with X-rays of the skull. It will only get more complicated if the victim isn't registered with either dentist here," I said.

"Well, until then, it could be anyone. It could be a man or a woman, so maybe we should call them Jo Doe. You know, because Jo can be Joanne or Joseph," David said with a grin.

I smiled. "You're not wrong." I took another bite of the lasagna and sighed. "And the police artist has sketched the guy who abducted Ryan O'Donohue."

"Oh yeah?" David sat very still, his eyes on his plate. "Do you recognize him? Did anyone?"

"He looked a little familiar, like I should know him, but not really." I laughed a little. "Honestly, he looked a bit like he might be related to you."

David raised his eyes and stared at me. "Stella, that isn't funny."

"What?" I looked at him, startled.

"You think the killer looks like me? So, what, you think

the killer is Dalton? Or wait ... you don't think it's me, do you?"

I gasped. "David, no, of course not! That's not what I meant. I just ... I thought maybe a distant cousin or something, not you or Dalton!" My heart was pounding at the foul look on his face.

He glared. "We don't have any other family, Stella."

I pressed my lips in a flat line to keep from angering him further. I didn't understand why he was so upset. I hadn't accused him of anything. "I'm sorry," I murmured. "I didn't mean to upset you. The guy in the picture just had similar features to you, that's all I meant."

David didn't say anything for a few moments, but then his shoulders relaxed, and he smiled. "Okay. I understand. There are a lot of men, I suppose, who have similar features to me. It doesn't make them a relative."

I nodded cautiously as I looked at him, still wary. "I know that. I didn't think me saying so would upset you."

He winced. "It's an old wound raising its head. I'm sorry I snapped at you, sweetheart."

My brow furrowed as I studied him. "An old wound? What do you mean?"

He shook his head. "I'd rather not speak about it, if you don't mind." He got up and cleared his plate, taking it to the sink.

It took me a moment, but I acquiesced. "Okay."

I finished my dinner, stood up, and put my plate and cutlery in the sink. I opened the fridge and grabbed a bottle of water. I opened it and drank half down.

"I need a shower," I said. "And then I think I might just go to bed."

David came over and kissed me, a quick kiss on the lips.

"Don't overdo things, Stella," he reminded me as he rubbed my stomach. "You're growing our child in there."

I smiled and put my hand over his. "I won't," I said. "Honestly, I've spent the thick of my day at my desk. I just fancied lying down and reading a book for a while."

"Okay," he said, smiling at me. "As long as you're looking after yourself and our little one."

"I am," I said, and then I hurried out of the kitchen and up the stairs to the bathroom. I was so curious to know what he'd been talking about, but I knew now was not the time to be asking those questions. The look in his eyes had been full of anger and hurt, and I didn't like all that being directed at me. It had been scary, if I was honest. For a moment there, I'd wondered if maybe he or Dalton actually was the killer and the artist had just not gotten the features quite right. I shivered at the thought.

I WOKE up to find my reading lamp still on and my book open beside me on the bed. I yawned and half sat up while I looked for my bookmark. It had fallen on the ground beside the bed. I picked it up, put it in my book, and put my book down on my nightstand. I figured I'd dozed off for a few minutes while I was reading, and I was surprised when I looked at the clock and saw it was almost three a.m.

I lay back down and turned the reading lamp off, wondering what had made me wake up. I heard the front door slam open and then close, and my breath caught in my throat as fear flooded through me.

"David?" I said, patting the bed next to me. "David, wake up."

Nothing. And now there were footsteps on the stairs. I reached over to shake him, and my horror turned to relief when I found his side of the bed empty. It had to be David on the stairs, and I guessed that it had been his car pulling up on the driveway that had woken me up originally. Where the hell had he been at this time of night, though? He hadn't mentioned that he was going out, had he? I thought back over the evening, but I couldn't recall him saying anything about having to go back to the office or that he'd planned to go out at all.

The bathroom door opened and closed, and a second later, the toilet flushed, and the tap came on. I heard David brushing his teeth, and then the bathroom door opened and closed again, and David's footsteps came toward the bedroom. He opened the door and came into the bedroom. He moved to the end of the bed and began to take his clothes off.

"Where have you been?" I asked.

"God, Stella, you scared me," David said with a jumpy half laugh. "I thought you were asleep."

"Sorry," I said. "I was, but I woke up when you came home."

"Oh, was it me slamming the bathroom door?" he asked. "I'm so sorry."

I shrugged although I wasn't sure he could see me. I didn't want him to feel like I was accusing him of waking me up just so we could argue about it. I wasn't bothered about that. I wanted to know where he had been, and I noticed he still hadn't responded to my question. "Not the bathroom. Actually, I don't think it was the doors at all, but when your car pulled up to the house."

"Oh." He nodded.

"So?" I said as he got into bed next to me and wrapped an arm around my waist.

"So what?" he asked.

He kissed my neck, but I wasn't about to let him distract me.

"Where have you been? It's three o'clock in the morning, David," I said.

He stopped kissing me, and his arm disappeared from my waist. I heard the shuffle of him turning onto his back, and I knew then that he was about to lie to me, I just didn't know why. "I didn't mean to wake you. I had to run to the office for another conference call with that Japanese client. Took longer than I thought it would."

I frowned. "You sure?"

He rolled over and looked at me in the dark. "What do you mean? What are you accusing me of?"

I waited a heartbeat and then said, "Nothing. I'm just … I didn't know you'd left, and you hadn't said you were going to. I got worried."

"I don't have to answer to you, Stella. I'm tired. I'm going to sleep. Good night." He rolled back over, facing away from me. His voice was hard and brittle, and I knew he was pissed at me again.

"Yeah. Good night," I said.

I lay awake long after David's breathing deepened with sleep. Where the hell had he been, and why had he lied to me? I didn't think he'd been with another woman. He didn't smell of perfume or sex, and surely, he would have showered before getting so close to me if he'd been with someone else. So why then did he lie to me? Because I knew with absolute certainty that he hadn't been at work. The question was, if he wasn't there, and he wasn't having an affair, then where the hell had he been? The possible answer sent a terrified chill through me.

When I finally fell asleep, the sun was starting to come up. And I still didn't have any satisfactory answer as to where David might have been and why he had lied to me about it.

28

David sent me a text from work to let me know he would be having another late-night meeting. He said it was a new client, this one in Australia, so like the Japanese client, it would be the middle of the afternoon for them.

> David: I'm going to sleep at the office so I don't wake you again.

I had to admit that I was becoming more and more suspicious that he might be having an affair. It just seemed too weird that suddenly he was leaving and coming home in the middle of the night, or not coming home at all. I didn't want to confront him until I had some evidence though, because I would look paranoid and stupid if I was wrong. And if I was right, he would deny it, and I would just be giving him a heads-up, and he would be more careful, and then I would never learn the truth. So I texted him back.

> Me: That's very thoughtful, but unnecessary.

He didn't answer, so instead of fussing about it, I headed over to my parents' house. It had been a few days since I'd been to see them, and if I was there, I wouldn't have to cook for myself. Dad had grilled steaks, and Mom had made baked potatoes and green beans. It was a nice relaxing evening except for the fact I couldn't get the idea that David was cheating on me out of my head.

I had driven myself mad the last few hours thinking about it, when I checked the time. It was almost midnight. If David was cheating on me, there was no way he would still be in the office now. It would be an easy way to check my theory. But was that too sad? Was I becoming one of those paranoid wives who checked their husband's pockets for receipts?

No, I told myself. It was just this once. And if he was in the office where he said he would be, I would let this nonsense go once and for all. And if he wasn't in the office ...? Well, I would worry about that if and when it came to it.

My mind made up, I reached for my cell phone and found David's work number. I listened to the phone ringing, and after a few rings, it got picked up.

"David Bell," he said.

I felt a strange mixture of embarrassment that I had actually checked up on him like this, and relief that he was exactly where he had said he would be.

"Hi, it's me," I said. "Sorry to bother you, but can you grab a carton of milk on your way home, please. We're almost out."

I made a mental note to check whether or not that was true, and if it wasn't, to pour some of the milk away.

"Yeah, sure," David said. "Why on earth did you ring the office for that and not my cell phone?"

"Oh, I didn't realize I had called the office," I lied.

"It's a good thing my personal extension calls divert to my cell phone, or I would have had to run all the way down to the main reception to take this call." He laughed.

"Sorry," I said. "Like I said, I'm sleepy and didn't realize I'd hit your office number instead of your cell."

"I'm joking, sweetheart. It's fine," David said.

"Oh yes. Yes, of course," I said, forcing a laugh. "Well, good night, then. Don't forget the milk."

I hung up before he said anything else, and I put the cell phone down, resting my head in my hands for a moment. I was no further forward. I didn't know that he could make his office line divert to his cell phone. And now I still had no idea whether or not he was in the office. But I was pretty sure he was, and the more I thought about it, the surer I was that I was right.

It wasn't just because I wanted to believe it either. It was because the background on the call had been quiet, for one thing. There was no one waiting for him to get back into bed. And if he was lying, why wouldn't he have kept that piece of information about his calls diverting to himself? He wouldn't have been making a joke about jogging to get my call. He'd have let me think he had answered his desk phone in the office. He was telling the truth. He really was at work, and I had to learn to trust him before I drove myself mad and destroyed our marriage.

I got up, went to the kitchen, and looked in the fridge. There was over half a carton of milk left, and feeling both guilty and a tad pathetic, I opened the carton, took a quick drink of the milk, and then poured almost all of it down the sink, leaving enough for if I wanted a cup of tea later on or in the morning before David came home. I rinsed the sink out more from habit than anything.

I was starting to think about heading up to bed when my cell phone pinged. A text. I picked it up and frowned when I saw Alan's name on the screen. It was hardly the sort of time I expected to hear from him, but my curiosity was piqued, so I read the message.

> Alan: Are you still awake? I have news.

Now my interest was well and truly grabbed. I sent a text back saying, yes, I was awake. Within seconds, my cell phone was ringing.

"Hi," I said quickly.

"Hi, sorry, I know it's really late, and I wouldn't have bothered you, but we have an ID on the beach body. I figured if you were up, you'd want to know."

"I would, you didn't guess wrong, and David's at work, so I was up anyway."

"The coroner hasn't done the full autopsy yet, but he did say that he's almost certain that the cause of death is drowning," Alan said. "And after we got the body out of the sand, we could see that he hadn't been butchered."

"But he would have to have been alive when he was buried since drowning was his cause of death, right?" I said, wincing.

"Yup," Alan agreed. "He didn't have a wallet or anything on him; in fact, he was naked. We used his teeth to identify him; he's a local. Name was Andrew Corbett, aged thirty-five.

He was single, no children, and his next of kin was his mother, who has been informed."

I gasped. My head was reeling. It couldn't be the same Andrew Corbett, surely? My stalker Andrew Corbett? Of course, how could it not be? Gull Island was a small place; there couldn't be two men with the name Andrew Corbett on the island and me not know it. It made sense. It explained why his stalking had stopped.

"You okay?" Alan asked, concern lacing his voice.

"Is his mother Noreen Corbett?" I said softly.

"Yes," Alan said. "How the hell did you know that?"

"I ... I know Andrew. Knew him, rather," I said. "He's my ex. I was seeing him before I met and married David."

"Oh shit. Stella, I'm sorry," he said.

"Don't be. It was long over, and I was well over him. I was just surprised to hear his name, that's all," I said. "I'll tell you now, he was stalking me."

"He what now?" Alan replied, sounding cautious.

"I broke up with him because he'd cheated on me. He didn't take that very well. He began stalking me, following me places, that kind of thing. He'd get mad if he saw me talking to another man. He threatened me a few times, but then he'd beg me to come back to him. He called me on my cell, at home and at work, and when I'd answer, he'd hang up."

"Did you get a restraining order?"

"No, I didn't think he would actually hurt me. Not until —" I broke off as I thought about him kicking in the door.

"Until?"

"Until he found out I was married, and he came to my house and tried to kick in the door."

"Why didn't you call me? Why didn't you call the cops?"

Alan sounded exasperated.

"David said he'd handle it."

"And did he?" Alan asked.

"He and Dalton had a talk with him, and the stalking ended, so yeah."

"Okay, well, that's good." He paused, clearly thinking things over. "So what do you think? Do you think Andrew fits the serial killer's criteria for a victim?"

"I mean, maybe? He did cheat on me, and he was a bit of a lady's man. I just thought I could change him, you know? When we were dating, I mean." I sighed. "Anyway, when I found out about him cheating, I left."

"So he definitely could fit. Maybe our killer is a local who knows these men and has watched them and their behavior?"

"I suppose if treating women badly is this guy's criteria, then yeah." I gave a half-laugh. "You know, if it weren't for the guy who kidnapped Ryan, I would have said maybe it was a woman looking for revenge."

"Huh, you make a good point." Alan paused. "Typically, women don't kill so brutally, but I suppose one could if they knocked them out first. It would be easy enough for them to get close to these guys, close enough to drug them with chloroform. The problem is the sketch and Ryan's testament of what happened."

"Yeah," I replied, frowning. A yawn overtook me. "Sorry, it's been a long day."

"It's late. I'll let you go. You need to get some rest. We'll talk more tomorrow."

"Sounds good," I said. "Good night, Alan."

"Night."

I hung up and let my cell phone fall from my hand. It

landed on the kitchen counter with a clank. The sound pulled me out of my thoughts, and I grabbed it back up off the counter, expecting the screen to be broken. I breathed a sigh of relief when I saw that it wasn't, but my sense of relief didn't last for long.

I thought back over what had happened to Andrew. Something was bugging me. I knew something, but I couldn't put my finger on it. Then it hit me. David had said he and Dalton had spoken to Andrew at the beach. Suddenly my chest hurt.

Was it possible? Had David killed Andrew? Surely not. Surely it was just coincidence that he had been murdered on the beach. It had to be, didn't it? I couldn't bear the thought of the love of my life being involved in killing someone. And the way it had been done too. That wasn't a fight that got out of hand. Burying someone neck deep in sand and leaving them to drown, that was some cold-ass premeditated-murder shit right there.

David had his weird moments, his dark moments. And he could be quite controlling. But was he capable of murder? No, I couldn't let myself believe it.

God, it had only been a few minutes ago that I had concocted this whole thing about him having an affair. Now I was thinking he had murdered someone. I was starting to think I was the problem here, not David. Maybe my hobby of looking at crime scenes and trying to solve cold crimes or going over other true crimes from history was affecting me. It had me seeing monsters where there weren't any.

When I finally got to bed, sleep was a long time coming, and my mind whirled with questions, the most prevalent one being:

What secret was my husband keeping from me?

29

I picked my cell phone up from the counter beside the coffee pot as it pinged. It was only half past seven in the morning. David hadn't shown up at all, which wasn't surprising since he'd said he was going to sleep at the office, but I'd missed him being here when I woke. I hoped the text was him, but instead it was Alan.

> Alan: We've got another body. Meet me at 2313 Birdstone Ave.

> Me: Okay, be there as soon as I can.

I hurried upstairs and quickly changed into a pair of maternity jeans I'd bought a week ago, and a top that flowed down to my hips. I brushed my hair, grabbed a pair of socks, and put them and my tennis shoes on. I looked around for my purse, but didn't see it upstairs, so I returned to the kitchen. I spotted it hanging on the back of one of the chairs, picked it up, and put my cell phone in it.

I was debating leaving David a note, with it being so

early, when he appeared in the kitchen doorway holding a gallon of milk. He saw my purse in my hand and frowned.

"You're surely not going into the office this early, are you?" he said as he opened the fridge and put the milk inside.

I shook my head. "No, Alan texted; there's another body."

"He does know you're pregnant, right?" David said, looking pointedly at my belly.

"Yes, of course he does." I smiled. "But I'm not an invalid, and I was already awake. I didn't sleep well with you gone."

David smiled. He stepped forward and gave me a quick kiss on the lips. "Sorry. I'm just being overprotective because I care about you and the baby," he said. "And I'm sorry I wasn't here last night. I missed you."

"I know, it's okay. I know you had to work," I replied, leaning into him, resting my head on his chest.

"I had hoped to come home and spend some time with you, but if you're going out, I guess I'll just change and head back to the office."

I bit my lip, torn. I really wanted to go, but I also wanted to spend time with David.

He chuckled. "I know, it's fine, sweetheart. Go. I know you're dying to see who was killed this time."

I looked at him curiously. "Is it morbid that I do?"

"Sweetheart, you love this stuff. Not the murders exactly, I know. But you love solving them. I've said it before, if anyone can solve it, it will be you." He smiled. "No, go before Detective Donut gets so frustrated that his head explodes because he can't solve it."

I rolled my eyes. "I'll call you later." I waved as I headed out of the house and got into my car. I typed the address from the text message into my GPS and headed on my way.

The directions took me to an area on the opposite side of the island to where David and I lived. It was a nice area, but not fancy.

I pulled up when my GPS informed me that I had reached my destination. I got out of the car and walked to the apartment building I had been brought to and rang the bell for number 2313. The door clicked without anyone speaking through the intercom, and I pulled it open and went inside.

The building foyer was small but tidy. Opposite me was a bank of mailboxes and, to my left, an elevator. To my right was a staircase with a bike beneath it. I figured number 2313 would be on the second floor, so I opted to take the stairs. They were clean and graffiti-free, which was always a good sign.

I reached the second floor and followed a narrow hallway to the right door, where I knocked.

The door opened, and Alan stood back and gestured for me to come in.

"So what do we have?"

"This way," he answered, directing me to the bedroom.

I followed him, but the scent of copper was thick and cloying. "Is that—" I felt myself gag.

"You okay?" he asked, concerned.

I put a hand to my mouth and my other to my stomach. "What am I walking into, Alan?"

"It's a gruesome scene, I'll admit. If you can't stomach it, what with being pregnant and all, I understand ... it's just, I'm hoping you'll recognize the guy."

I frowned, surprised. "Why would I?"

"He worked at Master Marketing with you," Alan said softly.

I felt like I'd been sucker punched. "Who?" I moved forward into the room and stared at the scene. My jaw dropped.

"Charlie Banks." Alan's voice sounded loud in the silent room.

"Who the hell ... why? Charlie was nice ... he wouldn't ... I don't—" I couldn't make sense of what I was seeing.

"How well were you acquainted with him, Stella?"

"We've worked together for years," I whispered.

Charlie's naked body was dismembered and nailed to the wall, all except for his head, which sat in the middle of his king-sized bed, his penis hanging from his mouth. Blood soaked the bed and ran down the walls. Whoever had done this was truly sick.

I had to get out of there. I couldn't look at that scene anymore. Alan followed me from the room. I kept going. I couldn't be there. Charlie had been a friend. A co-worker. I'd seen him two days ago at the office.

"Stella, I have to ask you a few questions."

"What? Why? What do you mean?"

Alan took a deep breath. "Were you involved with Charlie?"

I gasped, and my eyes flew to his as we stood in the outer hallway in front of Charlie's door. "What? No! I'm married, Alan. I would never!"

He raised his hands in a calming manner. "I know, but I have to ask. Were you ever involved with him?"

"No. Why are you asking these questions?" My heart was pounding so hard in my chest.

"Your husband. His name is David Bell?"

"Yes, why are you asking about David?" I stared at him,

fear walking down my spine. Suddenly I was dizzy, and I couldn't breathe. I started hyperventilating.

"Lean forward and put your head between your knees," Alan said.

There was a buzzing sound in my ears, a too bright white light covering my vision. I knew I was on the verge of fainting, and Alan's voice came to me as if it were being whispered from far away. I did as he said, and I felt the blood rush back to my head. I felt dizzy and nauseous for another moment, but then it passed, and I stood back up, not slumped, but not quite straight. I rested my elbows on my knees and held my head in my hands. Finally, the nausea faded, and I took my hands away from my face.

My worst fear had just been verbalized, and I was left reeling. Even when I'd had my suspicions about David, deep down, I had never truly believed he was capable of murder. But now I could no longer dismiss those thoughts.

"Are you okay?"

"Alan, why are you asking about my husband?" I asked shakily.

"So, when I realized you knew Andrew, and you told me David and Dalton spoke to him, I did a little digging."

I sucked in a breath. He was about to tell me there were witnesses or something. All my unspoken fears were about to come to life. I was married to a murderer. The man I loved, the man I was about to have a baby with, was a serial killer. I started shaking, unable to control it. My heart was pounding so hard in my chest I thought it might break through my rib cage at any moment, but I had to know. "What did you find out?"

"Did you know his father is a resident at Sandhurst Park?"

I nodded slowly, my eyes wide. "Yes," I murmured, my voice barely more than a whisper. I had a really bad feeling about where Alan was going with this, since I'd yet to find out why David's father was at that particular hospital.

"Do you know why he's a resident at Sandhurst Park?"

"No," I choked out, half afraid of what he was about to tell me. I knew that there was no acceptable reason for his dad to be there. He had to have done something heinous to end up there.

"He murdered several women. Including David and Dalton's mother. He eviscerated them and dismembered them. Except for his wife, they were all sex workers, so it didn't make any major news stories and is probably a footnote in the serial killer hall of fame, but he does qualify as one."

I stared at Alan, fear in my eyes. "And? Is he still there? Did he escape? Is he doing this to these men?"

Alan shook his head. "No, he hasn't left Sandhurst Park, he served his full sentence, but in the last year of it, he became ill and was sent there. He's still there because, according to court records, his sons had him committed, albeit voluntarily. He's actually very sick, bedridden mostly, and they don't think he's going to make it another month."

"Okay. So what are you saying?" My heartbeat had slowed a little, but it was still out of control as panic consumed me.

"I'm saying it's a bit of a coincidence, don't you think, that men you know are being murdered, and you're married to a man whose father qualifies as a serial killer."

"And you think David might be our killer ..." I whispered out my worst fear.

"I'm asking you if you think it's a possibility."

I stared at him, my throat tight. "I don't know. I honestly don't think so, but I can't say one hundred percent for sure that he's not, given what you've just told me." Tears filled my eyes and fell fast down my cheeks. "God, Alan, what if I'm married to a serial killer?"

AFTER ALAN CALMED me down by saying that I most likely wasn't in any danger, even if David did turn out to be the killer, I got back into the car. He'd sworn that he'd keep me updated on anything he could find out about David and Dalton so that I wouldn't have to worry. Of course, I still was, but it might all be just a coincidence. I folded my arms on top of the steering wheel, then leaned my head on them and sobbed again. I didn't know what to do. I didn't hold back. I let it all come. The hurt. The anger. The humiliation. The fear. It all poured out of my eyes and soaked into my sleeves.

When I finally finished crying, I lifted my head and pulled my mirror down in front of me. I looked terrible. My face was red and blotchy, my eyes were bloodshot, and there was black mascara smudged beneath them. My lips were so white they almost looked blue. I dug in my purse and got my makeup bag out. I applied a bit of powder foundation to cover the worst of the blotches, and I cleaned the black from beneath my eyes. I added a swipe of lipstick to my lips. I didn't feel any better on the inside, but at least I looked a little bit more presentable now.

I started my car, pulled out of the parking lot, and joined the traffic flow and headed home. I'd told Alan that my plan was to go in, pack a bag with the essentials, and get the hell out of there until we knew for sure if David was our killer or not. I didn't know what else to do. I hadn't thought that far ahead yet, but Alan had thought I would be safe enough even if he was the killer, since it was men who were being murdered, not women.

All I knew was that if David was the killer, I couldn't stay there. And how could I have a baby with a serial killer? What if it was genetic? What if there was some psychotic gene and our baby inherited it? Like it seemed David had from his father? I would be perpetuating the cycle. I couldn't do that.

I arrived at home, and my heart sank when I saw David's car in the driveway. I debated reversing out of the drive and driving away without any of my things and with very little money. But I didn't do it. As much as I couldn't bear the thought of being close to David right now, I was too afraid to up and leave with nothing.

I got out of my car, headed toward the house, and opened the front door. I stepped inside, closed the door, and listened. I couldn't hear David anywhere. Maybe he had walked to the office or had a car collect him. Maybe I could get packed now and leave after all.

I turned toward the stairs, but my relief at being alone in the house was short lived as footsteps sounded on the landing above me.

Then David's legs, his torso, his full body, and head came into sight. He smiled at first when he saw me, and then his smile melted away, replaced with a look of genuine concern. Was it genuine, though? Could it be possible he did care about me? Could a person be a monster who killed for sport yet still be capable of love?

"Stella, what happened? Are you okay?" he demanded.

He stepped off the bottom stair and took my elbow in his hand, and then he gently led me toward the living room.

"I'm fine," I said. "Really. I promise."

David looked at me like he wasn't convinced, but he let it go for now. "I'll go and make you a nice cup of tea," he said.

He disappeared into the kitchen, and I heard him moving around, cups clipping each other, the rattle of the spoon. He was back quickly with two large mugs of tea, one of which he put down on the coffee table in front of where I sat. The other one, he kept in his hand as he sat down beside me.

"I thought you were going back to the office?" I asked after I had sipped my tea a few times and thanked David for it.

"Well, I had planned to, but I decided to wait until you came back. I wanted to make sure you were okay." He looked at me closely and frowned. "But you don't look okay. What happened, sweetheart?"

My throat tightened. I couldn't decide if he was playing a game with me, or if he was genuinely concerned. I swallowed hard and just blurted out the first excuse I could think of. "Morning sickness, it's hit me pretty bad today."

"Oh, my poor girl," David said.

He opened his arms, and I hesitated for a moment before I let him hug me. He definitely noticed because I saw the way he looked at me. I had to say something to get him back on track and away from this suspicion of me.

"Sorry," I said, after hugging him. "I have done nothing but throw up all morning. I feel like I'm too gross to be hugging people."

"I could never see you as gross, but I guess it doesn't feel too nice for you. Let me go run you a bubble bath, and then I want you to go to bed and get some rest, okay?" he said. "You've been doing too much lately. All these crime scenes have to be taking a toll on your mental health too."

AFTER MY BATH, I actually managed to have a nap. It shocked me. I knew I was drained emotionally, physically, mentally, but I still didn't think I would have been able to let my guard down and relax enough to sleep.

When I went back downstairs, David was very attentive, fussing over me and insisting I rest and relax. Normally, I would have argued with him, reminded him that I'm pregnant not ill, but I didn't want to make him mad now that I suspected what he might be capable of, so I meekly followed his instructions. At one point I sensed that it was actually making him suspicious because I was doing as he said, so to make it a bit more believable that I was resting because I felt ill, I jumped up and ran for the bathroom, where I made a few retching sounds, then flushed the toilet and ran the tap.

David made sure I was okay, asking if I wanted to go to the doctor. He made me my favorite dinner and then announced that he would be staying in with me that evening. Of course, I tried to persuade him that such a thing wasn't necessary, that I would be fine on my own, but he wouldn't hear of it, and I knew if I kept pushing for him to go out, he would get suspicious again. It meant that I wouldn't be able to sneak away tonight, but as long as he was being the way he was right now, I could cope with one more night with him.

"Are you feeling any better?" David asked as we sat at the dinner table.

I nodded. Obviously, I was physically feeling better because I was eating everything he'd put in front of me like I hadn't eaten in a week.

"I'm glad," he replied, smiling at me. "So, you never said, how did it go this morning?"

Suddenly my heart was in my throat again. "What?"

David frowned. "The body? You ran out of here so fast this morning that you didn't even tell me where you were going except that Alan said there was another body."

"Oh. Yeah." I pressed my lips together and decided to tell him. "It was someone I worked with."

"What?"

I saw a flash of anger on his face that he quickly covered.

The sight of it surprised me. If he'd been the one to kill Charlie, why would he be angry at me telling him that was who it was?

"Why didn't you tell me it was someone you worked with? Hell, Stella, no wonder you've felt so awful today."

"I'm ... I was trying not to think about it," I whispered, afraid of making him angry.

David's face softened. "I'm sorry, I get that. Who was it?"

"Charlie Banks, one of the junior executives."

"The one who was hung all over your friend Brittany at the Christmas party last year, right?"

His words startled me. Had Charlie done that? "I don't know. I don't remember that."

"He had blond hair, a mustache and drank a lot?" David described.

"Yeah, that's him. I just didn't recall him hanging on Brit. I think I was too busy dancing with you." Thinking back over that Christmas party, I smiled. We'd had a great time; it was the first time I'd introduced David to the people

I worked with. It was actually the first time he'd met Brit too.

"I don't think your friend was too impressed by me," David said with a laugh. "She glared at me most of the night."

I looked at him, puzzled; then I sighed. "Well, I think she was still traumatized by what Jeff did to her; you remember I told you he was abusive?"

David nodded. "Yeah, I remember." He sighed. "You know, she still doesn't like me."

I frowned and shook my head. How had our conversation turned from Charlie's murder to him being sad because Brittany didn't like him? If he'd killed Charlie and all the others, wouldn't he be acting differently? Guilty even?

Was he playing a game? He'd said he enjoyed watching me solve crimes and that I was better at it than the entire Gull Island police department. He was excited when I spoke about all the crimes, like he was invested in some way. Was it because he was the killer and just messing with me?

"Stella?"

I glanced up at him, trying to figure out what was going on.

"Are you okay? You're not going to throw up again, are you?"

"No."

"That's good," David said after a moment. "I saw how pale and shaky you were earlier, and it looked like you were suffering from more than morning sickness. I don't want you having a relapse. Maybe you should take the day off tomorrow?"

"Maybe. I'll see how I feel in the morning." I was

desperate to know if my suspicions – Alan's suspicions – were real.

"Come on, let's go to bed." He picked up our empty plates and put them in the sink and then guided me upstairs to our bedroom and into bed.

David snuggled close to me, and I made a conscious effort not to let myself recoil from his touch. Instead, I lay awake, listening to David's breathing. I waited until his breathing deepened, becoming the long, slow breaths of sleep, and then I waited a bit longer. What I was about to do was going to be a big risk, and I wanted to make sure that David was in a deep sleep before I even attempted it.

When I was sure he was deeply asleep, I eased myself out of bed. He didn't stir, and I took that as a good sign. I moved slowly and quietly to the closet and opened it up. I crouched down and pulled a small duffel bag from the bottom. I stayed crouched while I considered what to pack. It would have to be the essentials only for now.

I chose a pair of sneakers, and then I straightened up and took two pairs of jeans and a skirt from their hangers and stuffed them into the bag. I added three tops. I went to my chest of drawers and threw in some panties, two bras and some socks, and then I snuck out of the bedroom. I relaxed more when I reached the bathroom and could lock the door behind me.

I started to gather my toiletries, but I realized David would see they had gone when he used the bathroom in the morning, so I put them all back and thought for a moment, and then I went to the storage cupboard. I took out a new toothbrush and tube of toothpaste, a bottle of shampoo and a deodorant. That would have to do for now. It was the basics that would allow me to go and buy some other stuff without drawing negative attention to myself.

I crept down the stairs with my duffel bag. I really wanted to sneak out into the driveway and put it in the trunk of my car now, but if David woke up, I had no way at all to explain that one. Instead, I chose to hide the bag in the closet underneath the stairs. I would have to find a way to smuggle it out of the house in the morning.

I climbed back up the stairs and headed for our bedroom. Exhaustion had crept up on me, taking me unawares, and I yawned as I reached the bedroom door.

"Where have you been?" David asked as I came into the room.

I didn't know how long he had been awake, so I decided to tell him exactly where I had been. I didn't have to say what I was doing. He would make his own assumptions about that.

"I went to the bathroom, and then I went downstairs," I said.

"You know, if you were thirsty, you could have woken me, and I would have gone downstairs and gotten you a drink," he said as he lifted the covers for me to get back in.

I slipped back into bed beside him, facing away from him, forcing myself to act naturally when he put his hand on my hip and kissed the side of my neck.

"I know," I muttered. "I wish I had now. I didn't realize how tired I was until I got downstairs."

This had the desired effect, and David stopped nuzzling my neck. He gave me one quick kiss on the cheek instead. "Get some sleep, sweetheart," he said.

I closed my eyes. I was sure I would be too on edge lying

beside a serial killer to sleep, but my body had other ideas, and I soon slipped into a deep sleep.

I WAS HIDING in the closet, my heart pounding hard. He was coming. I could hear him on the stairs. I held my breath and prayed like I'd never prayed before.

"Sweetheart, I know you're up here. It's time. We both know it."

Tears ran down my face. I didn't want to die.

The closet door opened, and he stood there, knife in hand; it flashed in the light, shining brightly as though he'd polished it just for this occasion.

"There you are, sweetheart. I promise I'll make it quick; you won't feel a thing. This has all been fun, but it's time to end the game."

He reached for me, and I screamed.

30

"Stella, wake up!" David shook me.

I screamed and scooted away from him, my eyes wide. "Stay away from me!"

David looked shocked. "Sweetheart, it's me, it's David; you're okay."

I was full of panic as I stared at him, not understanding what was happening. "Are you going to kill me?" I whispered, my breath coming out on a gasp.

"What? Why would I kill you? Stella, you were having a nightmare."

I took a couple of deep breaths and let his words sink in. He was right. That was all it had been, a nightmare. We were in bed; there was no closet, no knife glinting dangerously. I nodded slowly.

"Better?" he asked.

I nodded again. "Sorry. Yes, I'm better." I still didn't want him anywhere near me.

"Okay, I'm going to go downstairs and make you some tea."

"Thank you," I replied, my voice still sounding shaky to my ears. "I'm going to get dressed for work."

He turned around and stared hard at me. "Maybe you should stay home. Like we talked about last night? You're overdoing it, Stella. It's not good for you or the baby."

I took a deep breath and let it out. "I know we talked about it, but with Charlie—" I broke off and regathered my thoughts. "I need to be there to help pick up some of the accounts he left behind. I can't leave Lonnie in the lurch like that. And I'm okay. I don't feel sick like I did yesterday."

David sighed and moved back toward me. I had to stop myself from flinching as he gathered me in his arms. "Sweetheart, I'm worried about you."

I nodded. "I know. I'm okay though. I'm not an invalid."

He smiled. "I know. Just promise me you'll take it easy and not overwork yourself?"

I agreed, and he headed down to the kitchen. Once he was gone from the room, I relaxed more. I quickly got dressed. I had a plan to enact, and I didn't want to waste another minute in this house.

When I got downstairs, I saw that he'd made me toast to go with my tea. "Thank you," I murmured, all docile.

David kissed the top of my head. "I'm going to get ready for work."

"Okay, I'm going to eat and head out myself. Have a good day," I said, giving him a smile.

"You too. And don't overdo it." He left the kitchen, and I heard him on the stairs.

I quickly ate the toast, gulped my tea, and then put my plate and cup in the sink. When I heard the shower turn on, I went to the closet, grabbed my duffel bag, found my purse and laptop bag, and hurried from the house. I put it all in the back seat, climbed into the driver's seat, and pointed the car toward my parents' house.

Twenty minutes later, I got out of the car, grabbed my things from the back seat, and I went to the door and pushed it open. I stepped inside and closed the door behind me. "Mom? Dad? It's me, Stella," I called out.

My mom came into the hallway from the kitchen. "Hi, honey," she said. "This is a nice surprise. What's the occasion?"

"Is Dad home?" I asked. "I need to talk to you both."

"Yes," my mom replied, a frown of concern creasing her face for a second. She moved to the bottom of the stairs and called up them. "Perry? Come down, please, Stella is here, and she wants to talk to us." She moved back from the stairs and turned to me. "Where's David?"

"At work," I said, not ready to go into it until both of my parents were present. It was going to be hard enough to say all of this stuff once, let alone twice.

My dad appeared on the stairs. He smiled a greeting at me, and then the three of us went through to the living room. My mom left my dad and me alone for a moment while she went to grab us all drinks. She was back in a few moments with three mugs of tea. She set them down on the coffee table, and then she sat down beside my dad, and the pair of them watched me expectantly.

"I've left David," I started.

"What?" Mom exclaimed.

"Why, what happened?" my dad asked at the same time.

I sighed. How the hell was I supposed to explain that I thought I was married to a serial killer? "Well, you know the recent string of murders here on the island?"

My parents nodded.

"So, as you know, Alan has let me be involved in helping. Well, one of the men murdered was Andrew. Remember him?"

Mom nodded, her face turning a ghastly pale color. "What does that have to do with David?"

I shrugged. "I'm afraid he did it. When I told Alan about Andrew stalking me and how David and his brother had a conversation with Andrew around the time he went missing, well ... Alan did some digging and found his dad killed several women, prostitutes, and after serving his sentence, he was committed to Sandhurst Park."

"Okay, so because his dad was a killer, you think David is too?" my dad asked.

"I don't know, Dad. I mean." I blew out a breath, trying to organize my thoughts. "He's been acting weird lately. What if it's because he's been out killing these guys?"

"And what if it's not?" Dad questioned. "Where has he said he's been?"

I frowned. "He says he's been at work."

"Okay, now what if what he says is true and you're seeing things that aren't there?"

My brow furrowed, and I felt a quiver in my stomach; my hand went to my belly. I felt the baby shifting around a little, and it made me smile briefly. "I don't know."

"Look, why don't you stay the night here? You can tell David that I needed your help with something, maybe that your dad is sick, nothing major, just tell him it's kidney stones, and you'll be home in a day or two. That will give you time to figure this out."

"I don't know, Mom," I fretted. "Do you think that will work?"

"Maybe," she replied.

"I still think you're being ridiculous. David isn't a murderer. I think this pregnancy is messing with your head, honey. It happens. It's got you being irrational."

"Perry!" Mom gasped.

"Well, it's true. You know David isn't a murderer. He is a lot of things, but a murderer?"

"That doesn't mean Stella is being irrational because she's pregnant," Mom said. "She's following the evidence. Aren't you?"

That took me aback. Was I? Or, like Dad suggested, was I jumping to conclusions and being irrational? If I was, then Alan was too. However, maybe I needed to look at the whole picture again. "Honestly, I don't know. You could be right, but Alan has the same suspicions I do, because he's the one who told me about David and Dalton's dad. Either way, I think staying here might be my best option, at least for tonight, while I figure this out. I have more than me to think about now," I said, rubbing my stomach.

"You are welcome anytime, sweetie," Mom replied. "I'll get the guest room made up." She got up and went down the hall toward the bedrooms.

"Have you even talked to David at all?"

I shook my head. "No, how would I bring it up? Hey, David, are you the killer? Yeah, I don't think so. If I did that and he was, he'd kill me. If he wasn't, then my marriage would be over, don't you think?"

Dad sighed. "Yeah, I suppose that's true enough."

My phone pinged, and I saw a text pop up from Alan.

Alan: You good to meet with your friend and me to get that restraining order set up?

> Me: Yeah, wanna meet at her place? She took some vacation time, so she's not at work.

> Alan: We can do that. Send me the address.

I did as he asked and told him I'd see him there in thirty minutes. I glanced up at my dad. "I have to go help my friend Brittany file a restraining order. I'll see you later. And I'll text David and tell him you have kidney stones. You aren't going anywhere, are you?"

"No," Dad replied, shaking his head. "I'll be here. And should he call, I'll tell him the same." He sounded resigned, but willing to fib for me.

"Thanks, Dad." I got up and hugged him. "Mom, I'll be back later," I called down the hall. I picked up my purse and headed out the door. Before I left, I sent David a text.

> Me: Hey, got a call from Mom. She needs me to come stay the night tonight. Dad's got kidney stones, and she needs an extra pair of hands.

> David: Seriously? What about me?

I frowned. I didn't know what he was talking about. What about him?

> Me: What do you mean, what about me? Are you sick?

> David: No. What if I needed you home?

> Me: You're rarely home at night anymore anyway. Why would you need me?

David: You're being ridiculous. I am almost always home at night. Of course I need you.

Me: Look, I can't do this right now. I have to go meet Alan and Brittany. We're setting her up with a restraining order against her ex-boyfriend before he hits her again.

David: Where at?

I frowned again. Why would he need to know that? Was he planning to come yell at me? Maybe planning to kill me? Did he think I was making things up? Or was I jumping to conclusions again? I shook my head. Maybe I was being irrational, seeing things that weren't there, reading into things he wasn't saying. I sighed as I replied.

Me: At Brittany's place, why?

David: In case the asshole shows up, so I know where to come so I can protect you.

Me: That's sweet.

I added the address. Then sent another text.

Me: Don't know why I'd need protection, but thank you.

David: Sweetheart, it's my job, keeping you safe. I love you and our little one.

Suddenly I burst into tears. Here I'd been thinking awful thoughts of him, and he was out here loving me and wanting to protect me. He'd done nothing but be protective and loving and supportive. How could I think anything but kind things about him?

> Me: I love you too.

I wiped my face and put the car in drive as I headed toward Brittany's place. It took me a little longer than I thought it would to get there. I parked behind Alan's car and got out, seeing he'd been waiting for me. We walked up to the door together. I knocked and waited. I frowned when nobody answered. Had I even told Brittany we were coming? I hung my head.

"Alan, I'm sorry. I forgot to tell her we were doing this." I sighed. "I'll call her and see where she's at."

"Sure." He nodded.

I pulled out my phone and dialed her number. I waited as it rang and rang. I shook my head. "She's not answering."

"Leave her a message, and we'll do it as soon as we can," he suggested.

"Her voicemail isn't picking up ... oh, wait ..." I paused as it finally kicked in on the eighth ring. "Hey, Brit, I'm standing on your porch. Alan and I came by to set up the restraining order, but you're obviously not here, so call me so we can set up a time to do this, okay?" I hung up and looked at Alan. "Sorry I had you come all the way over here for nothing."

"No problem. There was something else I wanted to talk to you about, though."

"What's that?" I asked as we returned to the driveway.

"Your husband."

I froze. Was this where he was going to tell me that David was definitely the killer? My stomach tightened, and I knew my voice was quivering as I said, "What about him?"

"We're looking into the timeline for each of the killings and for Ryan's abduction, both for him and for his brother, Dalton."

"And?"

"Inconclusive so far. A team went to question them both, but they immediately shut them down. As wealthy as they are, they have a legion of lawyers on their side, so we're having to tread carefully."

"Lawyers? Why did they send the detectives to them if they were just asking them questions?"

Alan gritted his teeth and looked annoyed. "One of the detectives who conducted the interview jumped the gun and mentioned their father being a convicted murderer, and they went on the defense."

"Alan, why weren't you there conducting the interview?" I asked.

"I should have been, but I was unavailable at the time the captain sent them out." He sighed. "Look, we'll get it sorted one way or the other. In the meantime, I was wondering if David knew any of the other men who were murdered."

I thought about it and then winced. "I don't know about Cory, but James, he knew." I told Alan about the night in the restaurant when James had been drunk and hitting on me while David was in the bathroom.

"So he threatened the guy not to come near you again, did he?"

I shook my head. "I didn't see him again after that night. Our paths hadn't really crossed ever before. Just that one night at the restaurant."

"Okay, but they had that altercation. It does match what I'd been told by the girlfriend."

I looked at him with surprise. "You already knew?"

"It's my job, Stella." Alan shrugged. "Of course I've been doing my due diligence."

"Right. Of course you have. Sorry."

"It's fine. And you know nothing about any kind of altercation between him and Cory Elway?"

I shook my head again. It seemed I didn't know very much about David at all. That made me feel even worse. Whom exactly had I married? "Not that I know of," I said softly.

"Okay, so what about Dalton?"

That mystified me. "I don't really know Dalton all that well. He's quiet, always pleasant to me, but he's a bit stand-offish. He and David are close."

"Might Dalton be the kind of man to go after these men?"

"I couldn't say. I wouldn't think so, but then I wouldn't have thought that David would either." I frowned. I didn't know what to think. Maybe I wasn't as good an amateur detective as I'd thought.

"Maybe we should take a little trip and find out about them from someone who might know them better than you?"

I frowned. "What do you mean?"

"I think we should go speak to their father at Sandhurst Park."

31

I got out of Alan's car and looked around. The building didn't look like an asylum. I was expecting an old-fashioned, imposing building with graying bricks and an air of fear around it. Instead, I was met with a modern-looking building made from steel and glass, set in the center of some beautiful, manicured grounds. It still had an imposing feeling about it, but I was almost certain that was just my imagination playing with me, knowing why I was here.

"So what do you think?" Alan asked, coming to stand beside me. "Are we more likely to get in to see this man by playing the cop card or the family card?"

"Let's try the gentle approach of me being his daughter-in-law first, and then if that doesn't work, you can show them your badge," I suggested. I wanted answers, and I hoped this man would be able to give them to me.

Alan nodded, and we headed for the door of the facility. I reached it and tried to pull it open, but nothing happened. I tried to push the door instead, but still nothing happened. I looked around and spotted an intercom. I pressed the bell and waited.

"Hello," a voice said after a moment or two.

"Hi," I said. "My name is Stella Greene. I'm here to visit Ambrose Bell. I'm his daughter-in-law. I'm married to David Bell."

"Come in, Ms. Greene. Please wait in the seating area to your right," the voice said, and then the door clicked open, and this time when I pushed it, it opened. I stepped inside, followed by Alan, and we made our way to the seating area as instructed. We didn't have to wait long before a man dressed in black trousers and a white tunic-style top appeared and came over to us.

"Ms. Greene?" he said.

"Call me Stella," I told him.

He gave a barely perceptible nod, and I already knew he would ignore that instruction.

"I'm Samuel, one of the orderlies. May I ask why you're here? Just, he doesn't get a whole lot of visitors and—"

"As I said on the intercom, I'm his daughter-in-law, and this is Alan, a friend of mine," I blurted out, rudely cutting Samuel off mid-sentence as my nerves got the better of me. I felt my face coloring, and I looked down at my feet. "I'm sorry for interrupting you."

"Not to worry, I can understand you being intimidated being here," Samuel said. "As I said, Ambrose doesn't get many visitors, and we like to be sure when he does that they aren't going to be a danger to him or in danger from him."

"I see. Well, I ..." I paused and considered my words carefully. "I just have a couple of questions for him. David hasn't been all that forthcoming about his dad, and I thought maybe if I could just meet him, it would put my mind more at ease."

Samuel stood there for a moment, studying me. "Alright. If you'll both give me your IDs, I'll need to clear it with the doctor in residence and then check with Ambrose to see if he's willing to see you. It will be a few minutes."

I nodded and handed him my license. "We'll just wait over here," I said as Alan handed his over as well.

Ten minutes later, Samuel came back and returned our IDs. "If you would like to follow me, I'll take you up to Ambrose's room."

"Is he okay?" I asked as we followed Samuel through a maze of corridors. "Mentally, I mean. Like, will he be able to hold a conversation and have it make sense?"

"Oh, of course," Samuel said. "He is perfectly lucid. The only medication he is given is a sedative. It's not that strong, just enough to keep him calm."

"You've had problems with him in the past?" I said.

"Oh, well, that's an understatement," Samuel said. "He has viciously attacked several staff members, claiming that they got on his nerves. One young woman only asked if he would like a cup of tea, but Mr. Bell said her voice was annoying."

"So he can be violent, then?" I said, feeling my stomach tighten.

Samuel glanced at me from the corner of his eye as we walked. "Ms. Greene, you do realize that Mr. Bell is a certified psychopath, right? He served his time, and he may be here voluntarily, but he can still be violent when he wants to be. He can also be cruel and manipulative, and he has, over the time he has been here, reduced many a staff member to tears. If you're not prepared for that, then I would seriously suggest you reconsider your visit."

"No, no, it'll be fine," I said, more to convince myself than Samuel.

Samuel finally stopped outside a room. He knocked lightly on the door, then opened it and poked his head around the door. "Good morning, Mr. Bell, how's my favorite patient?"

"How should I know? I haven't left the room yet, let alone talked to anyone else," a deep harsh voice replied.

Samuel laughed and shook his head. "You know, if you behaved, you might get out of your room more often," he replied. "I have visitors for you."

"One of my boys? Have they finally deemed me worthy of their presence?"

The nastiness in his tone sent a chill down my spine.

"Actually no. Your daughter-in-law and one of her friends," Samuel replied.

"Well, this could be interesting," he said, and I felt I could hear a spiteful glee in his voice. "Do send them in."

Samuel turned back to us and smiled. He stood to one side and gestured for us to go in. "If at any time you feel unsafe, just call out. I'll be right outside this door." His voice was soft, barely a whisper.

I nodded and took a deep breath, then stepped into the room. I was expecting Ambrose to look a bit glassy-eyed due to his medication, but the piercing eyes that looked me up and down were far from glassy. They were David's eyes, Dalton's eyes too, in a different face, the skin around them paler than I was used to. Ambrose also had the same black hair as David and Dalton, although his was thinning, and he seemed to have a bald spot on the top of his head, which he had combed his thinning hair over. He didn't look like a psychopath, but I was fast learning that psychopaths didn't actually look crazy.

"Good morning," I said. "I'm Stella. David's wife."

"So that's who got married without a word to his old man. I suppose he didn't even tell you I was alive?" Ambrose stared at me, assessing me. "And it seems I'm to have a grandchild too; isn't that interesting?"

"So you didn't know David and I were married or that we were expecting a child?" I asked.

I sat down in one of the visitor's chairs without being asked to, and Alan took the other one beside me. Ambrose remained seated in the chair beside his bed.

"No, my sons don't like to tell me much about their lives," Ambrose said. "I can see why. You're a pretty little thing, aren't you?"

His gaze on me felt gross, and I had to keep from letting the shiver of fear I felt show. I swallowed hard and gave the man a smile. "Thank you."

"You know I killed little girls like you." His smile was feral, his eyes glittering with glee. "Sluts who thought they were better than me."

"Sir," Alan practically growled.

Ambrose ignored him and stared right at me. "So let me guess. You're wondering if you've married a psychopath like me, if either of my sons might be capable of killing anyone?" His smile reminded me of how a demon might look as he was trying to convince you that doing evil was actually good. "You do know it's genetic, don't you? You should have had a termination."

I bristled at the mere suggestion of it, and I shook my head. "Maybe being a psychopath is genetic. I'll take your word for it. But my baby will receive all the love and affection I can give them, and they won't be like you. And as far as I'm aware, David and Dalton aren't anything like you," I said.

"You think so? You said it's David you married?"

I nodded.

His smile grew even wider, like the Grinch's sinister grin; as he showed off lots of teeth that were surprisingly straight and white, his eyes blazed with menace. "David always was an interesting child. He and Dalton didn't play well with others, you know. Things always happened around them," Ambrose said, and I noticed how his voice held a darkness, an evil that wrapped around you and drew you close. "Nothing that could ever be proven, mind you. I suppose you could say, like father like sons."

"Is that you confessing to nurturing them into killing people as you did?" Alan asked.

Ambrose snorted out a laugh. "Calm down there, rent-a-cop. I killed whores, and I did my time for it." He turned his attention back to me, that demon still looking out through those familiar eyes. "I made David and Dalton watch me when I killed their mother. I hoped to inspire them into ridding the world of filthy disgusting sluts."

I frowned, confused. I'd known that Ambrose had killed prostitutes, and that he'd killed David and Dalton's mother, but I hadn't known they'd watched him do it. Nor did I understand the connection between Ambrose killing women and the serial killer we had who was killing men who treated women badly.

Ambrose laughed again. "What? That's why you're here, isn't it? There's a serial killer killing sluts running around wherever it is you people live, and you're wondering if it's one of my sons?"

"Not exactly," I said, hedging my answer.

Ambrose raised a brow and gave me a cynical look. "You're saying there isn't a serial killer? That's not why you showed up here with this rent-a-cop?" His eyes were barely slits, and he leaned forward and hissed, "Don't play with me, little girl; you'll end up like all the others I've killed."

"I'm saying yes, there is a serial killer, but it's not women who are dying."

"There now, was that so hard?" he replied.

"Do you think your sons are capable of killing anyone?"

"Aren't you his wife? Shouldn't you know the answer to that question?" Ambrose's evil grin was back.

"Yes, and I thought I did know him, but as it turns out, I don't know him as well as I thought," I replied. "He's told me nothing of his past. Of you."

"Well then, that makes two of us. I was locked up in prison for twenty years and then shoved in this place for the last number of years. I know nothing of either of my offspring. They don't visit me. You think I would know if they were capable of killing? Let me tell you a secret, little girl" – he leaned forward again, putting his face close to mine – "every man is, it just depends on the circumstances." He leaned back. "Some of us get locked up for it" – his eyes flashed to Alan and then back to me – "others get celebrated for it."

His words had my stomach twisting.

"You should seriously think about getting away from him and getting rid of the parasite in your belly." Ambrose smirked.

"You genuinely believe Stella is in danger?" Alan put in.

Ambrose shrugged. "All women are, if not from one of

my sons, then from the next man who comes along, maybe even from you."

Alan sighed.

"Now, if you'll excuse me, I do believe I have a book club meeting in around ten minutes. This month we read *We Need to Talk About Kevin*. My choice. You have to do something to keep this place lively, right?"

He stood up abruptly, and I was almost waiting for him to clap his hands together to get me and Alan moving. He reminded me of a principal in that moment, but despite him clearly being well educated and well read, there was no doubting that he was truly evil and dangerous. The question was, was David or Dalton like him? Were either of them the serial killer we were after?

"Thank you for your time, Mr. Bell," I said, standing up.

"Call me Ambrose. After all, we're family, even if it won't be for much longer. Goodbye, dear, so good to meet you," he said, gesturing for us to leave as he sank back down into his chair.

As the door closed behind us, I turned to Alan. We made our way back through the winding hallways, following Samuel until we were at the doors that led outside.

"I hope your visit went well," Samuel said. "I didn't hear any screaming, so it seemed to."

"It was fine," I answered.

"Will you be back?" he asked.

I shook my head, giving him a tight smile. "I doubt it."

Samuel gave me a wry smile in return. "Figured as much. Take care, Ms. Greene."

"Thank you," I answered.

Alan and I headed for the parking lot and got in his car. On the way back into town, we were approaching a food truck tucked into the side of the road. Alan nodded toward it. "Do you have time for a quick coffee and a bit of research?" he asked.

"Sure."

He parked, and we ordered, him an Americano, me a decaf latte. We sat on one of the ramshackle picnic benches behind the food truck, and Alan got his cell phone out.

I sat and sipped my drink, wishing like hell I could have caffeine, and waited until Alan looked up.

"I'm going to look a bit further into this as part of the official investigation," he said.

"What are you looking up?" I asked.

"Ambrose mentioned things happening around his sons, things that couldn't be proven. I want to know if there was anything suspicious I should be considering."

"You think they might have killed someone?"

"I don't know; let's just see what I can find." Alan began typing into his phone. "I'm looking up their time in Valley Hills."

"That's where they grew up," I replied, recalling David mentioning it once.

Alan nodded. "Yeah, that's where Ambrose was finally caught."

"I didn't know that."

"So, during the time they lived there, both boys were admitted to the hospital multiple times for fractured bones, which were passed off as accidents ... oh, and here's a couple of strange things ..."

"What things?"

"Looks like there were some sort of bullying incidents that happened, and David and Dalton were involved. Nothing too bad, some fights, and there was a missing girl when the boys were in their teens. Looks like she'd been dating David."

I swallowed hard. "Was she found?"

"No, she was never found." Alan shook his head. "She's still listed as missing."

A sliver of fear raced up my spine again.

"Stella, do you want to book into a hotel or something tonight? If money is a problem, don't worry, I'll sort it for you," Alan said.

"No, thank you," I said. "It's not the money. I've already told David I'm with my parents because my father took ill, and I think he believed me. If I'm not there and he comes looking for me, I'm terrified of what he might do to my parents if he is the one behind this."

"We could get them moved somewhere safe too," Alan said.

"No, I think we'll be okay."

"All right, if you're sure," he replied. "I wish we had something more concrete so I could bring your husband and Dalton in for questioning, or at least a twenty-four-hour hold, but we have no real evidence connecting them to any of this. Just suspicion because of who their father is, and their lawyers have filed harassment complaints against the department."

I knew he was right. There was nothing that really tied David or even Dalton to any of the murders. If you took out the fact their dad was a killer, then the only thing in common with our murderer was the fact that they fit the physical description of the killer like half the men on the island did.

We finished our coffees, and as we got up to throw our

cups away, my phone buzzed with a text message from
Brittany.

> Brittany: Hey. Sorry. I'm home now. Can
> you come by?

"It's Brittany; she wants to know if we can go do the
restraining order?"

"Sure, let's get this done so she can be safe."

> Me: Yeah, sure. I'm sure you saw my car
> parked outside your place. I'm with Alan,
> we had to go take care of something, so
> we'll be there soon.

I KNOCKED on Brittany's door and waited, standing with Alan
on her stoop. The house was dark, the curtains drawn,
letting very little light into or out of the house.

A moment later, I heard the locks turning on the door,
and then it opened.

"Come in," a voice slurred.

"Brit, what the hell happened?" I asked, seeing her face
as I stepped into the hallway.

In the little bit of sunlight that came through the door
with us, I could see her face was swollen, both eyes were
barely slits, and her lips were fat and cut and swollen to
twice their normal size. I reached for the hallway light
switch and turned on the overhead light to get a better look.
Her arms, which were covered in bruises, were wrapped
around her middle, her left wrist now in a cast.

"Jeff."

"Fuck, where's Roxy?" I asked, terrified.

"With my mom."

"You're sure she's okay?"

Brittany nodded and slowly started shuffling toward the kitchen.

"I can have him arrested for assault; do you know where he is?"

I glanced at Alan. I'd forgotten he was with me.

Brittany shook her head and gasped in pain at the movement.

"Why did he do this to you?" I asked, so worried about her. If I ever met this guy, I was going to kick his ass.

Brittany shrugged and winced. "Told him I was going to the cops."

"Damn it," I muttered.

"We'll get this paperwork filed, and I'll put out an APB on him," Alan said, pulling the papers from his jacket.

We helped her fill it out, and then she said, "This isn't really going to stop him from doing this again, is it?"

I patted her hand. "No, it's not, but if he comes here, and you call the cops, they can arrest him."

She nodded.

"We can try to get him off the street and locked up. With photos of what he's done to you, we can maybe get him put behind bars for a couple of years, depending on, well, previous convictions and—" Alan started to explain.

"I've tried that before," Brittany whispered. "He made bail, put me in the hospital. Once I got out, I grabbed Roxy and ran. That's how I ended up back here. I didn't know where else to go."

I sighed. One of these days Jeff was going to end up killing her. I wished our laws and the courts better protected women from abuse like this.

"Men like this ex of yours somehow always find a way to weasel out of charges." Alan shook his head, looking slightly pissed at the reality of how things worked. "Do you have a picture of him? It would help with the APB. I'll do everything in my power to get him off the street so you can feel safe again."

Brittany slowly got up, opened a drawer, and pulled out a framed photo of her, Jeff, and Roxy when she was a baby. I'd never seen the photo, and now, looking at it, I froze.

It was in full color, but I was staring at the sketch the police artist had drawn.

I was looking at a photo of our serial killer.

32

y nausea came back on strong, but I swallowed
it down, shock and fear making me able to
detach myself from the sickly feeling and fight
it. My eyes went straight to Alan, who met my gaze and
shook his head.

I pointed at the picture and said, "This is Jeff?"

Brittany nodded. "You never met him, did you?"

"No, I just remember you telling me you were dating a
really great guy, and the next thing I knew, you were dropping out and moving to Florida with him. You never introduced me to him."

"Count your blessings," she replied. "When you showed
me a picture of David, at first I thought it was Jeff. They have
a similar look. I guess that's why I never really liked him."
She shrugged.

"Yeah, I can see the similarities." Again, my eyes strayed
to Alan, who was still quiet.

"Can I take this?" Alan asked, lifting the picture.

"Sure. I only kept it for Roxy. It's one of the few pictures I have of her as a baby."

"I'll get it back to you," he said. "Stella, can I speak to you in the hallway?"

I patted Brittany's hand again. "I'll be right back," I said and followed Alan to the hall. "I'm not leaving her alone. Not with him on the loose."

"I figured as much. Be careful. We'll get him found." Alan shook his head. "Can't believe we were looking at the wrong fucking guy, but damn, they do look quite a bit alike."

I nodded. I'd nearly destroyed my marriage because of it. I needed to call and tell my parents they didn't need to worry anymore. "You'll let me know when you find him?"

"Of course." He started out the door. "I'll arrange with patrol to keep an eye on the neighborhood. I'll ask the captain if we can have a car come sit in front of the house, but I don't know if we have the manpower for that. In the meantime, be safe, and lock this door." He hesitated for a moment and then added, "Maybe I should take you both with me ..."

Frowning, I shook my head. "No, where would you take us? You need to get that APB out and find him. I don't think he'll be back here for a while; he's already beaten her up. Probably thinks she's at the hospital."

Alan lingered for a moment but then gave a slight nod. "Okay, but if you feel at any point that you might be in danger, you call me. And lock the door, got it?"

"Got it." I nodded, did as he asked, and returned to the kitchen. "Alan left. He went to file your paperwork and start the search for Jeff. They'll catch him."

Tears slid down her face. "I'm sorry I'm causing them so much trouble when they've got worse things to deal with."

I hated to do it, but I needed her to know and not be blindsided when the news broke of his capture, but first I had a few questions. "Brittany, did Jeff know Cory Elway?"

Her troubled gaze met mine. "No. Not that I know of, why?"

I started thinking about each man who was killed, working backwards. She'd been sort of involved with Charlie, and it dawned on me then that I wasn't even sure if she knew about his death. "You know about Charlie, right?"

Brittany looked at me, frowning. "No, what's wrong with Charlie?"

I covered my mouth, and my eyes started to fill with tears.

"You're scaring me, Stella; what about Charlie?"

"He's dead. He was murdered like the others."

Brittany's eyes, which were barely able to open, widened as much as they could, and her split lip began to tremble. "No, no, that's not possible. I just saw him ... we just ... no." She gasped and then jumped from her chair and booked it to the bathroom, where I heard her throw up.

As she did, I recalled that not only had she been seeing Charlie, but she'd also said that Andrew had hit on her and that he'd been friends with Jeff at one time. I knew James hit on anything in a skirt, so it was possible he'd tried it on with Brittany as well. Cory was the only one I couldn't figure out.

I held her hair back as she emptied her stomach. "Just breathe; it's going to be okay."

She shook her head, sobbing. "It's not. He killed them, didn't he?" Her swollen watery eyes met mine. "Jeff killed all of them."

I nodded slowly. "I think he did."

"I didn't even really know Cory. We went on one date before I started seeing Charlie," she said with a sob.

That explained her connection to Cory Elway, then. "And James?"

"He hit on me at the coffee shop. I told him to go away. I wasn't interested. I didn't even know Jeff was back in town at the time."

"And Ryan?"

She sniffled. "He was so sweet. I flirted with him when I took Roxy to look at the puppies. You know she's always wanted a dog. Ryan said he'd let me know when they got some Lab puppies in, because that was what Roxy wanted. I gave him my phone number. That was about a week before he went missing," she cried, her poor battered face a picture of distress and horror.

"It's going to be okay. Alan is going to find him and lock him up. I'm going to stay here with you. Unless you want to come stay at my parents' place?" I offered.

"No. I'd rather be here," she whispered. "I don't want anyone seeing me like this."

"Okay. Why don't you take a nice relaxing bath, and I'll fix us some dinner," I offered.

She nodded.

I left her alone and headed for the kitchen. Once I was out of earshot, I called my mom. "Hi, Mom. Can you put me on speaker with you and Dad?"

"Sure, is everything okay?"

She sounded worried, and I supposed since I had left them earlier thinking David was a serial killer, I couldn't blame her. "It's fine; everything's fine, I promise. More than fine, actually."

"Perry, dear, it's Stella; she wants to talk to us."

"Honey, are you all right? You left here in a hurry, and we haven't heard a word from you."

"Yes, I'm good. Look, everything I said this morning, I was wrong. It wasn't David. It's not David. I was being irrational and jumping to conclusions I shouldn't have."

"Oh, honey, I'm so glad. So are you going home tonight, then? Is that why you're calling?"

"Well, no, there's been a complication in that. I'm going to call David and tell him that you've passed the kidney stones quicker than expected, and Mom doesn't need me to stay, but that Brittany does."

"What's wrong with Brittany?" Mom asked.

I looked over my shoulder toward the bathroom, which now had the door closed. "Turns out, we're thinking her ex-boyfriend is the serial killer," I said quietly. "He beat her up pretty bad too."

"Stella, that's terrible. I don't know that I like you being there alone."

"I know. I'm going to call David and let him know where I am and why."

"Okay, sweetie. Be safe."

"I will, Mom." I smiled. "Bye. I'll come by tomorrow if I can."

I hung up and set my phone down, then opened the fridge and looked for ingredients. I saw some ground beef and decided I'd keep it simple. I set it on the counter and opened the freezer, pulling out a bag of French fries.

I picked up my phone again and dialed David.

"Did you have a good time at Sandhurst?" he questioned, sounding pissed.

I froze. "Ummm—"

"Don't deny it, Stella. They called to confirm who you were. Why did you go there?" he asked.

Tears slid from my eyes. "Alan dug into your past after finding out Andrew had been stalking me and you'd confronted him. He also knew about the altercation at the restaurant with James," I whispered.

"So you and he thought what? That I might be the serial killer because of course I would be since my father was?" His voice was full of rage and hurt.

"No. No, I never believed that," I lied, but I couldn't tell him that I had thought it was possible. I was suddenly glad I'd never said those words at Sandhurst.

"No? You just asked if my father thought it possible if I could kill someone."

I sighed. "That doesn't mean I thought you could be, but you kept so much hidden about your past from me, and Alan wanted to rule you out ..."

"We're married, Stella; you're supposed to trust me. I didn't tell you because I was protecting you from him. From what he did and what he's capable of," David replied, his voice now sounding simply sad. "Maybe it's a good thing you're staying at your parents' house tonight."

I started crying harder. "David, I do trust you. I'm so sorry you think I don't. I—"

"I've got to go."

"Wait, please. I'm not staying at my parents'. I need to tell you—"

"I don't want to hear it," he snapped. "Goodbye, Stella."

He hung up, and I felt my heart break into a million pieces.

I blew out a breath and tried to calm down as I dialed David's number again. It didn't ring. It merely went straight to voicemail. He wasn't going to talk to me. He was too angry. I doubted he'd even listen if I left a message, but I had to try. My voice was too shaky, so I decided to hang up and try a text message.

> Me: David, I know you're angry at me. I need you to know that I do love you, and I trust you. I'm over at Brittany's, her ex beat her up again, and there is an APB out on him. I'm hoping he's caught soon, and we can talk tomorrow. I love you.

Sighing, I set my phone on the counter and washed my hands. I turned to the cabinet and pulled out a baking sheet. I dumped some fries on it and turned on the oven. Then I got started on the ground beef.

I heard a creak of the floor and called out, "Did you have a good bath?" without turning around.

The next thing I knew, a cloth was over my mouth and nose, and a thick arm was wrapped around my middle. I struggled to get free, but my eyes started to close, and I couldn't fight the darkness. I was terrified for myself and my baby, and most of all I feared I was going to die before David and I could make up.

No, please, no, I begged silently as I fell unconscious.

33

M y head was pounding, and I couldn't move my arms or my legs. I felt a sting to my cheek, and I startled, my eyes opening as I threw my head up and looked around.

"Finally, you fucking nosy-ass bitch!"

I stared into the dark corner of the cement room I was in. A single bulb hung overhead, giving off barely any light. "Jeff?" I questioned.

"Give the girl a prize," he snarled. "Welcome to the final round."

I shook my head, trying to figure out what was going on. "Where am I?"

He laughed. "You don't need to worry about that."

"Where's Brittany?" I asked, looking around. "What have you done to her?"

"Brittany's being punished right now, bitch," he snarled. "You should be more worried about yourself and contestant number one."

I frowned, unsure of what he was talking about. My head

was killing me, and I was seeing black spots in my vision. I wondered if that had anything to do with whatever was on that cloth he'd put over my nose. How long ago had that even been? Did anyone even know I was missing? Did David? Had he gotten my text message? Had he forgiven me? Had he come to find me? I had so many questions, but there was one I urgently needed to know, and Jeff was the one with an answer.

"Did you hurt her again? Where is she?" I asked, frantically worried about Brittany even more so than myself.

"Shut the fuck up! Brittany is my business, not yours, you interfering bitch! You should have left well enough alone. This didn't have to happen. But no, you just had to stick your fucking nose in my business, so now you have to pay the price."

"What are you talking about?" I asked, trying not to freak out. I could feel that my wrists were bound behind my back in the chair I was seated in. My feet, too, were tied to the chair legs.

Jeff got in my face. His eyes were dead; there was no life there as he stared at me. "I'm talking about you getting her that job. Making her think she was too fucking good for me. Introducing her to that pencil dick she worked with. The one she started fucking behind my back. She defiled herself with that scum. You're going to pay for that. But first, I have a little surprise for you."

My heart raced. I needed to get out of here. Maybe if I could keep him talking, David would get that text and come find me. Maybe he was already looking for me. I had to hope he was because otherwise I didn't know how I was going to get out of this. "I don't know what you're talking about. I didn't do anything."

He slapped me, and I realized that he'd already done that before; that was why my cheek was stinging a minute ago. "Shut the fuck up. Don't you want to know what your surprise is?"

I shook my head. Any kind of surprise he had wasn't going to be good. "No thanks, I'd like to leave."

He laughed darkly. "Funny. Glad you got jokes. See how you like this one." He shoved a chair forward into the light.

Suddenly I wanted to puke. David was tied up in the chair he'd just brought forward. He was still out cold, though. "No! Don't hurt him!"

"You don't call the shots here. I do. And both of you losers have pissed me off no end. So yeah, you both have to pay, but first, shall we hear from the man of the hour?"

"Please," I begged, "please don't hurt him. He had nothing to do with this. He's never hit on Brittany. He doesn't even know you're the serial killer. Please—"

"Stop your whining; this has nothing to do with Brittany. This has to do with him and his fucking brother."

His words had me shutting my mouth. I didn't understand what Dalton suddenly had to do with any of this. Was there something I didn't know? Did David, Dalton and Jeff have a history? Was this part of the past I was unaware of?

"What? Did I surprise you?" He smirked at me, then turned to dump a bucket of water over David's head.

David sputtered as he came awake.

"David!" I cried.

"Stella? What the hell?" He looked around and tried to get up but realized he couldn't stand; his legs were tied to the chair, same as mine were. "What the fuck is going on here?" he demanded as he struggled in his bindings.

"Welcome to the party. I suggest you say your goodbyes

now, there's going to be a lot of screaming in a few minutes, and I'm pretty sure you'll forget. Oh, and don't worry, there won't be anyone to hear us. Neither of the neighbors are home." Jeff grinned manically.

"Stella, sweetheart, what's going on?"

"That's not a goodbye ..."

David glared at him. "Who the fuck are you? What's going on here?"

"See, that's a good question. Here's the gist of it. Your bitch wife stuck her fucking nose in my business, and you, asshole, murdered my best friend."

My eyes flew from him to David. "What?"

Jeff chuckled. "Didn't know that, did you? Thought I did it. Naw. Andrew was a good guy. And your asshole husband and his brother fucked him up; then his brother dumped him in a hole and left him there to drown."

My heart was pounding in my chest. David had murdered Andrew? "I don't understand ..."

"Shut the fuck up, asshole," David growled at Jeff as if he were the one in control.

"Go on, tell her. Tell her what you did."

David looked at me, and I could see the sorrow in his eyes. "I was protecting you the best way I knew how. He wouldn't listen to reason." He narrowed his eyes at Jeff. "How the fuck did you know Dalton put him in that hole?"

"I watched him do it." He shrugged, a smirk on his lips. "Got that idea from the Crypt Keeper, did you?" He pointed a sharp knife at him.

David didn't say anything about where they got the idea; instead he said, "If you watched us do that to your friend, why didn't you rescue him?" He glared at Jeff.

Jeff's grin widened. "The asshole hit on my woman, and I

wasn't going to let that go. He got what was coming to him. That doesn't excuse you, though." He glanced at me, then back to David. "One more minute to make your goodbyes."

David stared across at me, his eyes full of love and sorrow. "I love you. I would do anything to protect you, Stella. Anything."

34

I wasn't sure what was about to happen, but I knew David was about to do something, and I was terrified. I kept my eyes on him as I said, "I love you so much."

"So touching," Jeff said sarcastically, turning his evil gaze toward me as his hand with the knife dropped to his side.

It seemed that was enough to give David the chance he was looking for. I felt my heart rip in half as David pushed himself to his feet at an angle. As he stood, the chair kind of fell back to the ground with a clatter, and he ripped his legs forward, breaking off the wooden legs of the chair he was tied to. He charged toward Jeff, crashing into him with his head impacting into Jeff's middle.

I screamed and tried to jump as he'd done, but only succeeded in knocking my chair to the ground with a crash. As I fell, I heard David cry out in pain. My pain from the fall was nothing compared to the anguish I heard in his voice. I didn't care about anything except getting free and helping him.

"David!" I screamed, desperately wanting to go to him.

"Get out of here, Stella!" he shouted as he pinned Jeff with his body.

I couldn't tell what was going on from my prone position on the floor. I couldn't see either of them, and my hands ached now from being crushed between the floor and the back of the chair. I heard David cry out again in agonizing pain. It didn't matter anymore how badly my hands hurt; I wiggled my body around, trying to find a way to see them. I shifted again and got the chair to fall on its side and used my feet to turn me enough to catch sight of them. It was then I saw the flash of a knife covered in blood.

"Oh my God! David!" I screamed in panic. We needed help. He needed help, and I was fucking stuck here just watching Jeff stab the shit out of him.

"Run, Stella!" he shouted harshly again.

I couldn't. It wasn't possible with the way I was still tied to the chair. I began to struggle anew, yanking my ankles against the rope, trying like hell to loosen it as David continued to cry out in pain.

"Please, Stella ... go ..." I could hear that he was struggling to breathe and get words out now.

Every word was a stab in my own heart. My vision was so blurry I could barely see. My heart was lying three feet from me, dying, and I couldn't do the one thing he was asking of me. I took a deep breath, and with renewed resilience, I slammed my ankles forward against the rope and finally felt it give. I was able to use the bottom of the chair leg to slide my feet from my shoes and then slip my feet free of the rope. With them free, I was able to slide my torso free of the chair, then struggle to stand. I looked at David, wanting to go to him, but I didn't know what to do to save him.

"Stella, leave me! Go!" David said harshly, his gaze meeting mine with desperation. "Get out of here!"

Tears raced down my cheeks, and my lips trembled as I said, "I love you," and then I spun around to run for the stairs with my hands still behind my back. The stairs were wooden slats with open spaces between them. I stumbled as I tried to get up them.

"Bitch! You're not going to get away!" Jeff called, but he was still trapped underneath David's body.

David grunted, but called out, "Save ... our child ... get out of here!" before screaming again in pain.

I finally made it up the stairs and shoved the door wide with my shoulder. As I looked around, I could see we were still in Brittany's house. I didn't have time to look for her. I needed to get my hands free and grab my phone, which was still on the counter. I needed to get us help. I needed to save David. But first I needed something to get my hands free.

Earlier when I'd been looking for things to use while cooking, I'd seen a drawer with heavy-duty kitchen knives in it. Now, I put my back to the cabinets and drawers so I could use my hands to yank open the drawer. I managed to get my hands on a large butcher knife. I cut my fingers on the blade, but I was able to manipulate it enough to shut the handle half in the drawer with the sharp end pointed out. I wrapped my wrists around the blade and began to saw at the rope.

I could hear Jeff shouting from downstairs. David's voice was silent, and I feared what that meant. Still, I tried to remain calm, at least as calm as I could because I knew I needed to get free and call Alan and the entire Gull Island police department. I had to if I was going to have any chance in hell of saving David. If he was even still alive. I didn't care that he'd murdered Andrew, or had helped his brother kill him, not at the moment anyway. All I cared about was saving my baby's father. And besides, Jeff had sort of admitted that he would have killed Andrew, so Andrew would have died anyway. Maybe in an even worse way than drowning. Yes, I was rationalizing, but I didn't care. All I wanted was to get us help and save David.

Finally, I felt the rope come apart, and my wrists fell free. I rushed across the room toward my phone. I was so focused as I ran across the kitchen and grabbed up my phone, using my fingerprint to open it. I found Alan's number and hit dial, but as I did, I felt a hand in my hair, yanking me backwards. My phone clattered to the floor as I screamed. I didn't even know if Alan had answered. I hoped he had, that maybe he'd hear everything going on and trace the call.

"Fucking bitch!" Jeff dragged me backwards through the kitchen as I struggled not to fall.

"Let me go!" I screamed and clawed at his hands as I tried to keep my feet under me.

He was strong, and I couldn't break free. "Shut the fuck up! All you bitches do is fucking scream! Can't get a minute of peace and quiet!"

He dragged me down the hall toward the bedrooms, and I tried hooking my foot in the bathroom doorframe to stop our progression, but he was unbelievably strong, pumped up on some adrenaline high. I scratched his hands, clawing at him as I tried to twist out of his grip. I felt my nails break, but I finally managed to use the wall to push myself and turn around so I could face forward as he dragged me, his fingers tangled tightly in my hair. I kicked out at him, hitting the back of his calf, making him grunt, but my feet were bare and didn't really do much damage, so he still didn't let me go.

He slammed me face-first into the wall, causing stars to appear behind my eyelids and my nose to bleed, then he shoved me into the bedroom, and I fell to the floor hard. A moment later he was on my back, slamming my face into the floor. I continued to scream, but there was another voice screaming too, and just before I passed out, I saw Brittany tied to the bed.

The last thing I saw was her breaking free, and then there was nothing.

35

My blackout didn't last long. It seemed it had only been seconds. I could still hear Brittany screaming, and Jeff yelling unintelligible things. I pushed myself up from the floor and shoved my hair from my face, which felt like it was on fire. I felt my nose, which was getting puffy, and I hoped it wasn't broken, but I knew it probably was.

I turned around so I could sit on my butt and take in what was going on. As soon as I realized that Jeff was pinning Brittany to the bed, I was back on my feet. I grabbed him from behind and tried to pull him off of her, but he elbowed me in the cheek hard. I lost my grip on him and fell backwards to the floor again, landing on my butt.

As I started to get up, I heard someone yell, "Stella, stay down!"

A moment later, there was a loud bark of a gun going off, and Jeff cried out and fell to his side off of Brittany. "You fucking shot me!" he screamed.

Alan and a couple of officers came through the door, filling the room with their presence and firepower.

Brittany scrambled to cover herself with the bed linens as I pushed myself to my feet. "David!" I cried and started to the door, pushing and shoving my way through.

I felt an arm wrap around my waist, pulling me back. "Wait." Alan's voice was in my ear.

"But he's hurt! Jeff stabbed him multiple times," I sobbed. "I have to go help him."

"Where is he?" Alan asked, his voice calm.

"In the basement," I said, tears pouring down my cheeks. "Please, you have to save him."

"Ain't no saving that asshole." Jeff laughed and then cried out in pain again as he was handcuffed.

I yanked myself from Alan's arm hold and rounded on Jeff. "What did you do to him?"

Jeff grinned like a maniac; his eyes were crazy, his pupils blown so wide that they almost made his eyes completely black. He looked demonic in that moment. "What that fucker deserved."

I hauled back and punched him in the face as hard as I could, and blood poured from his nose. I shook my hand because it hurt like a bitch, but if Alan hadn't grabbed me and pulled me back, I might have hit him again.

Jeff licked his lips, then spit the blood at me. His gaze went from me to Alan. "I'm not the only murderer around here. That asshole and his brother killed my friend Andrew Corbett," he said, spitting again. His sinister gaze returned to me, and then he grinned. "If I'm going down, I'm taking them with me."

I hated him. I had never wished anyone dead in my life, but in that moment, I wanted him dead. Yes, what David and

Dalton had done was awful and couldn't be changed, but I had my child to think of, and I didn't want them to be tainted by this monster's words.

"Get him out of here and get the medics in to see to these two," Alan ordered. He kept his grip on me so I couldn't go anywhere.

"Let me go," I said, trying to be calm. "I want to go to David."

"I'm sorry, Stella, but I can't let you do that," Alan replied.

I broke down again and started sobbing. I needed to see him. I needed to see my husband with my own eyes. Just one last time if that was all it was going to be.

"Please," I begged, but my desperate word fell on deaf ears.

36

I was a sobbing mess as Alan handed me off to one of
the paramedics who came into the room to look at me
and Brittany. I was made to sit on the end of the bed as
Alan started toward the doorway. He paused and looked
back at me. His mouth opened and closed a few times, the
look in his eyes troubled. Finally, he came back over to me
and put a hand on my shoulder.

"I'll go see to David, and I'll let you know what I find, but
until I know what you'll be walking into, I'm not going to let
you see him. Not until he's cleaned up and looking like you
remember him. You don't need to see him if—" He broke off
there.

I knew exactly what he was saying. He was saying that I
didn't need to see David, the man I loved, cut up and muti-
lated in the same way I'd seen Elway and Walker. He was
right, that would be completely traumatizing, and my
rational brain agreed with him; however, my heart and the
rest of my brain were screaming at me to go to him. I
couldn't come to terms with the fact that he was indeed

gone. That he'd died at the hands of the serial killer. And that it was my fault.

Alan shook his head. "It's not your fault, Stella. Don't be taking on any kind of guilt over this. Over any of it. Not one bit of it is on you. You didn't kill anyone. You didn't get anyone killed. You taking the blame would be the same as putting the blame on Brittany for all the other murders and for being beaten by the actual responsible party."

I knew he was right. Again, the rational part of my head completely agreed with him. I hadn't done anything to be guilty about, but my heart ... my heart told me that if I hadn't said anything to David about Andrew, Andrew would still be alive, or at least David and Dalton wouldn't have killed him, and David would still be alive.

Then a thought popped in my head. It wouldn't have mattered. David would still be dead. Jeff was going to kill him anyway, as a punishment to me for interfering in his "relationship" with Brittany. The man was insane. He blamed me for Brittany coming to work at the marketing firm and meeting Charlie. He blamed me for her getting a restraining order against him. If David hadn't done what he'd done down in the basement, our child and I would probably both be dead too.

"He saved my life," I murmured, looking up at Alan.

"Who?"

"David." I sniffled as more tears spilled. I didn't know how I had more tears to spill, but there they were. "He saved me. He gave me a chance to get away, to get to my phone and call you."

"He loved you," Alan acknowledged.

I nodded, and my face crumpled in pain. "He loved me so much he made sure that Andrew could never hurt me," I whispered. "Does it make me a horrible person that I don't care that he caused Andrew's death?"

Alan shrugged. "Not at all, but we will have to talk about that death later, Stella. I need to know what you know."

I sniffled again and gave him a nod.

Alan looked at the paramedic, who was waiting patiently for us to finish our conversation. "She's pregnant; be gentle." With that, he moved his hand from me and walked out of the room.

"Hello, Stella, I'm Martin. I'll be taking care of you."

I nodded.

"Can you tell me how far along you are?" Martin asked as he put his stethoscope up to his ears.

"About five and a half months," I murmured.

"Okay, that's good. I'm going to listen to your heartbeat and then see if I can hear the baby."

Again, I nodded. I took breaths as he listened and prayed that everything with the baby was okay. If I lost them after this, I didn't know if I would recover.

"Both your and the baby's heartbeats are strong. Still, I think we should get you into the hospital for a complete check-up and get some of this trauma seen to. I want to make sure you don't have a concussion or any internal bleeding that might cause you to lose the baby or deliver early, okay?"

"Yes, that's fine." I felt my eyes closing. Now that things had calmed down and the adrenaline was wearing off, I just felt so exhausted.

"They may want to keep you overnight or even for a few days, considering there is the baby to think about. Is there anyone you'd like me to call for you?"

I blinked, and my eyes drifted closed again. "Hmmm?"

"Stay with me, Stella." Martin patted my cheek. "I'm

going to need you to stay awake for just a little while longer, okay?"

"Sure."

"Now, is there anyone I can call to meet you at the hospital?"

David was the first name I thought of, but I'd never be able to call him again. David was gone. Stolen from me by the serial killer. I started to cry again.

"Shit, what did I say?" Martin muttered; then he took a long, loud breath and said, "Breathe with me, Stella; stay calm. I need you to stay calm, okay?"

I tried to do as he asked as I thought about who else to call. After a moment I said, "My parents. Call my parents."

"Good, that's good, Stella. I'll call them and make sure they meet us at the hospital." He gently put an arm around me. "Can you stand? Do you think you can walk outside to the ambulance, or do I need to get a stretcher in here?"

"I can walk."

I stood up with him, and together we headed out the door and down the hall. We passed through the kitchen and past the CSI team bagging evidence. My gaze slid to the basement door, where I could hear voices floating up from downstairs, but I couldn't make out their words. I longed to break free from Martin's hold on me and rush down there to see David, but I didn't have the strength to do it. My body felt like I'd just run a 5K marathon at top speed. Every muscle, every bone was sore.

We passed through the rest of the house, and outside, the neighborhood was filled with various cop cars, the fire department, a couple of ambulances and news trucks. There were crowds of people clustered around, watching the scene unfold, and I ducked my head, not wanting to be seen. I wanted them all to go away.

Of course, that wasn't going to happen. This was the end result of the case that had plagued us; everyone wanted to know what was going on. If I hadn't been involved, I would probably be one of those people.

"Just two steps up, and we'll get you settled on a gurney," Martin murmured.

I followed his directions, and a moment later I was lying on the narrow bed, and he was covering me with a sheet and pulling seatbelt-like straps over me to hold me in place. He attached an oxygen mask to my face.

"I'm just going to call ahead and let them know we're bringing you in. Before we head out, I want to make sure they don't want me to start an IV on you. Give me a moment."

The oxygen in the mask was waking me up more, but with it on my face, I couldn't really answer well, so I just nodded.

Martin called in and spoke in a soft tone, getting directions from the ER, I assumed. He nodded a few times, checked my pulse, and looked in my puffy, blackening eyes. Even his tender touch had me wincing at the pain that was starting to settle in on me. He murmured a few more times into the phone and then banged his hand on the back wall of the ambulance that connected to the driver.

"Let's go," he called as the small window between us and the driver opened.

I heard the siren flip on, and the next thing I knew, we were pulling away from the scene and flying at top speed toward the hospital.

37

R iding on the gurney as Martin and the other medics rushed me through to the ER was just like you could see on any medical drama show on TV. The nurses and doctors all gathered around, along with the medics, each calling out codes that sounded confusing to my ears.

I seemed to fade in and out of consciousness. Blinking as the lights overhead passed by in a whirl as I was rolled down the sterile hallway. I didn't know what was happening or why. I rolled my eyes to the side, trying to catch someone's attention, but the oxygen mask was still on me, and they were too busy speaking to each other to pay attention to me wanting to ask questions.

A minute later, I was in a room, and a group of people were lifting me, sheet and all, from the gurney onto a bed. I didn't know anything else for a few minutes, I just recall shutting my eyes as they were all gathered around me and then, a moment later, waking up to find it calm as could be with just the sound of the heart machine beeping softly next to me.

I blinked, looking around, and realized I was in a private hospital room. There was an IV in my arm, and I had a heart monitor hooked up to my chest. I was also wearing nothing but a hospital gown, and I wondered who had changed my clothes. I supposed it didn't matter. These were the professionals: they did this on a regular basis, so I figured I was in good hands.

I heard movement in the corner of the room, and for a moment I froze in shock. And then I realized it wasn't David. I started to cry as Dalton came forward, looking as traumatized as I felt. I wasn't afraid of him, even knowing he'd killed someone. He'd done it to protect me, and I couldn't hold that against him, even if the cops would. He leaned down and hugged me.

"I'm so sorry," I whispered as we held each other, mourning the loss of David.

"It's not your fault," he replied, sounding so much like David it hurt my heart.

He drew back a few moments later and pulled a chair up to the side of the bed. "I sent your parents down to the cafeteria to get something to eat. We don't have very long to talk."

I nodded.

"Can you tell me what happened?"

I wasn't going to deny him. I told him everything I knew, including the fact that he and David had killed Andrew and that the cops knew because Jeff had told them. He didn't seem surprised.

"David wasn't the one who put him in that hole. It was me. I'd do it again in a heartbeat too."

His eyes took on the rage and fury I'd seen in David's

eyes before, but it didn't scare me. I'd looked into the eyes of someone truly evil, and this wasn't that. I reached a hand out to him, and he took it.

"David and I set up a contingency plan in case things went wrong. You and the baby will be taken care of. The company is in your name, and the board will now answer to you. There are people we trust who will take care of the day-to-day operations for you. And if you want to sell, that's fine, just talk to Jacob Shelling, he's the board president, and he has a list of potential buyers. There's a trust set up with plenty for the child, which will only grow as they grow."

I looked at him in sheer confusion. "What do you mean, the company is in my name?"

"The house too. Nearly everything is yours. We didn't want you struggling if our assets were frozen, and we didn't want our father contesting any kind of will or anything, so we took care of fixing it before anything happened." He glanced over his shoulder toward the doorway, then back to me. "And don't worry about our father's expenses; those are taken care of as well. Please don't ever go back there." He paused. "In fact, don't answer any calls from Sandhurst Park."

I nodded.

"I have to go. Goodbye, Stella. Take care of that angel." He nodded toward my stomach and then leaned down and kissed my forehead. As he headed for the doorway, he glanced back and said, "You know he loved you more than anything in this life, and he was so proud of you. He'd want you to find a way to be happy."

And with that, he left.

I blinked back tears, unsure of what I was feeling. I thought back over everything that Dalton had just told me. I didn't understand how he and David had set all that up, just on the off chance that they'd either be caught or dead.

A knock sounded at the door, and my parents and Alan walked in. I smiled to see them, and Mom rushed to my side. "Hi, Mom," I murmured as she enveloped me in a hug.

"Sweetie, you had me so worried," she said, tears streaming down her face.

Dad came over and kissed my brow. "Glad you're all right, honey." He brushed a hand over my hair. "I'm so sorry about David."

I nodded, unable to put into words how I felt about him being gone.

"Dalton was here earlier," I said. "Did you see him?"

Alan glanced at my dad, a look of consternation on his face. "Dalton Bell was here?"

"Yeah, why?" I tried to be nonchalant about it, not wanting to see Dalton caught. He and David had only done what they'd done to protect me from Andrew.

"How long ago? Did you speak to him, Stella?"

I didn't want to tell him, but I knew I had to. "He left a few minutes before you all got here."

"Damn it," Alan cried and rushed from the room, pulling his phone from his pocket.

"What was that about?" Dad asked.

"You know how Andrew's body was different than the others Jeff murdered?" I said, looking at my dad.

He nodded. "Yeah, still a horrible death though, drowning like that."

I took a breath and blew it out. "David and Dalton did it."

"What!" Mom exclaimed. "What a thing to accuse them of. Stella, how could you?"

I shook my head. "David admitted it right before Jeff

killed him. Jeff watched him and Dalton do it. They did it to protect me. I'm not sure what went down on that beach, but, yeah, they did it to protect me." I knew I was justifying Andrew's death at their hands, but it was how I felt. Andrew had scared me, and I honestly thought he might have continued to elevate his stalking to harming me, so I didn't really feel all that sorry that he was gone.

Dad glanced toward the doorway. "So Alan's going after Dalton to arrest him."

"I don't think he's going to catch him. I think Dalton's going to disappear." I went on to explain what he'd told me. "He didn't say he was going to disappear, but it was the feeling I got."

Dad ran a hand through his hair and sighed. "I can't say I'm happy about what they did, but as your dad, I can understand the urge to protect you at all costs, even at the expense of someone else's life."

I gave my dad a half-hearted smile.

"I'm really sorry about David, honey."

I sniffled. "Me too. I feel awful for being so suspicious of him. My head is kind of a mess about the whole thing." I would probably need therapy to sort through everything that happened, but not right now.

"That is understandable, given the circumstances," Dad replied.

I feigned a yawn. I wasn't really all that tired, but I really missed David, and I wanted to be alone. I had a lot to think about, and I knew they would only leave me alone if they thought I needed rest.

"Oh, you're sleepy. Perry, we should let Stella rest."

"Okay, dear." Dad leaned down and kissed my head

again. "We'll be back in the morning, honey. You get some sleep."

"Okay," I answered as Mom hugged me.

"We love you, sweetie."

"Love you too, Mom."

When they were gone, I surrendered myself to my feelings and sobbed into my pillow until I fell into a deep, but restless sleep.

38

TWELVE WEEKS LATER

"Congratulations, Stella. Your work on these accounts has brought their sales up thirty percent or more, which I feel is no coincidence," Lonnie said as I sat across her desk from her. "Our clients are ecstatic at the uptick in revenue, and you've brought national recognition to the firm."

I beamed at her, pleased that my work had been so well received.

I supposed the notoriety I'd gained from having been one of the survivors in a serial killer's rampage had helped a little. Lonnie had closed the office for a few days once the killer was caught and the news about Charlie came out, and she'd had a grief counselor come in for those who needed to talk. Once the dust had settled and everyone was back to work, she'd fielded numerous business calls from people who wanted to work with us because they'd seen me on the news.

It hadn't been just the news, though. There were film directors and screenwriters who wanted to tell the story, and

Brittany, who was still grieving Charlie, and I had needed to hire an agent just to go through all of the offers. I didn't exactly need the money with what David had left me. I had known that he was rich, that we'd never had to worry about money, but I'd never known the full extent of it until it was all in my hands. It was actually pretty staggering to discover I was worth several hundred million, and that was prior to selling the company, which was currently in the works. Jacob Shelling, the president of the board of directors, had put me in touch with the Japanese client David had worked with, who was over the moon to make an offer on the company.

I turned my thoughts back to Lonnie and smiled. "I've loved every second of working on those campaigns."

"I'm sure going to miss you while you're on your maternity leave," Lonnie said.

"I'll miss you too. All of you. But I'll be around," I said. I loved my job, and I wasn't going to give it up despite all the money.

Lonnie nodded. "Make sure you bring that cute little noodle along to meet Auntie Lonnie and the rest of the gang."

"I will," I promised as I rubbed my huge belly. These last several months had seen my stomach grow large with the baby.

"And what about you? What are you going to do with yourself for almost a year?" Lonnie asked. "And don't think I don't get it. I know being a single mom is more than enough to fill your time. But I know you. You'll miss the thrill of creating ads and following marketing trends."

I grinned. "Hopefully, after the trial, Brit and I will decide on which offers to accept, and we'll be involved in the book and movie process over the next year. We're planning to dedicate the book to Charlie and David to honor their memories."

"I'll be first in line to buy the book from you guys when it comes out," Lonnie said.

"Shut up," I told her with a laugh. "You'll be the first on my list for a free copy. And I expect a nice review on Amazon, obviously."

"Done."

"We're going to make sure half the proceeds go to support women's shelters and treatment for abused women and children."

"That's brilliant." Lonnie smiled at me as she leaned back in her chair. "When does the trial start, do you know?"

"Next week. Monday morning at nine, in fact."

"Are you ready to relive all that?"

I'd spent the last three months coming to terms with everything that had happened. Burying David had been the hardest part. Jeff had stabbed him in the face multiple times after I'd run up the stairs, so I'd not gotten to see him a final time. Per his wishes, David had been cremated and then his ashes buried in a plot he'd already paid for. There was a spot reserved next to him for me and our little one too, when the time came.

After that, there'd been so much to deal with as far as finances and the company went. Then there was the manhunt for Dalton, which had turned into a nationwide hunt. He was still on the run, at least according to Alan. I personally didn't think Dalton was running anymore. He was somewhere else, another country, probably one without extradition, living a whole new life. I'd heard from him a few times, just postcards, but still, he wasn't quite gone from my life for good, and although I knew it was wrong in many ways, that actually made me happy.

As for the trial and everything that was going to entail, I was as ready as I could be, honestly. "I think so. I just want to get it over with."

"Yeah, I don't blame you there." Lonnie nodded. "Oh, hey, did you hear about Olive Casden?"

I frowned. The name was familiar, but at first, I couldn't place it. Then it hit me. David, my dad, and I had discussed her what now felt like a lifetime ago. The missing woman from about two years ago. "Did they find her?"

"Yeah, she turned up in Michigan."

"Alive?" I asked, surprised.

Lonnie nodded. "She'd been dating some shady guy, and she was going to turn state's evidence against him, but he'd threatened her life, so they chucked her in witness protection, and then the paperwork got mislaid, and there was this whole screw-up, which meant she didn't even testify."

"Sounds like a mess."

"Yeah, she's suing the state for putting her through all of that for nothing." Lonnie shrugged.

"Wow." The baby kicked, and I smiled as I rested my hand on the spot. "I should probably go," I said. "I've still got to pick up a few more things before we get the nursery set up this weekend."

"Okay, take care."

Lonnie stood up with me, and we hugged each other, and then I left her office. I said my goodbyes to some of the others in the office, telling them I'd see them soon. I didn't think many of them believed I would come back to work, seeing as I was rich and famous now, but the fame part of it I honestly wished I could give back. I didn't want to be famous because a serial killer murdered my husband and tried to kill me. Brittany had it far worse, though. She'd had a kid with the guy. I glanced over at her desk and smiled. She was still raw from losing Charlie, but after Jeff was arrested, Ryan had been released from the safehouse, and he'd come to the hospital to see her. The trauma they'd both been through at Jeff's hands had led them to a connection, and it looked like they might be working toward starting a relationship.

Brittany saw me and got up. She walked over and hugged me. "We're going to miss you around here." She grinned.

"Thanks, I'm going to miss being here." I smiled.

"See you this weekend," she said, pulling me into another hug and holding me tightly.

We'd gotten even closer, almost like sisters, after what we'd been through. Brit and Roxy were coming over to the house this weekend to help me decorate the nursery. I had dragged my feet on getting the house ready, but time was creeping up on me, and I knew I needed to get it done before the little one arrived.

David and I had wanted to wait till I gave birth to know whether the baby was a boy or a girl, so I'd honored that wish, and I still didn't know what I was having. Because of that, I'd chosen neutral green and yellow colors for the nursery. My mother was crocheting blankets in those colors, and she and my dad were coming over as well to help paint and put furniture together too.

"I'll have Roxy's favorite treats," I said, grinning.

"That's why you're her favorite aunt." Brittany laughed.

I waved, and a few minutes later I stepped out of the office building, and Alan was waiting for me on the sidewalk. I smiled and went toward him.

"Hi, Alan, what's up?" I said.

He laughed.

"What?" I said with a frown.

"Nothing, just happy to see you looking chipper."

"Fair enough." I grinned.

"How are you really doing, Stella?" he asked, eyeing me.

I thought about it for a minute. Losing David hurt a lot, and I missed him every day, but it was also getting easier. My heart was mending bit by bit. There would never be anyone like him in my life again, but that didn't mean I would be alone forever. He wouldn't want that. Dalton had even said as much. "I'm doing good, just taking it one day at a time."

He nodded. "Heard from Dalton?"

I had. "Just a postcard from Rio. No return address."

"Trial starts next week; you going to be up to testify?"

"As long as I'm not in the hospital with this one," I said, rubbing my belly.

He nodded. "If you are, I think it will be all right with Ryan's and Brittany's testimonies. Plus my own."

We reached the coffee shop, and Alan opened the door for me. I thanked him and stepped inside, and as I did, I felt a rush of warm wetness between my legs. Fuck. I turned back to Alan.

"Umm, any chance of a ride to the hospital?" I said. "I think my water just broke."

Alan looked startled at first and then wrapped an arm around my back and quickly got me to his car as the contractions started to hit me. "Just hang in there; we'll be there in no time," he murmured.

True to his word, Alan got me to the hospital just in time, and he stayed by my side until the nurse took me back to the maternity ward.

Seven hours later, I'd delivered the most perfect baby girl

in the world. I smiled as I snuggled her to my breast. I kissed her sweet little head and whispered, "We have a beautiful baby girl, David. She's got your eyes." I wished with all my heart that he could be there with us.

"So adorable," my mom gasped as she came into the room.

She and Dad rushed to my side, and Dad leaned down and kissed my head. "You've done good, honey." He beamed at me and my new baby. "And don't you worry, we'll have that nursery ready for when you bring her home in a few days."

"Thanks, Dad," I said, grinning up at him. It was a good thing I'd already shown everyone pictures of what I wanted to do in there.

"What name did you decide on?" Mom asked.

"Davina." I smiled up at her. "Davina Louise Bell. After David and his mother."

"That's beautiful, sweetie." Mom smiled, her eyes on my precious new daughter. "May I hold her?"

I lifted my gorgeous daughter toward her grandmother.

I couldn't believe everything that had happened over the last year, both the horrible and the amazing. I prayed that the coming years would be filled with more blessings than horrors. As I stared at my daughter, I vowed that, just like her father, I would protect her with every last breath in my body. God forbid anyone would try to harm her. She would be loved as strongly as he'd loved me.

THANK YOU FOR READING

Did you enjoy reading *The Hollow Husband*? Please consider leaving a review on Amazon. Your review will help other readers to discover the novel.

ABOUT THE AUTHOR

Cole Baxter loves writing psychological suspense thrillers. It's all about that last reveal that he loves shocking readers with.

He grew up in New York, where there was crime all around. He decided to turn that into something positive with his fiction.

His stories will have you reading through the night—they are very addictive!

ALSO BY COLE BAXTER

Inkubator Books Titles

The Perfect Suitor

The Betrayal

I Won't Let You Go

The Night Nurse

The Doppelganger

The Couple Next Door

The Patient

The Hollow Husband

Other Titles

Prime Suspect

What She Witnessed

Deadly Truth

Finding The Other Woman

Trust A Stranger

Follow You

Did He Do It

What Happened Last Night

Perfect Obsession

Going Insane

She's Missing

The Perfect Nanny

What She Forgot

Stolen Son

Before She's Gone